Affairs of the Heart

By: Kevin Elliott

CHAPTER 1

Christian Walker was three years old and held up three fingers whenever anyone asked him his age. Christian was big for his size. Sometimes, he was mistaken for being five, and he possessed the ability to speak pretty damn good sentences for a toddler. Kendall, Christian's mother, phone rang, and Christian yelled "Daddy!" He associated his father with fun. His daddy tickled him and tossed him high in the air before catching him. He would blow on his belly and make funny noises. Christian loved his mother too, but he wanted to be like his Daddy, like most little boys did.

Kendall had been logged onto her Facebook page, scanning the profiles of her old high school classmates, and she was amazed at how many of them were too damn huge to be only thirty years old.

Baby Christian sprinted toward Kendall and screamed "Daddy!"

"Christian, it's not Daddy."

Christian frowned in disappointment.

Kendall tossed him a Spiderman figure and instructed, "Play with your toy, while I talk to Godmama Chrissy."

Chrissy Johnson and Kendall White had met at Sunday School at Weeping Willow Baptist Church as eighth graders. Chrissy's family had relocated to Charlotte from Pittsburgh after her father's job had transferred him. Kendall was the first girl that Chrissy had met, and they hit it off right away. They liked the same kind of music, and they were members of the Praise and Worship dance team in church. Each were the only girl in their families. Chrissy's family was ecstatic that she'd been so fortunate to find a good friend, and sixteen years later they were still best friends, Kendall had even named her son after Chrissy.

Though they had a lot of things in common, they contrasted in appearance. Kendall had a large Ethiopian forehead, sensuous lips, and long natural hair and minuscule waist and womanly figure. Kendall's resembled East Africans so much, they'd often approached her yelling Selam. She would simply laugh and say that she was American. One cab driver had said she was denying her heritage and said that she was East African, and she would respond "My parents are from South Carolina."

"I want my Daddy," Christian whined.

"I don't know where your daddy is. This is Godmama. Now go play."

"Godmama?" He repeated.

"Yeah, Godmama. Play with Spiderman while I talk to Godmama."

He sat on the floor, pitting his figures against each other, while Kendall resumed her conversation.

"My bad girl. My phone was in the other room when you called earlier." She paused before continuing, "I was watching these dumb ass hoes on the reality shows."

Kendall knew and she knew this girl could talk forever about nothing. Before she could cut Chrissy off, she'd started talking again.

"I mean every episode, I don't care if its New York, LA, or Atlanta, it's the same plot. Throw a fuckboy into a love triangle, with two desperate chicks and the ratings go through the roof."

"Hey, hey, hey!"

"What's wrong?" Chrissy asked.

"I called to vent, not hear about these recycled reality TV chicks."

Chrissy laughed, "Yeah, I was the one returning the call. My bad."

Kendall sighed. "It's all good."

"What's on your mind, boo?"

"Dre hasn't been answering his phone."

"He's a busy man. No man is going to stop to answer your calls every time you call. He has to pay for that house and Range Rover that you're driving somehow. The man is working. He's staying busy, that's how. My mama always told me don't bother a man while he is at work. I mean he could be not doing shit with his life—"

Kendall sat the phone down then stared at the ceiling; Chrissy was on another tangent. Kendall strolled to the fridge, snatching a cranberry Snapple as a rubber ball whizzed past her face. Christian was laughing as he picked up the ball and was about to throw it again. She snatched the ball away from him and said, "We don't throw balls in the house, okay?"

He frowned and said, "I sorry Mommy!"

She kissed his forehead, then said, "It's okay, baby."

Kendall picked up the phone and pressed it to her ear. Chrissy was still yapping. "Will you shut the fuck up? I called to talk to you about something, and you keep making this about you and what you know and what you have heard. Can you please be a good best friend today and listen?"

"I'm so sorry, girl. I'll be quiet." Even though Kendall couldn't see her, she mimed zipping her lips together.

"Dre has a girlfriend."

"Daddy?" Christian asked after hearing his father's name.

"No its not Daddy. It's Godmama like I just told you. Go play."

"Dre is a married man!"

"He's cheating. He has a ho on the side. Someone that's not me. Want me to spell it out for you?" Kendall snapped.

"How do you know this?"

"A couple of nights ago, he came home and he smelled of Classique by Jean Paul Gaultier. He doesn't wear that, obviously."

"Did you ask him about it?"

"Don't need to. The signs are there." Kendall paused. "He doesn't answer my calls half the time, he comes home smelling like another woman, and when he doesn't smell like another woman, he hops in the shower before getting in the bed. Sometimes he'll come in at 3 am and he'll go in the guest bedroom to shower, giving some lame excuse that he didn't want to wake me up."

"But it is 3 am, Kendall," Chrissy laughed. "Do you want to be woken up at 3 am?"

"I'm up because I'm waiting on my man, and he knows I'm up because I've called him twenty eight times."

"I can't say that I know the signs. I haven't had a boyfriend in two years. I don't even deal with niggas anymore. Slim, who comes by and gives me head then leaves in the middle of the night... I can't keep holding out waiting on him to get his shit together and leave his mama house. The man is thirty-five—"

"Listen, please." Kendall was getting irritated.

"So Dre's cheating?"

"I'm certain."

"But what are you prepared to do about it?"

"What can I do? I don't have a job; I can't leave him. I have a baby, and I'm broke."

Chrissy had an idea. "Go back to school, you were always the smart one."

"I hate school. I hated everything about school."

"What about fashion? You can be a stylist."

"And what do I do while I pursue this stylist thing? You want me to just stay put while Dre just run around cheating on me?"

Chrissy rolled her eyes. "They're all going to cheat, like this meme on Instagram said, you might as well be crying in a mansion than be crying somewhere in the projects."

"You think all men cheat?"

"Most do." Chrissy nodded.

"You think your daddy cheats?"

"They don't make them like my daddy no more," Chrissy laughed. "Who says he didn't cheat when he was younger?"

"Did he?"

"I don't know, but I know when my Uncle Leroy died and we went back to Pittsburgh to go to the funeral, we discovered that I had two cousins that I didn't know existed."

Kendall gasped, "He had another woman?"

"Two women."

"Damn."

"But your daddy don't seem like the cheating type, obviously Uncle Leroy was thotting around..."

"Uncle Leroy didn't seem like a cheater either. He was a deacon in the church and a track and field coach at the high school. Word was it that Uncle Leroy had gotten one of his ex-runners pregnant."

"Oh wow. Damn. Uncle Leroy was a savage. So she had two kids by Uncle Leroy?"

Chrissy laughed, "That's just it. Uncle Leroy had two baby mamas."

"Who was the other baby mama?"

"The girl's sister."

"Stop it."

"I'm serious."

"So your cousins are sisters."

"Yeah. Really nice girls. But my point is there are skeletons in everybody's closet."

"So all men cheat?"

"I think most people cheat," Chrissy said matter-of-factly. "Or will cheat if the opportunity

presents itself."

"Scandalous."

"Yeah, but I wouldn't have ever thought that about him. But that made me realize if Uncle Leroy could cheat, then anyone is capable of cheating. But you have it made with Dre."

Kendall laughed; she couldn't believe what she was hearing. "Since I got it made with Dre, I should just look over it. What's a little cheating right?"

"No, I didn't mean it like that."

"I'd rather have real love than material things," Kendall sighed.

There was silence on the other end of the phone, then Chrissy stated, "You don't think Dre loves you."

Kendall all but whispered, "I do."

"So do I."

"But why do I feel so alone?"

"But you're married."

"Marriage ain't nothing but a piece of paper nowadays."

"You're right."

Kendall looked at the 2.16 carat canary yellow diamond ring. She'd initially hated the ring; the damn thing costed too much—almost fifty thousand dollars—but then she'd grown to love what it represented: the union between her and the man of her life. She began to sob. "He's cheating

Chrissy. I think it's just time for me to accept the fact that he's a cheater, and I'm going to be alone."

Chrissy, who usually had a lot to say, could only say, "You're not alone. I'm here for you."

Christian waddled up to her, and she looked in her son's eyes as he said, "Don't cry, Mommy."

She smiled at Christian and said, "Mommy is going to be okay, son. Don't worry about Mommy." She pinched his chubby jaws and then gathered him into her arms.

* * * *

Her iPhone charging on the nightstand read 4:12 am. She heard the water bustling from the shower of the guest bedroom. She'd guessed that Dre probably arrived about ten minutes ago, and it also told her that he had been with some woman and they had probably gone out to eat at some fancy steakhouse, perhaps Upstream or Flemings. One of the reasons she liked him is because he loved to eat. He'd teased her that he was going to get her fat so nobody else would want her. Even after they had eaten, he'd probably taken her to the Ritz Carlton or perhaps her place, but if her place wasn't nice enough for him, she knew that they were in a five-star hotel. Though Dre was from the hood, he had become bougie. Money had a tendency to make hood niggas that way.

When she met Dre, she had to teach him the difference between a salad fork and a dinner fork. She taught him how to hold a fork. She taught him a man was supposed to walk on the outside of a woman. Taught him not to place his elbows on the table. Taught him to look the waiter in the eye and acknowledge him and not to talk to service or professional people with slang or hood jargon. She had taught him that Gucci was not the best cologne. She bought him Tom Ford Tobacco Vanille and a small bottle of Creed Aventis with her waitress check. She'd taught him how to dress. She was more cultured than him—but not because she came from a higher social economic class.

Kendall was a girl from the hood, but she had big ambitions. She spent hours watching YouTube videos about fashion, etiquette, and how to be a lady. She had dreamed of being a creative. A designer or a writer or a stylist for the stars, she'd style Beyonce and Rihanna, move to New York, and buy herself a Brownstone. She'd also have a place in Paris. When she first met Dre, she thought he was cute, but he was not her type. He was a nice boy, but he didn't have dreams. Well, his dreams were not as big or ambitious as hers. He was a small-time hustler, and she hated hustlers, but Dre wouldn't go away. He gave her attention and showered her with gifts. They weren't expensive gifts, but he was the only one that ever bought her anything, and she appreciated him.

A year after their first date, she'd given in and had sex with him. Two years later she had gotten pregnant with Christian, and now that Christian was here, those dreams had to be put on hold. She fought back the tears as she thought about how much of herself she had sacrificed for him, but was it his fault? She had become lazy, and she had gotten to the point where she didn't want to work. Why get a job? Her man had so much money, he had taken her on so many vacations, and he had showed her so much that there was no point in working. Plus, she had been with him in the beginning.

She was with him the first day he'd met the plug. Dre had gone from a street hustler getting a couple pounds of exotic weed to a kingpin, and she remembered the day a strange Mexican knocked on his door in their little run-down apartment in the hood. She remembered because she was scared as hell.

The tattooed Mexican man had showed up at the door wearing a wife beater, Dickies, and a t-shirt and asking for Dre, who was in the bedroom asleep. Kendall had lied to the man that Dre wasn't home and closed the door, then dashed into the bedroom to wake him.

Dre sat up on the bed, as she asked, "Do you owe someone some money?"

He cleaned his eyes. "Hell no... Why?"

"A Mexican just knocked on the door and asked for you, and I told him that you wasn't home."

"What? Asked for me?"

"Yeah, he asked for Dre."

Dre dashed through the living room with his 9mm stuffed in his pocket, ran out into the parking lot, and stopped the man who had been driving a Red BMW X5. "Hey, amigo."

The man lowered the window.

"You looking for Dre?" Dre asked, his hand inside his pocket, caressing his weapon.

The man smiled and said, "Yeah." He turned off the ignition. "Can we talk inside?"

"What the fuck it is we need to talk about?"

"I came to help."

"Help me do what?" Dre was furious now wondering who this strange motherfucker was.

"Carlos got locked up a week ago, and he told me to call you."

Carlos had been Dre's connect and his homeboy for a while. Carlos was big time, and he'd always consigned Dre small amounts of weed and coke, and Dre had always paid him.

"He got locked up for what?"

"The feds picked him up."

"And who the fuck are you?"

"I'm Carlos' connect, Juan."

"I don't believe you."

"Carlos is going to call you tonight."

"So what do you want from me?"

"Can we go inside?" the Mexican asked again.

Dre looked around before agreeing. "Yeah."

Dre and Juan disappeared inside his apartment and sat on opposite ends of the sofa. Juan Marco explained to him that he'd been working with Carlos for five years. He'd already known about him, and Carlos had explained that Dre was very trustworthy. After Carlos had gotten arrested, he'd asked for Dre's information, but Carlos was hesitant at first, he didn't want to be cut out; he wanted a piece of the proceeds. Juan would have to put aside ten percent of his profits for Carlos if Dre wanted the opportunity. Dre jumped at the opportunity to supply the Carolinas. Two years later, he was a millionaire.

Kendall had counted so much money with him, that her hands ached. They would sometimes count money for hours. Dre was a young man, but he possessed an old soul and always mimicked the ways the ways of older people; his father had been a small-time hustler, too. He taught Dre that money counters were bad luck. His father had grown up in a small town called Rock Hill in South Carolina, and he was superstitious and believed in

Root Workers. But Kendall had been so sick of counting so much money all they time, she convinced Dre to buy a money counter, and it had made their life that much easier.

She would never forget the day he had he proclaimed he was worth a million dollars, and they had counted the money like they had did so many times before. This time when they'd finished, he'd sealed it, and there was a big, silly smile on his face.

She asked, "Why are you so damn happy?"

"I finally have it."

"You have what?"

Dre's grin widened. "I've made a million dollars!"

"Are you going to quit?" Kendall asked.

"Why would I do that?"

"Because I'm pregnant."

"You are?"

Kendall nodded. "Yeah."

"Are you being serious right now?"

"Why would I lie about a thing like that?"

He tossed the pile of money and sprinted around the apartment in his drawers. "Imma be a daddy. Imma be a daddy!"

His joy was infectious, and Kendall broke out in a matching smile. She'd been kind of nervous about telling him; she didn't know how he would react. After he'd finished his celebration, he stated, "We have to get married."

"No, we don't."

He winced, slumped, then frowned.

She said, "I don't want you to marry me because we have a baby on the way." Then, she asked, "If I wasn't pregnant, would you have asked me?"

His eyes narrowed as he said, "I haven't really thought about it."

"Exactly."

A year later, he proposed. Christian was three months old. They had their parents, Chrissy, and her off-and-on-again boyfriend, Slim, over for what was supposed to be a Super Bowl party. He surprised her by proposing and presenting her with a beautiful 2.2 halo engagement ring, that she'd felt had been over the top. But of course she accepted because he was the only man that she had ever really loved.

A year after that, they had a small wedding of about 50 in Turks and Caicos.

She heard the buzzing of the Dre's toothbrush interrupting her memory and thought about the other woman. Was she taller? Was she prettier? Did she have a better body? Was she better in bed? The toilet flushed twice, she heard running water from the sink, then Dre's bare feet tiptoe across the floor. He pulled the covers back and slid underneath them. He smelled like coconut oil and soap, not like that whore that he'd left in the street. Kendall stared at the wall on her side of the bed, her back turned towards him as he crawled in the bed. This was her side of the bed, and it had been for years. He scooted his body over next to her, and she felt him against her butt. He slid his arm underneath hers, grabbed her waist, and held onto her. He'd always gone to sleep holding her, but that day, Kendall escaped his grip.

"What's wrong?" he asked.

"I'm hot, baby," she lied. She didn't want him to touch her; she wanted no parts of him.

He scooted across the bed, and minutes later, he was snoring. He didn't hear her cry.

* * * * *

The next morning at the kitchen table, they ate scrambled eggs, turkey bacon and toast. She'd prepared grits for Dre. He loved cheese grits, but they were out of cheese, so he would have to settle for plain ones. Christian was eating cereal from his highchair when Dre came in from behind him, grabbed the toddler, and made a monster sound. A trail of milk dribbled from his mouth onto his chin. He looked up at Dre, laughed, knocked his cereal bowl over, and held his arms up. Dre picked held him up and tossed him in the air three times, and Christian giggled the whole time. Dre was a man of average height, he was stocky and he had skin the color of creamy coffee, with a slight mustache and a short afro, faded around the temple.

Kendall cleaned up the wasted cereal and milk, observing the interaction between Dre and Christian.

Dre asked, "Did you miss, Daddy?" He cut his eye over at Kendall. "Good morning, baby."

"Morning," Kendall replied.

Christian responded with giggles.

Dre sat him back down in the high chair, and Christian was still laughing. When Dre stepped away, he sobbed.

"Daddy ain't going anywhere. I'm just fixing me a plate of food," he said, holding a plate up. Christian realized that Dre wasn't going anywhere and stopped crying. Dre fixed himself a plate of grits, eggs, and turkey bacon, then poured a glass of cranberry juice. He sat down beside Christian, who smiled again with his hands toward wanting Dre to scoop him from the high chair again. Kendall placed another bowl of cereal and a blue Sippy-Cup filled with orange juice in it in front of the toddler.

"Eat your food, Christian." Kendall ordered.

Dre flexed his biceps. "Eat your food so you can grow up big and strong like Daddy."

"Strong." Christian held his arm up and pretended to flex his baby muscles, too.

When Kendall sat down across from him, and the couple made eye contact, she asked, "Where were you last night?"

"You know me, out in the street. Had business to take care of."

"You couldn't answer your phone?" She asked.

"Was it an emergency?"

"No, but I would think a married man with a child would answer his phone if his wife called," his wife snapped.

Dre stuck a spoonful of grits in his mouth, then quickly swallowed. "How do you think shit gets paid around here?"

Kendall rolled her eyes. "Dre, cut the bullshit. We have enough money to last us for years."

"But I can't stopping making money until Christian's kids have money."

"I want us to create a life together."

"Me too, baby! But there is so much more I want for my son. I see the white folks sending their kids to the best school, making the best connections. That's what I want for Christian. I'm just saying." Dre took a swig from his juice.

"How is the deal with the shopping center going?" Kendall asked. Dre had been trying for months to purchase a shopping center on the west side of town.

"We are close to closing on it."

"What is the hold up?"

"Since I work for myself, it's harder to get things they want like bank statements and tax documents and shit."

"So give them your bank statements," she said as if it was the easiest thing in the world.

"I'm going to do that," Dre snapped, "I know what I'm doing."

"Hey, I was just trying to help. That's the problem, Dre. You act like you don't want me to help you anymore."

"I'm sorry, babe, but I know what I'm doing."

He continued to eat his grits as if the conversation never happened. She stood then disappeared into the other room. Dre picked Christian up from his highchair, carried him into his room, and turned on Soul Pancake, a kid friendly YouTube show. When he entered the bedroom, Kendall sat on the edge of the bed crying. She looked up when she saw him.

"You've changed so much, Dre."

Dre sprang to the bed and said "It's not like that, K."

Dre called her K or Ken. Short for Kendall.

She looked up at him. "How long do you think I can take it?"

Dre threw his hands up. "Take what? Take living in luxury? Take buying whatever bag and jewelry you want? Going places you've never even imagined? Driving a Range Rover? Yeah, you live a pretty fucked up life." He laughed.

Kendall stood and pointed at him. "Motherfucka, you really just tried me. Acting like I'm some kind of gold-digger. You know I met you when you didn't have shit. I did not ask for this life. I was with you and you still ain't have shit. Remember we used to buy foodstamps from crackheads?" She paused. "It's crazy how quick motherfuckers forget."

"That's not what I'm saying at all."

"What was the point of you saying that shit then?"

"I'm trying to make sure that we don't ever have to go back to that life of being without."

"We were happy. I was happy with you. Happy when you were selling your little weed and we spent time together. We were inseparable. The money came, and then the baby came, and everything changed."

"You didn't want Christian?"

"Andre, you know damn well that's not what I'm saying. I wanted Christian and many more with you. You're the man I love."

"So *I've* changed?"

"You know all I care about is me, you, and Christian. Material shit don't mean nothing to me."

"You know you don't want to go back in that ratty westside apartment though."

"I don't."

"Well, you have changed too."

Kendall shrugged. "I've always wanted nice things."

"Now, you have them, and you're still bitching."

"Is that what I'm doing?" Kendall was furious.

"Sounds like it to me."

"I won't say a damn thing else then."

"No. I want you to speak your piece."

"Why can't you come in at a decent time? I don't really know if you are fucking around or not, but it sure as hell look like it."

He avoided her eyes.

There was a long silence as she looked at him and waited on him to respond.

Finally, he said, "I'll do better."

CHAPTER 2

Her name was Catherine Smith. Dre had teased her when he first met her, saying that she had the whitest name he'd ever heard. She'd then said, "Maybe because I'm white."

Catherine worked for her father's real estate firm. She grew up in a well to do neighborhood and attended private schools and boarding schools before graduating from the Ivy League school, University of Pennsylvania, with a business degree from the prestigious Wharton Business School. Dre met her as she'd been presenting a townhome, a place he could use as a bachelor pad as he kept the place for his family in the suburbs. He was attracted to her as soon as he saw her. She had a slender but curvy build, with bee-stung lips and straight ivory teeth. Her eye-popping runners legs were highlighted in the heels that she wore that clacked across the hardwood floors. Her boyish short haircut had him pegging her for a feminist lesbian until she said, "I would be so turned on if my man had a place like this."

As she led him into the foyer, he watched her little, perky ass slink up the stairs, thinking "Skinny ass Catherine will get fucked if she made one false move." The townhome was breathtaking, with the cathedral ceilings and private balcony that offered an excellent view of Charlotte. Dre appeared relaxed until she asked for his credit. He frowned. He didn't know about all of that. Kendall had taken care of all of that kind of stuff. They had always used her credit to get what they needed. She knew how to get things on credit. He never needed credit. Dre had millions of dollars of cold hard cash.

Catherine stood with her hands on her hips, a silly ass, naive ass white girl. She smiled very unassuming, and he liked that.

"Look, I don't know how my credit is looking. I haven't used it in a while."

"No problem." Catherine said. "Let's just run it."

She passed him a questionnaire and a black ballpoint pen. He stepped into the kitchen and leaned against the marble island counter to fill out the paperwork. When he passed the application back to Catherine, she snapped a picture of the application with her smart phone and then emailed it to the office. She smiled at him, and his penis awakened. Her nipples peeked through her fuchsia blouse.

She explained, "This will only take five minutes. Glenda, my Dad's secretary, will run your credit and get right back with us."

She sashayed her perky ass across the room and peeked through the window. For the first time in a very long time he had been turned on by a white girl. He imagined what that little frame looked like naked. Catherine Smith was the type of girl that went to Soul Cycle, did Pilates and yoga, ate Greek salads with feta cheese, and drank water with lemon. She was not the kind of white girl who had fucked black men—at least a black man like Dre—but perhaps some cornball nice guy that dressed in khakis and loafers. She turned and caught him staring at her and smiled back, the kind of smile that said "I know you find me attractive but I'm just going to be nice and acknowledge it. But you're not going to get any pussy."

Her phone rang, breaking the pair's unintentional stare-down.

"Glenda." She smiled, nodded twice, and then frowned before ending the call, and she said. "Mr. Walker, I've got some bad news."

"What is it?"

"You don't have any credit. Glenda said it's like you don't exist. I don't understand it. Do you think it's a mistake? Do you think you wrote down the wrong social perhaps?"

"I don't use credit."

Her left eyebrow rose. She tiptoed back across the room and faced him.

"I really want this place. What if I pay for a year in advance?"

She rubbed her chin. "You do realize that's over fifty thousand dollars, right?"

She pulled up her calculator app and punched in a few numbers.

Before she could calculate it, he said, "Its $55,200."

"Good with numbers, I see."

"I'm better with blondes."

She giggled. She didn't find him funny, but it seemed like the polite thing to do. "I mean if you can afford to pay it up for a year, I don't see why not."

She glanced back at the application then her left eyebrow rose. "You own a car wash?"

"A detail shop."

"You know, I've never understood the difference between a car wash and a detail shop. I thought they were the same thing."

"Well that's like saying a gym and a fitness studio is the same thing."

"I suppose so." She paused. "Is that all you do?"

"Yes, why?"

"Only one car wash. I mean 'detail shop.'"

"Yes." He was wondering why this bitch was asking all the questions. Seemingly the same question over and over, all of the questions were about his job. His business. His occupation.

"And you are going to give me fifty thousand dollars to rent a townhome?"

"$55,200."

"Whatever it is. That's a lot of money. You must wash an awful lot of cars."

"Detail."

"Excuse me?"

He laughed, "What are you getting at, Catherine?"

"Hey, listen, I'm not insinuating anything. When can you give me the check?"

"I never said I was going to give you a check."

She smirked and spat out, "Cash?"

"Yes. Is that a problem for you?"

"No, it's just rarely do I see people doing business with that kind of cash nowadays."

He smiled. "You know what they say. Cash is king, right?"

"I guess so."

"Look—" she glanced at the application searching for his name "—Andre, this is not adding up."

"What do you mean?"

"You own one detail shop, and you're going to give me fifty-five thousand dollars in cash. Are you doing something illegal?"

He chuckled, "So you want to racially profile me because I'm black? Ask yourself Catherine Smith." He paused, his words exploding off the walls of the hollow building. "If I were white, would you have asked me all of these questions?"

She thought for a second. And though she knew if he was white, there wouldn't have been extra scrutiny—or perhaps no scrutiny—but he wasn't white. He was a black man that had zero credit, owned a car wash, and had fifty-five thousand dollars in cash to give her to rent a townhome.

"Look, Andre, you're right. I'll rent you the place, but only after a background check."

"Fine."

Two days after he'd submitted his background check, a possession of marijuana charge came up, but it was a misdemeanor and was nothing to be too concerned about. Catherine met with him and he'd given her the cash. She handed him the keys and told him that she needed her car washed and wanted to know the location of the car wash. He responded that it was on the application, then he told her that he would give her a free car wash if she let him take her to lunch.

She was startled at his bold move. What could they possibly have had in common except youth? And though she'd never ever gone out with a black guy, she found Andre attractive, very savvy, and mysterious.

They had gone out three times, and she found him charming. He was surprised that Catherine liked trap music. One night after they left the movies, he asked if she was going to spend the night with him.

"What? I can't spend the night with you. I have to be at work in the morning."

"Bring your clothes. You can shower at my place."

"I'm doing no such thing," she exclaimed, "but I will come by for a few."

Inside the townhome, he offered her a drink. She asked for wine, and he had a bottle of cheap red wine that some girl he'd met had left in the refrigerator. Catherine frowned when she read the bottle, "Santiago 1541."

He knew it was cheap; he'd remembered paying under ten dollars for it.

"Hey, I'm not much of a wine drinker."

"I see," she said stiffly.

She drank the wine and relaxed a little as they sat on his sofa, watching an episode of Game of Thrones. Midway through the show, he leaned toward her and planted a kiss on her lips. Her hands traveled his thigh, and she gripped the hardening bulge in his pants. His tool was thick and rigid. She excited him and knowing this aroused her.

He stood and removed his boxers. His dick swung wildly, and she appreciated his nice rounded chocolate ass and his chiseled body. She'd never been with a black man before, not like this. She'd kissed a guy in college, but he was a black dude that pronounced words like her and was a well-off nerd whose father was a neurosurgeon. Andre was a real black guy that came from the hood and looked and dressed like a rapper.

He motioned for her to follow him into the bedroom. She glanced at her watch knowing she had to be up at seven in the morning. Maybe she'd be late this once.

* * * * *

After they fucked, they were lying in the bed. He was fully exposed, but for a kelly green sheet draped over her tanned legs, her pear-shaped breasts were on full display. She turned to him, and they exchanged smiles. "You know, I've never thought I would be with a black man."

"How was it?"

She smiled. "I don't wanna weird you out, but I'm starting to like you a lot."

"Weird me out?" He laughed.

She smiled. "What's so funny?"

"The way you talk."

She shot him a glare that quickly faltered. "Quit dancing around the subject, Andre."

"What subject?" He knew what she wanted to talk about but didn't know if he was prepared to go there with her.

"I like you."

"And I like you."

"So does that mean we're an item?"

"An item?" He laughed again. "I really gotta get used to your vocab."

She crossed her arms and frowned. "So I guess you just think I'm some dumb, white valley girl that you can hook up with every now and then?"

"Not at all."

"So where do we stand, Andre? I mean, I'm not a whore. I can't be coming through and sleeping with you whenever it's convenient for you."

"I have a confession." He sat up on the bed and avoided her gaze.

"What is it?" She sat up and tried to make eye contact with him.

"I live with a woman."

She laughed. "You're joking right?"

"No." His face was very serious.

Her chest tightened. "What do you mean you live with a woman? You live here alone. That's pretty obvious."

"I have another place. I have a son and wife."

She choked up; there were so many things that she wanted to say but the words wouldn't come, finally tears spilled from her eyes. "You have a wife? What the fuck, Andre? How can you do this to me? You think I'm just going to be some car wash guy's mistress? If you were a billionaire sure, but I'm young. I'm attractive. No way I'm going be your little side boo."

"I'm not asking you to be my mistress."

"I will not continue to sleep with a married man."

"That's not what I'm asking at all."

She stood, slid on her jeans, and beelined to the door, and he trailed her. She stopped at the bedroom door and faced him.

"Andre, I can't be number 2."

"You will not be number 2."

"But I *am* number 2."

"Not for long."

"Is there anything else you want to tell me while I'm here?"

"Yes."

Catherine waited for him to open his mouth again.

"I'm not totally legit."

"What do you mean you're not totally legit? First the wife and kid, now what? I don't understand this."

"I'm a drug dealer."

"A drug dealer? You mean you sell like dime bags of weed?"

"...Not quite."

"What then?"

"Just say it's a little bit more than weed."

"Oh my god! I should have known. The lump sum of cash." She placed her hands over head. "How did I get myself involved in this?" She turned her head before he placed his hand underneath her chin and forced her to face him.

"You like me, right?"

"Of course."

"Help me go legit. I want to invest in real estate. I want to be legal."

Ever since that day, Andre and Catherine had been inseparable, and she even introduced him to her father. John Smith was a tall, thin, fresh-faced man with glasses, who looked to be in his late forties though he was sixty-two. He greeted Andre as they entered the corridor of the massive Victorian home. Catherine had wanted Andre to make an impression on her father so she asked him to dress down. He showed up wearing Stan Smith Adidas, jeans, a black t-shirt, and a jacket.

Her father led them into his study. A book shelf hovered behind his head.

Catherine and Andre sat across from him.

John said, "Cat, you didn't offer Andre anything to drink."

"I'm fine, sir."

"So... You and Cat are friends."

Andre looked at Catherine then back at John. He was not sure how to answer the question, not knowing how this man would react if he knew that he was fucking his daughter like a wild savage.

Catherine interjected, "Yeah we're friends."

"Did you meet in school?"

"Yeah," Catherine repeated.

"No." Andre said.

John lowered his glasses.

"We've known each other since high school, sir."

"Oh."

Dre looked annoyed at the lies in the conversation and said, "Sir, with all due respect, me and Cat are more than friends."

Mr. Smith looked at Catherine. "What is he saying?"

Catherine shrugged. "I guess he's saying that he's my boyfriend."

"Your boyfriend?"

"Yes."

Mr. Smith laughed, "Why didn't you just say so?"

"I didn't know how to tell you." Catherine hung her head.

"Why? Because Andre is black?"

"Exactly."

"Do you think I'm racist, Catherine? Times have changed a lot since my day."

"No, of course not. I just didn't know how you would react."

John smiled at Andre. "I would like a word with my daughter alone if you don't mind."

"No problem," Dre said, then stood, heading for the door.

"You can just go through the double doors in the hallway, and it leads to the den. There is a TV in there if you wanted to keep yourself occupied. We won't be long."

When Andre left the study, Catherine's father hissed, "Are you out of your mind?"

Catherine grimaced and swallowed hard.

"Catherine, you know I don't approve of this shit. Why would you put me on the spot like that? You think I worked this hard for you to send you to these nice schools so you to go off and have some mulatto children with some baboon?"

Catherine gasped, "What the fuck, Daddy! I can't believe you just called Andre a baboon."

"What has gotten into you? Does your mother know about this?"

"Not yet. I thought she would be at home. I planned on introducing Andre to both of you."

"Don't even bother upsetting her with this news."

"I can't believe you're acting like this."

"Believe me, this is not an act."

He stood and asked, "Have you slept with this man?"

"That's none of your business."

"Jesus Christ Catherine, please don't tell me you've slept with that ape, next thing you know you're pregnant then bringing some mulatto child in the world that he's not going to take care of and you're supporting him and the kid."

"Daddy, I can't believe what I'm hearing." She looked at him angrily. "FYI Dre has his own money."

"Dre," He laughed. "Not Connor, or Thomas or Phillip. My daughter's boyfriend's name is Dre and what does "Dre" do for a living?"

"He's owns a chain of car washes, and he's an investor."

Her father knew what that meant immediately. "He's trying to launder money."

Catherine avoided her father's gaze.

"Oh my god Catherine, is this guy doing something illegal?"

"Look, Daddy, it's not like everybody that comes to us to do business is on the up and up."

John asked, "What are you talking about?"

"What about Filepe Torres?"

"What about him?"

"Have you'd forgotten that we'd counted 1.8 million dollars in cash when I was eighteen. Who has that kind of money?"

"That monkey certainly doesn't have that kind of money, so I don't know if dealing with him is worth it."

"First of all, he's not a monkey, and he has more money than you think."

"He's doesn't have Filepe Torres money."

"You want to bet? Possibly more."

Mr. Smith's eyebrows raised. "Oh really?"

The next day, Dre visited John Smith's office dressed more casually than he'd been before. John stood and shook his hand, then offered him a cup of coffee, which Andre declined. "Cat tells me that you have money that you want to invest."

"I do."

John Smith stood and walked around the rich mahogany grained desk, approached Dre, and frisked him.

Dre jerked away from the man. "What the hell are you doing?"

"I'm just trying to make sure I'm safe."

Dre laughed. "You think I'm bugged?"

"I don't know you."

Dre was wearing a black t-shirt with Drake's face plastered across the front. He raised his t-shirt and rolled his eyes.

John relaxed a little then resumed his position on the other side of the desk.

"My daughter likes you."

"And I like her, I like her a lot."

"What do you want from us?"

"I'm not after your money, but I was just thinking that you could help me go legitimate."

"What do you mean go legitimate?" He paused, then picked up a Mont Blank pen, passed it to Dre, and shoved a yellow legal pad to Dre's side of the desk.

"What is this for?"

"I need you to write down how much money you're trying to invest."

"Why do you want me to write it down? Can't I just tell you?"

"Can you do what I asked, please?"

Dre scribbled a number then pushed it back to the other side of the desk.

John Smith yelped, then his mouth flew open. "You have 4.5 million dollars in cash?"

"Yeah," Dre replied, now wondering why he'd asked him to write the figure, down if he was going to turn around and blurt it out.

John Smith stood and started pacing before he sat back down. Then, he'd made eye contact with Dre. "How old are you, son?"

"I just turned 30."

"Why do you want to invest this? I'm sure this is not all you have."

"I don't understand."

"You're already a millionaire."

"I know, but I don't like my career. Do you understand? Plus there was this shopping center that I was trying to purchase, but I couldn't prove my income in order to buy it."

"I can imagine. Why don't you just get a job?"

"I don't want a job. A job wouldn't enable me to buy the property. Why don't you get a job?" John Smith let out a hardy chuckle.

John Smith was perspiring, and he was trying his best not to look nervous, while analyzing Andre at the same time. "Look, I don't want to know where you get your money. Don't ever tell me and don't tell Cat."

"Cat ain't all up on my business like that."

"Keep it that way."

"I plan to."

"Don't just plan to. Make sure you don't tell her shit. I don't even want her to know what I plan to do with you. Do you understand?"

"Yes."

"Do you really understand?"

What else was there to understand? "Yes."

"You realize that we both can be charged with U.S.C. 1956, right?"

"What the hell is that?"

"The money laundering statute."

"Sounds serious. I mean, when you say the statute and all."

"It sounds serious because it is serious, son."

"I understand. I have a friend with the feds right now," Dre said as he thought about Carlos.

"What's he in there for?"

"I'm not sure." Dre lied, but that was none of John's business.

"But it doesn't have anything to do with you?"

"It doesn't. I'm sure of that."

"Good." John Smith settled back down in chair before snatching up the pen, stuck it into his mouth, then removed it. He scribbled on the legal pad, then scratched out the 4.5 million dollar figure.

"So what did you have in mind?"

"I wanted to invest in commercial real estate. That's where I heard the money is."

"I have better idea."

"What is it?"

"You're going to start a company that specializes in fixer uppers, and you're going to buy a series of fixer uppers and invest in REITS. Then I will use some of the money to invest in affordable housing. I will write you a check at the end of the year for your investments, and you can slowly show how you have profited. There is no way that I can take that 4.5 million and double it. But I'm sure we can give you ten percent return on your money—about 450,000 dollars a year."

"Wait a minute? I give you $4.5 million, and you give me $450,000?"

"That is the return. The profit. You will still have your 4.5 million. I will give it back to you at any time with advance notice."

"Okay."

"This will be legitimate income. You will be making $450,000 dollars a year. Andre, this is not the drug business; this is great money for the average person."

"I know." Dre laughed. "I came from nothing."

"Me too."

"Really?"

"I married up. I came from a small town right outside of Greenville, South Carolina. I got lucky enough to meet Cat's mother, and her father was a real estate tycoon. He taught me all I know."

"Oh yeah?"

"Listen, we have to be careful."

"I understand."

"Don't tell Cat shit about this."

"You have my word."

The men shook hands.

CHAPTER 3

Christian was at the park with the nanny. Kendall was cleaning the interior of her Range Rover as she often had to do; she had a toddler for Christ's sake. McDonald's French fries, action figures, and Legos blanketed the floor. She gathered most of it and stuffed in a Hefty bag. When she slid the seat up searching for more Legos, she stumbled upon a greeting card scented with J'Adore by Christian Dior—the same scent that had been on Andre's shirt. She sat the trash bag down on the floor and disappeared into the kitchen to read the note.

Last night was amazing, then again, every day is amazing. I can still feel your hands around my waist. I love the way you manhandled me, the way you made love to me, the way you whispered you love me, and the way that you treat me. I've never had a man give me the attention that you give me—the right kind of attention. I love you. Every day is amazing. I can't imagine life getting much better than it is now. I can't wait to spend the rest of my life with you. Who knew that when I showed up to show you the townhouse that it would be the start of something magical? Who knew that the same townhome I rented you would be the one where we share so many amazing memories. I can't wait to become your wife, the future Mrs. Walker. I know we will make each other happy and I can't wait to meet Christian. I just know he's going to like me. I love you so much, beloved. Happy birthday. And I hope to spend the next birthday as a couple, a real couple.

Kendall gasped. She didn't want to believe what she'd just read, but she knew it in her soul that he was stepping outside of the relationship. A woman always knew; this just confirmed it. She felt that something was wrong, and her intuition was right. She hated that she had been right. Thinking it was one thing, but reading intimate details of the affair was like someone had taken a machete, stabbed her in the chest, and ripped her heart out.

She glanced at the fuchsia-colored lipstick plastered on the inside of the card, then sniffed the it. The perfumed lingered, and she was reminded of his hour-long showers at four in the morning. Who the hell was this Catherine bitch? What did she have on her? Why was she trying to steal her man? And why in the fuck was she mentioning her son? There was only one way she could have known: Andre had been running his mouth about her and Christian. She was sure of that. Otherwise, the bitch would not be alluding to his next birthday. By that time, Andre would have dumped her, and Catherine could be Mrs. Walker.

She stepped into her bedroom and plopped down on the bed. She sunk into the mattress and covered her face. She was too stunned to cry; she just laid on the bed, her head spinning with so many unanswered questions, and she was sure that she was not going to get any truth from Andre. Determined not to cry, she bounced from her bed and searched for her cell phone, then she remembered it was on the kitchen table. She called Dre.

He answered, "Hello."

She didn't bother with the niceties. "Who the fuck is Catherine?"

"Who?"

"Catherine Smith."

"I'm on my way home."

Kendall wanted to kill Dre's ass. It had taken him fifteen minutes to get home, and as soon as he walked in the door, she demanded again, "Who the fuck is Catherine Smith?"

Dre looked confused.

"Don't play dumb, motherfucker."

"I'm not playing dumb. That name don't ring a bell."

"Dre, you've been fucking Catherine Smith. I read the fucking birthday card. Now you can stop acting stupid."

"Oh, Catherine. I didn't know her last name was Smith."

"Who the fuck is she?"

"Just someone I had sex with."

"You say that shit very nonchalantly." She shoved him and removed the engagement ring and wedding band and slung them at him. "Don't come near me, Dre. I want to know one thing, and the only thing that you need to be answering is: who in the fuck is she?"

"It's not what you think."

"And what the fuck do I think?"

"Catherine means nothing to me."

"First, you didn't know what I was talking about. Now she means nothing to you." Kendall picked up the card from the counter, held it to her face, and began to read it. "'Last night was amazing, but then again, every day is amazing.'"

Dre tried to yank the card, but she was too fast for him.

"Don't snatch a motherfuckin thang from my hand, you punk bitch."

He inched toward her, and she snatched an empty wine bottle from the counter and cocked it back, waiting to throw it. "Don't come near me motherfucka."

"You called me over here to talk, but you don't want to talk."

"I called you. I didn't ask you to come home. You decided to come home. Furthermore, it's too late to talk unless you want to tell me about this secret home that you and Catherine got together."

"What are you talking about?"

Dre bit his bottom lip. What the fuck did the card say? How did she know that? He had only glanced at the card briefly; Catherine was always giving him cards that he never bothered to read.

"And for the record. Catherine will never get to meet my son. So tell your little girlfriend it ain't happening."

"You are overreacting to a situation that is nothing."

"Look Dre, I preferred that you were faithful, but I think I could deal with you fucking a chick and moving on—a one night stand—but this girl has clearly been around for a while. You have feelings for her."

Dre bowed his head. She was right. He did have feelings for Catherine, but there was no way in the hell he was going to admit that right now. Kendall would kill him.

"So you are going to tell me how I feel about another person? Like you know what I feel better than me?"

"You like the woman."

"I love you, Ken."

"'I love you, Ken' my ass, I don't want to hear that shit. Dre, you are pissing me the fuck off."

Dre tried to inch closer, but Kendall held her hand up like a stop sign.

"Stop it boy. I can read, this was written by a woman that is in love."

"But I'm not in love with her."

"Who is she?"

"A realtor I use to get rentals. She accepts cash, so it was easier for me to rent there."

"What kind of place? Spaces where you go fuck other chicks?"

He sat down, and he shifted in his seat before lowering his gaze. He was trying to think of an answer to her question. A good lie.

"Why is this the first time I'm hearing about these rentals?"

He sighed, they made eye contact briefly before he looked away. "They stash houses, and you didn't need to know about them. I just wanted to keep you out of it just in case something happened to me. I didn't want you involved." He paused, then he looked away again. "We have a son, and I can't risk both your lives by letting you know too much."

What he said made perfect sense, but Catherine Smith was in love with him. She couldn't let that rest.

"Did you sleep with this Catherine person?"

"Huh?"

"Did you fuck Catherine, Dre?"

"No."

"A few minutes ago, you told me you did."

"Yeah, I slept with her, but it meant nothing."

"You're lying."

"Fuck you, Dre, and I want you to get the hell out of this house."

He laughed, "You want me to get out of a house that I pay for? Try again."

"If you don't leave, me and Christian are leaving."

"Look—"

The doorbell rang, and Kendall scurried to answer. It was Miss. Ortiz, the nanny. Miss Ortiz was a short rotund woman with a button nose and horn-rimmed glasses. She could pass for a librarian. Christian seemed to like her, but what Kendall liked most about her was that she taught Christian basic Spanish.

Kendall grinned when she saw Christian, who was wearing blue and white shorts and was holding tightly onto a big red balloon.

"Did you behave yourself today, son?"

"I was good, Mommy."

Kendall looked at Miss Ortiz, who nodded. "He was good, and he learned to count to ten in Spanish."

Christian spotted Dre and ran into his daddy's arms. "I missed you, Daddy."

Dre kissed his son and said, "Daddy missed you too." Then he turned to Kendall and asked, "You still want me to leave?"

"Yes, I want you to go and go right now."

* * * * *

The next day, Kendall dropped Christian off at her mother's, then she called Chrissy, who had called in sick from work, not because she actually was, but because she hated the petty customer service job. Kendall spoke briefly about the conversation between her and Dre and drove to Chrissy's house.

When Kendall entered the house, Chrissy hugged her. A man named Cato was there. Cato was a tall, thin, coal-colored man with nappy locs. Cato trailed Chrissy from the kitchen carrying a bottle of Hennessy in a brown paper bag. He offered to pour Kendall a shot of liquor, but she declined. The three of them sat in Chrissy's small living room.

Kendall looked at Cato. "I didn't know you were going to be here."

"I was in the neighborhood and just dropped by."

"With a bottle of Henny at 1pm? What the fuck? Who drinks in the middle of the day?"

Cato smiled. "I'm what you call a good friend."

Chrissy looked between them and sensed that Kendall wanted to speak to her alone. She turned to Cato and sweetly asked, "Can you come back later? Me and Ken want to have a girl chat."

Cato stood. "Hell, I ain't want to share my drank in the first place."

"He can stay. I want to hear what he has to say about the situation. Since he's a man," Kendall spat.

Cato sat back down and smirked. "I'll be glad to offer my expertise." He unscrewed the top and sipped it before sitting it on the coffee table.

Chrissy frowned.

"Hell, y'all didn't want any, so I'm drinking it from the bottle." He turned to Kendall and asked, "What happened, Ken?"

"Same ole shit! Niggas don't know how to act when they have a good woman. This shit has been going on since the bible days."

Cato laughed, "When are y'all going to learn? We really ain't shit."

"Y'all really ain't," Chrissy agreed.

A pensive expression covered Kendall's face. "Seriously. I found out Dre been running around on me, and I put him out, but I feel bad because now my son is separated from his father, so I don't really know if it's the right thing to do."

Cato took another swig from the liquor before sucking his teeth. "You got proof or is this just speculation?"

"I found a birthday card from another woman."

"That don't mean shit. Dre is getting paid. Of course women are going to try go get at him." Cato shrugged.

"But Dre admitted it."

Cato spat out the liquor.

"Oh hell no nigga, you ain't going to spit all over my furniture," Chrissy hissed.

Cato removed a hundred-dollar bill from his pocket and tossed it on the table.

"I don't want yo petty ass hundred dollars." she lied. "Don't you dare spit on my shit." She scooped the hundred, stuffing it into her bra anyways.

Cato then turned back to Kendall. "I wouldn't have admitted to shit."

Kendall and Chrissy both wished he would shut the fuck up, but Kendall did ask him to stay.

"Dre had some bullshit excuse for that. Said the woman helped him get rentals and shit. Saying it was nothing to it."

"Maybe it was nothing," Cato said.

"If you would shut up and let me finish." She sighed. "I told you I found a card from her..."

"Who?"

"Catherine."

"What kind of name is that? Does she spell it with a C or a K?"

"C. Why?"

"Is she white?" Cato asked.

"I don't think so. Why do you ask?"

"I don't know any black chicks named Catherine."

"Janet Jackson's mother's name is Catherine."

"No, that was Katherine with a K, and she's old as fuck. I suppose back in the day, they named black girls Catherine and Margaret and Annie and shit like that. 'Iont know nobody named Catherine that was born after '85."

They laughed their asses off.

"What did the card say?" Cato asked, getting back to the matter at hand.

"She was saying shit like she had an amazing time with him last night and how she always enjoyed being with him. She proclaimed her love for him and how she couldn't wait to meet my son and how she looked forward to living a life with him."

"Damn, shawty." Cato said. "I'm sorry, I mean I talk a lot of shit, but you know you are my homegirl. I'm sure that shit must have hurt."

"Damn right it hurt, but don't feel sorry for me. I just hate that I have a son by this man and I can't get my time back, but I'll be okay. It's my son that I'm worried about. He idolizes this man that ain't shit. Clearly not the man that I thought he was."

"The good thing is that your son is so young. I think he can get used to not seeing his daddy right now. Trust me, it would be a lot harder if he was seven or eight." Cato said.

"Yeah, but how long can I tell him his daddy is at work?" She paused. "You know what he told me the other day? He said 'I don't want Daddy to go to work' and 'Daddy is like a grandma.'"

Cato and Chrissy looked confused.

"I think what he was saying in his own little way was that he sees his Daddy as much as he sees his Grandma." She made eye contact with Chrissy again. "I don't think you understand. His daddy is his best friend."

"As with all boys," Cato noted.

"I don't give a damn about all boys. I'm just worried about my son and when he realizes that we are not together."

"He's three, he'll be fine," Chrissy said.

"You don't understand—"

"I know I don't have kids—you keep telling me that all the time—but you only have one, and you have only been a parent three years. So how much more about parenting can you possibly know than me?"

Kendall cut her eyes at Cato, who had four kids by three different women.

"She is right. A bond between a father and son is sacred. And that is the worst part about not being with any of my baby mamas—I don't wake up to my kids." Cato added.

Kendall paused. She wanted to curse Chrissy the fuck out, but she knew her friend was only trying to be helpful. She knew she was right, but that didn't make her feel better.

"So who is Catherine?"

"I don't know anything about her."

Cato took another drink. "I bet she's white."

"I just assumed she's black. I don't know what color she is. All I know is that she is a real estate agent, she wears J'Adore by Christian Dior and she paints her lips."

"I love that perfume," Chrissy interjected.

Kendall frowned.

"Catherine, the real estate agent... Well that could be every other woman in Charlotte."

"Exactly."

"Pull his phone record."

"He has two, and one is a burner."

"What?"

Kendall frowned. "Dre is a hustler."

"So you think he called her on his work phone? You think Catherine knows that he is a hustler?"

"I don't know any of that," Kendall said, staring at Chrissy.

"Are you two on the same phone plan?"

"We are."

"Well, maybe he's called her."

"I'm sure he's called her."

Cato spoke for the first time in a while, "He damn sure ain't called her ass on his work phone."

"How do you know that?" Chrissy asked.

"Cuz I'm a hustler, and I got a work phone. I ain't calling no chick that don't know what I'm up to on my burner."

"Is that what you call what you are doing? Hustling?" Chrissy asked.

Cato removed a roll of money with two crisp one hundred dollar bills over a wad of one dollar bills. "I got money."

"Bruh, you call that hustling? You sell grams of loud, and you are still staying at yo' mama house!"

"I gets my money." Cato said. He stuffed the bills back into his pockets."

Kendall and Chrissy laughed.

Kendall became serious. "What are you thinking?"

"How do you know I'm thinking anything?"

"Bitch, I'm your best friend, I know that look."

Chrissy laughed, then offered, "Maybe—maybe—you should pull the phone record to see all the numbers that he has been in contact with repeatedly."

"Bitches are so damn scandalous," Cato said.

"I'm getting cheated on, and I'm scandalous." Kendall scoffed.

"That is just how warped his thinking is. Men are just selfish."

"I'm always a step ahead of the game. That's why I got my own phone. No plan with a woman. For snoops like y'all."

"Bruh, you got a thirty-five dollar a month Metro PCS plan."

"A phone is a phone. When you call me on that Verizon phone, my phone does the same shit yours do, but I'm smart cuz I ain't paying but thirty-five dollars a month."

"You damn kingpin, you," Kendall laughed.

"You can laugh all you want, but it's called 'wealth building.'"

"Whatever, bruh, you act like you're one of those dudes on *Narcos*."

Chrissy disappeared into her bedroom, returned with her laptop, passing it over to Kendall, and ordered, "Pull the phone record up."

Kendall did as she was told. She logged into her Verizon account and pulled up the phone record and examined the record looking for repeat numbers.

Cato sat on the sofa, flipping through pics of thick Latinas with fake asses on Instagram.

There were two numbers that he called over and over that Kendall did not recognize and she scribbled the numbers down.

Kendall's heart raced as she asked, "What do we do next, Chrissy?"

"We have two options."

Before Chrissy could explain further, Kendall cut her off. "I'm not calling that woman, do you realize how desperate that will make me look?"

Cato looked up from his phone and said, "Yo, just let it go. You might find out something that you ain't prepared to handle."

"Gimme one reason she should let it go?" Chrissy demanded.

"Because she said that she has already broken up with him. He has left the home already. Do you think this shit is going to make her feel better? Trust me, she's going to feel much worse once she knows for sure that Dre's been lying to her."

"She deserves to know who Catherine is. Why are you defending this, Cato? You're supposed to be our homeboy."

"I'm *your* homeboy. Kendall said she wanted a man's perspective, and I'm just telling her not to go looking for something that she ain't prepared to deal with."

Kendall ignored Cato and turned her attention to Chrissy. "What are my options?"

"Well since the first option is out the window, we need to just use people finder to find out who these numbers belong to."

"What's people finder?"

"There is a service online that you can use to find out who the numbers belong to. It costs twenty dollars."

"Let's do it," Kendall quickly agreed.

Chrissy logged into her account. She'd used the service plenty of times to find out the background of men that she had met on Tinder and Bumble. After she logged in, she gave them permission to run her credit card, and seconds later, there was a match for the number: "John Smith."

She looked at Kendall and asked, "Do you know who this man is?"

"I have no idea. Hell, I have no idea who Catherine is either."

Cato glanced over Chrissy's shoulder. "Damn, dude is white. I told you Catherine is white."

"No fucking shit," Chrissy spat.

"Bruh really is kicking it with a snow bunny," Cato laughed.

"Maybe this is the guy that he was partnering with to buy the shopping center. I don't know. He had told me about some guy that was supposed to be his partner. There has to be a reason."

"Call the damn number and if its a man that answers the phone. Just tell him that you have the wrong number. "

"I don't want to." Kendall said.

Chrissy dialed the number for her and waited for someone to answer.

"Smith Realty. Joanne speaking, how may I direct your call?"

"Can I speak to Catherine, please?" Chrissy asked.

"Catherine stepped out of the office for a few. May I ask who's calling?"

"When do you expect her to return?" Chrissy asked, ignoring Joanne's request.

"She should be back around two," Joanne replied, "Do you have her cell phone number?"

"No. Can you give it to me? If you could, that would be awesome," Chrissy said.

Joanne rattled off the number—the same number as the second number. Just as they had suspected.

"Thank you, I just have one more question."

"Yes?"

"What is Catherine's last name?"

"Smith, just like the owner of the firm." Joanne thought it was a weird question, but shook the thought quickly out of her head.

"Thanks Joanne, you're the best."

Chrissy terminated the call before Joanne could say anything else.

Cato chuckled, "Damn, that was a bad white bitch right there."

Chrissy and Kendall raised their eyebrows at him. Kendall spat, "Boy what the hell are you talking about?"

"I'm talking about Chrissy's white woman voice. Damn, I didn't even know who the fuck you was, you were talking so goddamned proper."

The girls busted out laughing. "Look, you have to play the game. Gotta be versatile in this white man's world."

Kendall fumed inside. Just imagining Dre leaving her for a white girl had her very uneasy.

"Dre don't look like the kind that would fuck with a white girl," Chrissy said, as if reading Kendall's mind.

Cato said, "Have you seen these white bitches nowadays? These ain't the white girls that your granddaddy used to see. They got lots of ass." He took a swig of liquor then said "Google Catherine Smith and let's see what comes up."

Chrissy googled Catherine. There were twenty-four people on LinkedIn alone with Catherine Smith's name.

Chrissy then googled "Catherine Smith real estate agency."

The first result that came up was a Catherine Smith from Amhurst, Massachusetts. The next Catherine Smith was of Huntersville, North

Carolina. The link led to a headshot of a pretty blonde with ice blue eyes and sparkling teeth.

Chrissy looked at Kendall. "Do you think it's her?"

"Has to be," Kendall said faintly, and the reality that her man, in fact had been seeking a white woman made the situation worse.

"So what are you going to do?" Chrissy asked.

Kendall pretended it didn't bother her, but Chrissy knew it did and embraced her.

"There is nothing else to do," Kendall said dully. "I asked him to leave and he did."

Cato said, "I know you wanna kill her, but you have to admit that is one beautiful white girl. I wonder what that body look like."

"Probably some skinny ass white chick that does Pilates," Chrissy said.

Kendall tried her best to keep a straight face. "She has Dre."

"Dre lost on this one," Chrissy said trying to make her friend feel better.

"Maybe it ain't about the looks. Maybe she's submissive. Maybe she brings brains to the table. Maybe she doesn't nag," Cato said.

"Typical ass black man in 2018." Chrissy said, cutting her eyes at Cato. "What the fuck are you saying? Are you saying Ken don't have brains?"

"Look, I'm not saying that at all." Cato put his hands up in defense. "I'm just trying to think of why he might have started fucking with her in the first place. I'm on your side, home girl."

"I'm not mad at you, but it's unfortunate that this is how society has brainwashed black men to think that all black women do is nag and complain and make black men's lives hard. And we don't have brains? What the fuck?"

Catherine Smith's Instagram page was private, but they found her on Facebook, and they scrolled down her page. The first thing they saw was John Smith, the owner of the real estate agency.

There were a few more public pictures on her wall of her holding a yoga mat, and then there was a slice of carrot cake with a single candle, captioned "Happy birthday to Bae. You are indeed an amazing man." There were no pics of the two together. A girl named Bethany Hobbs commented "When are we going to get to meet Andre?"

Kendall covered her eyes. Bethany Hobbs' words stung, and the words made her nightmare real. Andre and Catherine Smith were in a real relationship.

* * * * *

Carlos Jacobs was Puerto Rican and black, and he spoke fluent Spanish because of his summers in Puerto Rico, where his father's side of the family had lived. After the summer, he came back to live with his mother, in the Clanton Park neighborhood, a primarily black neighborhood. Carlos had been in and out of reform schools as an adolescent for petty drug charges. When he was eighteen, he'd gotten locked up for assault and battery with intent to kill, but those charges were later dismissed, because the witness didn't show up for court but instead was seen in Miami vacationing according to his Instagram photos. While in jail Carlos had befriended a Mexican Cartel member named Jesus, who had been arrested for international drug trafficking and guns.

Inside Pod 3B, Jesus was the only Mexican, and he'd spoken little English. Weeks went by before he'd gotten any money on his books. During his time of being broke and destitute, he'd been unsuccessful in begging his fellow inmates to buy him any snacks from the commissary—or even hygiene products for that matter—until Carlos was assigned to the pod. Carlos shared his Jack Mackerel, crackers, and soups and bought Jesus deodorant and soap.

When Jesus' money finally arrived from Mexico, he paid Carlos back, and two days later, he'd had Carlos bonded out. A week after that, Jesus had sent 21 kilos to Carlos because Jesus' only child had just turned twenty-one, and he'd hoped this would bring Carlos good luck. Jesus got sentenced to life in prison but arranged for Carlos to keep the connect. And the good fortune Jesus wished for his friend had come to pass; Carlos had been successful for six years, making a lot of money in the drug business. He bought car lots, night clubs, and land.

He had made millions of dollars, and he was on a yacht in Miami when the feds rolled up beside him and arrested everyone. Carlos was then flown to Charlotte and charged with drug conspiracy. He passed his connect on to a friend named Dre, who'd grown up in his neighborhood in exchange for a percentage of his profits. He'd shelled out almost three hundred thousand dollars in legal fees and he plead to ten years. The Obama administration reduced his sentence going into his fifth year, giving him a 2018 release date. Now Carlos was a free man. His first order of business was to find out where Dre was so he could collect the money he was owed. During the first two years of his incarceration, Dre had been faithful giving him ten percent of the profits, but after that, Dre changed his number and Carlos hadn't heard from him. After going to the old neighborhood barbershop, he'd learned that Dre had lived out in Ballantyne. He'd found the address online by doing a search on Kendall's last name. He rang the bell of their sprawling Mediterranean style home.

Kendall appeared wearing workout tights and sports bra and New Balance running shoes.

She stepped back, she was startled at first but when she realized that it was Carlos, they exchanged smiles as he tried his very best not to stare at her camel toe, but it was very hard not to stare; hell he'd been locked up without pussy for five years.

She hugged him, and he held onto her for a long time inhaling her fragrance, which had taken him back to the flamboyant trees in Puerto Rico.

Just that fast, his dick had sprung to life and he wanted her. He wanted her right now.

Before she could feel it, he released her and smiled.

She invited him in. She didn't offer him a seat so they stood in the living room.

He commented, "Looks like you're about to hit the gym."

"Trying to motivate myself. I don't go enough. She laughed "But look at you, you're all muscle, Carlos."

"Yeah, it's very easy to be all muscle in a place like that."

"I didn't know you were out."

"Obama freed me. Well, he cut my time." Carlos shrugged.

"Good, I'm glad to see you out."

"Glad to be out." Carlos scanned the luxurious home filled beautiful black and white photography and he remembered he'd once had all these things.

"Where is Dre?"

"Did you call him?"

"I don't have his number."

Kendall's mouth flew open. "You don't have his number?"

"Ken, I haven't had Dre's number for the last two years. I know you know that. I've written him and tried to email him. He doesn't respond to me. I guess money changes people."

"Tell me about it," Kendall muttered.

Carlos raised his eyebrow. "What is that supposed to mean?"

"Dre's changed that's all."

"Can you call him?"

She dialed the number she had for him, and it went straight to voicemail.

"Can I have his number?"

Kendall didn't know how to respond. Obviously, Dre was avoiding Carlos, but she wondered why. She was no fool; she knew Carlos was the reason they were living so lavish. If he hadn't given Dre the connect, God knows where they would be. She rattled off the phone number, and Carlos punched the number into his Boost mobile phone.

"Thanks, Ken."

"No problem."

Carlos turned to walk away, but before he reached the door, he turned and faced Kendall. "Ken can you do me a favor?"

"What is it, Carlos?"

"Can you drop me off at the bus stop. The nearest one is about a mile. I don't have my license yet. I mean if you're going that way, that would help me out a lot."

"Yeah, I'll take you."

Carlos hopped in the passenger side of the Range Rover, and he occasionally glanced over at Kendall's thighs, trying his best not to be creepy. Kendall really wasn't his type, but he'd fuck her right now if he got the chance. Her thighs were turning him the fuck on. Before he'd left, he would have never thought of fucking with a friend's woman, but Dre had not paid him his dues for the last two and a half years. He'd certainly fuck Kendall for that.

"Carlos," Kendall said and snapped Carlos out of his dream of fucking her doggy-style.

His eyes rose from her thighs and he made eye contact with her. "Yeah, what's up Ken?"

"Do you and Dre have a problem?"

"Oh no. Well, not that I know of."

"So why is he avoiding you?"

"I don't know. I thought I was his friend."

"Does he owe you some money?"

"Ken, now you know it's total disrespect for me to discuss a man's business with his woman."

"I see," she said sharply.

Kendall approached the bus stop, then dug into her purse and handed Carlos a wad of 15 one-hundred dollar bills."

He swallowed hard.

She smiled. "Just a little something to help you get on your feet."

She stopped at the bus stop and hugged Carlos again, and he inhaled the scent of her perfume. It was good for him to be inhaling the scent of a woman again. He held onto Kendall for a long time. After a while, he let go of her.

"Ken." He hopped out of the car and stole one last look at her inviting thighs. "You're a real one. Dre is lucky to have you."

"He doesn't think so."

He closed the door.

Kendall rolled down the window and bid him farewell. "Good to see you, Carlos. You take care of yourself."

Kendall telephoned Dre and informed him that Carlos was looking for him.

CHAPTER 4

Two days later, Carlos paid his barber, TaTa, two hundred dollars to tell him the next time Dre visited the barbershop. The very next Saturday, TaTa called saying that Dre was inside the barbershop. Carlos hustled up to the barbershop and peeked inside, and Dre was sitting in the chair, so Carlos waited outside smoking an E-cigarette occasionally glancing inside as TaTa trimmed Dre's head.

TaTa and Timmy, another barber, argued about who was the highest scorer in NBA history.

"I'm telling you," TaTa said. "Jordan is the leading scorer."

"Naw, bruh. I'm telling you, Kareem is the highest scorer."

"What do you think, Dre?" TaTa asked.

"I don't know. Probably some old school ass baller before our time, like Bill Russell or Wilt Chamberlin. I really don't know."

"Google it, nigga," Timmy suggested.

"Okay," TaTa agreed. "I'll google it."

He stopped cutting Dre's head. Dre was getting annoyed as hell, but this was the kind of shit that went on weekly in the barbershop. TaTa googled it only to find out it was Kareem. "Tim, you were right."

"I know my stats," Timmy said. He was a short fat man who looked like he'd never dribbled a ball in his life.

A half hour later, Dre stood, paid TaTa, and headed out of the door. When he walked around the corner, Carlos approached him. "If it isn't the world famous Dre."

Dre stepped back, startled, but he tried his best not to look surprised.

"Hey, Andre."

"Los." Dre nodded.

"Yup it's me in the flesh."

"Ken told me you were home."

Carlos inhaled the cigarette, then continued, "I'm sure she did, but it didn't seem like you wanted to hear from me. You didn't try to get in touch with me."

"I've been busy."

"I'm sure you have." He paused then took another drag from the E-cig. "I haven't heard from you since the third year of my bid."

"Hey man, you know I don't like talking on the fed phones."

"I don't blame you."

Dre looked over his shoulder and wondered who in the fuck told Carlos he was in the barbershop, before deciding it could have been anyone or it could have been nobody. They were all from the same neighborhood, and this could have been clearly coincidence.

Dre asked, "Can we talk in the car?"

"Sure."

Carlos and Dre got into Dre's Maserati.

"Doing well for yourself."

"Yeah. Thanks to you."

"Thanks to who?"

"Thanks to you."

"I thought you forgot."

"Oh no. How could I forget that?"

"Well I haven't been paid in three years."

"I know."

"Why not?"

"I don't know."

"Dre, you know that I'm no pussy."

"I know."

"So you know what that means."

"No."

"Look, I want my money. That's all I'm here for."

"You'll get it."

"Well, I estimate on the low end, you made at least ten million dollars in the last two years, but I'm sure it was more than that. Either way, I will settle for a million dollars and be on my merry way."

"A million?"

"Come on, Dre. I plugged you with the fucking cartel. Give me a million, and we're good. I'll never fuck with you, but at least there won't be any blood shed amongst two neighborhood friends you feel me?"

"Give me a week and I'll get you half of the money, then in another two weeks, I'll give you the other half."

"You need a month?"

"Yeah." Dre said, avoiding eye contact with Carlos.

Carlos lowered the heat. "This thing heats up really fast."

"Yeah," Dre said lamely.

"So you really need a month?"

"Is that a problem?"

"Not at all." He shook Dre's hand, sealing the deal. "What's your phone number?"

"704-909-0900."

Carlos removed his cell phone and dialed the number, and Dre's phone rang.

"Lock my number in."

* * * * *

Dre had called to ask if he could come over and bring Christian a puppy. Kendall agreed. Dre entered the home, and Kendall made a beeline for him. "Catherine Smith is white," she said.

Dre took a step backward. "What?" He yanked the leash on the tiny brown and white beagle then closed the door shut and sat on the love chair.

"Stand up."

He stood and shrugged.

"You don't live here."

"I can't sit down?"

46

He was rubbing the now panting beagle's head and said "Don't worry, Lad. It's not you that's not welcome; it's me."

"You damn right it's you."

"Where is Christian?"

"He is in his bedroom, watching a show on Netflix."

"Can you get him for me?"

The pup jerked the leash.

"So Catherine Smith is white?"

Dre kneeled and took a hold of the beagle. Dre was stalling. How was he going to respond to the question when it was obvious that she already knew that Catherine was white?

"Will you answer the question, Andre?"

"What question?"

"Catherine Smith is a white girl."

"You know this already, Ken."

"You cheated on me with a white girl? You're so fucking pathetic."

"Its about business, that's all it is."

Her nostrils flared. "I'm supposed to be stupid? Catherine Smith is the naive little white girl, not me."

"I've told you that we're networking," he said, clenching his jaw.

"Her and her rich ass daddy."

"Can I give my son his puppy?" He inched toward Christian's bedroom. Kendall stepped in front of him, cutting him off.

Dre sat the puppy on the floor and said, "Move, Ken." He lowered his voice. "I still pay all the bills here."

"I can pay my own shit as a matter of fact. I don't want you to pay nothing."

"If I don't pay shit here, who is going to pay? Where are you going to go?"

"I'll go to my mother's house."

"Can I give my son the puppy?"

"Leave, Dre." Kendall spat. "How is he supposed to keep up with this stupid dog anyway?"

"The dog collar has G.P.S." He passed her some paperwork that would teach her how to pair it with her phone.

"And if I don't?"

"I'll call the police."

"You wouldn't do that."

"Don't try me, Andre. I'm not the one to play with right about now."

"So you would actually try to get me arrested in front of my son?" He laughed. "But what are you going to call the police for? I live here. I have clothes here. There is nothing they can do to me."

Kendall froze; she really didn't want Christian to have a memory of the police escorting Dre away in handcuffs.

Dre yelled. "Christian!"

The sound of his father's voice had Christian sprinting from his room. The puppy scurried and scratched the floor. His face lit up and he barreled into his daddy's arms. Then he asked if he could play with the puppy."

"This is your puppy. Daddy bought it for you."

"My puppy?"

"Yeah it's your puppy, and his name is Lad. Unless you want to name him something else."

"I'm calling him Frank."

"Frank?" Dre laughed. "Why Frank?"

"My granddaddy's name is Frank."

"Your granddaddy's name is not Frank."

Kendall interjected. "He's talking about my daddy's daddy. I showed him a picture of him the other day."

Dre laughed "Well his name is Frank, and he is your dog, son, and you can name him whatever you want to name him."

Kendall stared blankly. She was happy that Christian was excited about the pup, but she wanted nothing more than for Dre to get the fuck out.

Kendall interjected again, "Christian, Daddy has to leave. He has to go to work now."

Dre glared at her. "So you're really going to do this to me?"

"Give Daddy a hug so he can leave."

Christian rubbed Frank's hair. The two of them looked adorable together, Kendall had to admit. Christian sat Frank down on the floor. "I don't want Daddy to go to work. He always goes to work."

"Kendall, so you're really going there right now?"

"Dre you didn't think about nobody but yourself, when you stepped out of this relationship."

During an awkward silence, Christian took hold of Dre's leg. "I don't want you to go to work."

Dre brushed his son's hair, then eyeballed Kendall again. "You're really going to ruin this moment between me and my son?"

"You ruined it, Dre. You ruined the life that we were supposed to have together."

"Daddy, don't go to work."

Dre hoisted Christian up on his side and kissed him on the forehead. "Daddy will be back."

"I don't want you to go to work," Christian whined.

"I need you to be a big boy. I want you and Frank to take care of Mommy, okay?" Dre said.

"Okay."

Dre kissed Christian on the forehead and sat him back down onto the floor, then turned to walk away without saying a word to Kendall. Right before Dre made it to the front door, Christian latched on to his leg and began to cry and startled Frank, who began to bark and scurried around Christian's leg.

"I don't want you to go, Daddy. Stay and play with me. Stay and play with me and Frank, Daddy."

Dre faced Kendall and asked, "So this is what you want?"

Frank barked and ran in circles, his tail wagging, as Christian gripped Dre's leg. Dre tried to pry Christian off his leg, but he couldn't; the toddler was too strong. Kendall pried her son's hands from Dre's legs, and he was bawling. Frank continued to bark.

"So, is this what you want Kendall? Is this what the fuck you want?" His eyes were now bloodshot, trying his best to swallow his anger.

"Leave now, Dre."

Dre exited the house, and Kendall inched toward the door to try to close it. Christian tried his best to break free. She closed the door and placed him on the floor, and he sat down and cried. Frank licked Christian's face, trying to cheer up his new friend.

* * * * *

Catherine had prepared Dre's favorite, spaghetti, though she'd given up meat four years ago. She was happy to cook for her man. She sat across the rustic farmhouse styled kitchen table from, plucking green olives from her salad bowl while sipping red wine.

Catherine noticed that Dre was unusually subdued. "Is there something bothering you honey?" She paused and tossed an olive into her mouth. "You're not eating."

"It's my son. I was just thinking about him and how all of this is going to effect him."

"Affect him, you mean?"

"Now is not the time to be a grammar expert."

"I'm sorry."

"What did he think of the puppy?"

Dre smiled, remembering that brief but happy moment. "He named him Frank."

"Frank?"

"Yeah, after his maternal great-grandfather."

"Do you have pictures?" She smiled. "I'd love to see his face."

Dre frowned. "No, that's just it. Ken ran me off before I could see my son enjoy the dog. I was there for five minutes. As soon as I stepped into the house, she told me about you. She said 'Catherine Smith is white.'"

Catherine dropped the fork on her saucer. "OMG, she knows who I am?"

"Yes."

"How does she know that?"

"I don't know. Perhaps it was the card. I don't know. All women need is one clue, and they will go digging until the find out what they are looking for."

"Are you angry at me, Andre?"

"I'm not angry. I'm just wondering if you left that card in there for her to find it." He forced a smile, as if it was a joke.

She sighed, "You were sloppy, Andre. I told you a long time ago that you needed to tell her that you were leaving. I would be pissed, too, having to find out that my man is in love with another woman through a birthday card."

"And you being white makes it that much more harder to accept."

"I don't understand why race has to be an issue, so if I was black, it would make it better?" She flinched, and her tiny nose wrinkled. "But I should have known; race always matters to black people."

"Race always matters to black people?" Dre repeated. He couldn't believe Catherine was so naive, but he should have known. Catherine had never had a tough day in her privileged little life. "You're living in a bubble if you don't think race matters."

"Maybe."

Dre folded his arms and pursed his lips as he tried to understand why she didn't know that race always mattered.

"Sounds like you're married to a racist. She has the problem with race. Not me," Catherine said.

"No more than anyone else." Dre sipped more water.

"Why is it a big deal? So what I'm white?"

Today both a black woman and a white woman had gotten on Dre's nerves.

"Its not a big deal that you are white. Love is love, but understand black women will always be upset when they view that a white woman has taken 'a good black man.' A lot of black men view white women as an ultimate prize of success."

"But it's not like it's that way between you and I, Andre. We love each other. I'm not some trophy for you to flaunt."

"Kendall doesn't know that."

"This is a very interesting conversation you and I are having. I never knew black women felt like that." She paused. "I shouldn't generalize, but I never knew some black women felt like that. What about all these black women with white men?"

"Now that's different."

"How so?"

"That is viewed as the black man's fault for not dating his own."

"You've got to be kidding me." Her mouth flew open.

"Look, I don't want to get into this whole race thing. What matters is that you're with me, and I'm with you."

"So when are we going to be official? When are we moving in together?"

"You are over here every day. You have a key."

"That's not what I'm talking about. That's not what you promised me."

"I don't know. I have to think about my son. If you could have seen his face... I can still see him crying."

She stood, gathering the dishes from the table. She'd just lost her appetite. She walked over to the trash can, pressed the button to open steel can, and tossed the leftover salad into the waste. Then, she finished off the rest of her wine and placed her dishes into the dishwasher before gathering Dre's and placing them inside the dishwasher too.

He could sense that she was mad. He stood and approached her. Her J'adore scent lingered. Her earrings highlighted her high cheekbones. Catherine could have been a model for sure. She certainly could be someone's trophy wife; he'd never thought about her in that context. He had also never set out to fall in love with a white woman. It just happened. She had helped him in a way that nobody had ever helped him. She taught him about real estate investing. And more than anything else, she didn't need him. He slid his arms around her tiny waist. She gave him three small pecks on the cheek before he forced his tongue into her mouth, and he held unto her before gripping her ass.

She faked a smile and said, "Not today."

He frowned and his head dropped. "Visitor?"

Catherine nodded. "I came on yesterday."

"I love you, Catherine."

"When are we going to make it official? When are you going to tell your friends about me?"

"Just give it some time."

"I know you will do the right thing."

CHAPTER 5

It was one o'clock, and Christian was with the nanny at the park again. Kendall had removed her shoes and was about to doze on the sofa when the doorbell rang. She stood, thinking that perhaps it was some package she'd ordered from Amazon. She opened the door without asking who it was.

Catherine Smith stood before her smiling pleasantly, and Kendall had to admit she was a very attractive woman. Catherine Smith was beautiful, but not in the traditional sense of beauty. It was an odd beauty with her boyish haircut and slender figure. She was nothing like Kendall, and she wondered what the fuck had Dre seen in her. Catherine was wearing a grey pencil skirt and a matching shirt with exorbitant black Jimmy Choo shoe pumps. Kendall owned the exact same shoes. Perhaps Dre had paid for both of them.

Kendall faked a smile. "How can I help you?"

"Hi, I'm Catherine."

"I know who you are." Kendall said.

"May I come in?"

Kendall sighed, still watching her, and wondered what the fuck had Dre seen in her. They were nothing alike, and maybe this is what Dre wanted all along. But she didn't want to seem ghetto or like the bitter ex-girlfriend that still wanted her man even though she was exactly that. She remained calm.

"Can I come in?" Catherine asked again pleasantly.

Kendall stepped aside, and Catherine strolled inside and when the door closed Kendall faced her. "How can I help you?"

"You found the birthday card?" Catherine smirked, looking as if she knew something that Kendall didn't.

"I found the card."

"You want to talk about it?"

"Why?" Kendall studied Catherine, who looked skinny but physically fit, but Kendall was pretty sure she could whip her ass if it came down to a fight.

"I don't know. I just thought you might want to have a conversation with the other woman."

"I spoke to *my* husband. There is nothing for us to talk about. Besides I don't want to hear all of that 'it's not what I think' bullshit."

Catherine laughed, and her blue eyes twinkled. "I'm here to tell you it's exactly what you think."

"Okay," Kendall sighed, trying her best to be civil.

"I love Andre, and he loves me," Catherine said.

"So I need to know that?" Kendall shrugged. "Why?"

Catherine cut her eyes to leather Chesterfield sofa in the corner of the living room. "Can I sit down?"

"You won't be here long enough for all of that."

"Where's your manners? I would have offered you a seat. Offered some water. I see some of us weren't taught any better."

"You cannot be fucking serious."

"I thought we could sit down like grown adults and be civil, but I see I was way out of line for thinking that. I've often wondered what Andre saw in you. And I'm still wondering it. I thought he liked a certain type of woman. Perhaps classy and elegant, but I see you and I are nothing alike, and I'm not speaking of race."

Kendall pointed her finger at Catherine. "Look. You don't know me. I'm not the one you want to play with." She paused. "Why are you even here?"

Catherine shifted from one foot to the other, then clasped her hands.

"Would you stop that you are making me nervous," Kendall spat.

Catherine stopped. "I love Andre, and he loves me."

"Is that so?"

"We have plans to move in together, but *you* are in the way."

Kendall raised her eyebrows. "Please tell me how I am in the way of your plans."

"Look, he loves his son, and he knows that in order to see his son, that he has to go through you, 'the baby mama' and you being a little bitter that he is with a white girl is making it hard for him, but let me tell you race has nothing to do with us being together. We're two people in love."

"You think I'm racist?"

"You are. Andre and I see no colors."

Kendall's nostrils flared when Catherine said Andre and I. "Okay well, I'm not racist. I can't be racist because I don't own anything. I didn't set anything in place. I don't make decisions in this country."

"If you don't like this country, why don't you just leave?" Catherine laughed.

"What? Bitch, this is my country too, and I never said that I didn't like this country."

"You seem kind of bitter that he's with me."

"White girl, if you don't get the fuck out of my house, I will hurt yo' ass," Kendall threatened.

"But acting out like that is exactly what makes me think that you're bitter Kendall. You're not going to get over this easy by being bitter. You just need to accept the fact that Andre loves someone else and just move on."

"You telling me to accept the fact that *my* husband loves someone else and move on?"

"Soon to be ex-husband."

"Why'd you even come here?"

"I need you to get in line so me and Andre can move forward with our future. I don't think that is a hard thing to do."

"And I want you to go. Get out of my house. Right now." Kendall walked to the door and opened it for Catherine, then escorted her outside.

* * * * *

"Catherine Smith *is* beautiful," Kendall said to Chrissy.

"I saw that white girl's Facebook page, and I ain't impressed. Typical white girl. Actually... she kinda looks like a boy to me, but if that's what Dre wants."

They were eating lemon pepper wings at a Wingstop. Kendall dipped a wing in a pool of ranch dressing then bit into it.

"Some nerve of her to come to your house in the first place. That couldn't have been me." Chrissy shook her head at the thought. "I would have beat the brakes off her little skinny ass, talmbout I need to get in line so she and Andre can move forward. Did she really say that?"

Kendall and Chrissy laughed their asses off.

Kendall plucked a white napkin from the dispenser and polished her fingers.

Chrissy saw something cloud her friend's mind and asked, "What's wrong?"

"What do you think she has on me?"

"Nothing. Men just want different pussy." She took hold of Kendall's face. "You are perfect, baby. Nobody can figure out how and why men cheat."

Kendall guzzled her watermelon iced tea. "I just hate that I'm so dependent on Dre, that I don't know how to do nothing myself. I mean the money that I have is his. I mean I got a little that I'd put aside, but how long do you think that is going to last? I'm sure he's not going to support me forever."

Chrissy flagged the waitress and ordered a Heineken.

"Yeah you know how some dudes can get when they are not getting the pussy, how they like to cut the money off. I don't think Dre will be like that though."

"I didn't think Dre would be planning a life without me. I mean the man has a place I didn't know about with a woman I didn't know about. Who knows what else Dre will do?"

The waitress dropped the Heineken off, and Chrissy took a swig of the beer almost as soon as it landed on the table. "So what's your next move?"

"I gotta get a job, I guess, but I don't know how to do shit. I haven't worked in years, so I have no skills."

"I know, but at least you have the thirty five thousand."

"Thirty five thousand?" Kendall looked at Chrissy like she was crazy. "What's thirty five thousand dollars compared to a million?"

Chrissy suggested, "You could sell the Range Rover."

"I've already thought about that. No use in me riding around in a hundred thousand dollar car but broke as fuck."

"It's not the end of the world. This shit could have happened much later in life. You're young. You will survive this. Trust me, but you're going to have to invest in you. Quit putting Dre first. Quit putting others first. You have to be selfish with your time."

"I understand."

"Do you?"

Kendall nodded. "Yes."

"Well, if you understand that. You wouldn't ever wonder what Catherine Smith has on you. Catherine Smith is not your competition. You are your own competition, baby girl. So what you might have to get a job. Get one. Go back to school. Get in shape. Better yourself. Don't feel sorry for yourself."

Kendall smiled. Chrissy was right. She had always thought about going back to school, she definitely wanted to get in shape, and she didn't have a choice but to get a job before the money ran out.

Chrissy slid to her side of the booth and hugged her.

* * * * *

The next day, Kendall joined Best Body Fitness center, a local gym about a mile away from her home, but she didn't have the courage to work out that day. Instead, she had driven to the outlet and bought a couple of cute Under Armour outfits, though she didn't know what she would be doing; she'd never worked out in her life, but here she was, nervous with purple leggings, a matching purple sports bra, and Nike Air Max Flyknit. She detested wearing Nikes with Under Armour workout gear, but it would have to work.

The locker room was full of body types. Fat women. Skinny woman. Elderly women. Women with big booties and some with no ass at all. Kendall felt at ease being around the women in the locker room, though nobody spoke to her until a cute black girl with dreadlocks said she loved the purple Under Armour gear. Kendall thanked her, and she had hoped that someone would talk to her. She wanted to kill time in the locker room because God knows she didn't know what the fuck she was doing.

She approached the naked girl who was walking to the shower. It was a little awkward, but Kendall told her where she could get the same outfit from.

The girl looked surprised. "Thanks."

"No problem. I'm Kendall."

"I'm Aria."

"See you around, then."

Aria nodded then walked the shower. The stalling was over now. Time to face her fears. She didn't know what to do first. Then she thought she should have hired a personal trainer. She remembered the day that she joined, they'd offered her a free training session if she was interested. Kendall approached the desk to inquire about the training, and there was a very fit black guy with a friendly face, a sexy ass beard, and nice, sculpted ass wearing the black gym-t-shirt. He had a sleeve tattoo of an angel. His name tag read Rashad.

Kendall bet that Rashad got all kinds of ass. He was probably single and texted multiple women, but never planned to get serious with any of them. Probably broke as hell with a 460 credit score, but Kendall had to admit he was a sexy motherfucka. He smiled at her, and his eyes focused on her breasts. Why was he looking so hard? Were her nipples hard?

"Can I help you?" Rashad asked.

"Hi! When I signed up I was told about personal training sessions."

"Are you interested?"

Now why in the fuck would she be standing at the desk if she wasn't interested in the training sessions? Well, Rashad's name tag did say 'Trainer' not 'neurologist.'

"Yes I'm interested." She smiled.

"They are sold in blocks of twelve at 90 dollars per session."

"Yes, I know. I was told I get the first one for free."

Rashad licked his lips, and chills traveled her spine. "Honestly, I wouldn't change a damn thing about that body," he chuckled.

She smiled again, thinking that he was unprofessional as fuck, though she appreciated his candidness. "I'm getting in shape for me."

"I'm your guy."

"Are you a good trainer?"

"You think I'm going to say no? Look at my body." He lifted the Under Armour shirt and revealed an eight pack. She imagined herself licking ice cream off those abs before snapping back to reality.

"I guess you are," she smiled.

Rashad stepped away from the desk. "Are you ready for your free session?"

"Yeah."

"Let's go."

"You mean right now?"

"Why not?"

"Who is going to train me?"

"I am. Unless you want my man Brian to train you."

"Who is Brian?"

He pointed over to a white guy with glasses that looked like he would be way too serious.

"Look I've never lifted weights before, and I'm not—"

He cut her off. "You're not trying to have muscles like a man."

She laughed, "You've heard that before."

"You wouldn't believe how many times I hear it. I had one woman who came in here and worked out with another trainer, and she refused to do arms at all, though I don't like that look either on a woman," Rashad said.

"But you're in shape," Kendall commented.

"I like what I like. A little toned, but I like the softness of a woman." He grinned as he looked at her ass.

Rashad was one unprofessional motherfucker, but she had to admit she liked the attention.

He smiled, revealing incredible teeth. "Now I know you're ready to workout, wearing all this nice new athletic gear. You look like you might know what you are doing. Well at least you look good in your new outfit." He laughed, and she was annoyed by him but she didn't let him know.

He said, "Shorty, this is the wrong place to be acting all soft."

She got a closer look at tattoo of an angel on his forearm with the word 'Mya'

"Look, you just need to be professional." She tried to pretend like she wasn't enjoying the attention.

He apologized, "You're right. I'm sorry." He offered her his hand and she shook it. "We are going to have a good working relationship."

"Good." She paused, then said, "I don't want you to think I'm all uptight, but I believe in starting a working relationship out a certain way."

"You're right, and I won't call you 'shorty.'"

She laughed, "Well at least not while we are working out."

"I can see you are a professional woman and all, and I should have been more thoughtful about that."

"It's okay, Rashad."

"Is there a look you are going for?"

She hadn't really thought about that.

"What do you think?"

"I think you look great."

"Come on, now. You're a trainer. Tell me what you really think."

Rashad shook his head. "I'm not going down that road. I can't tell a woman what I think. I've learned that when you say something women take it personally."

She laughed. "I suppose I would like a nicer butt and toned legs, maybe some inches off my waist."

"I hear that a lot."

"That means we're doing squats, right?"

"That will be part of the workout, but not the whole workout."

"I understand. You're not going to work me too hard, are you?"

"I'll go kind of easy on you since you're cute," he said with a wink.

She smiled.

"Oh, you do know how to smile?" He chuckled.

This flirting ass nigga Rashad just didn't know how to be professional. They stepped inside the gym, and he had given her a full body workout, starting with stretching, then box jumps, squats, lunges, dumbbell press, kettle bell swings, and then finally ab work. After the workout was done, Kendall laid on the floor, agonizing. She'd never been through anything like that before.

He took hold of her arm and pulled her up from the floor. "Are you coming back?"

"Yes." She paused, thinking. "But not tomorrow."

He laughed, "Why not tomorrow?"

"I'm sure I'll be sore," Kendall whined.

"Yeah, you'll be sore for the next couple of days. So do you want to sign up for the twelve pack?"

"So how much does it cost again?"

"Usually a session costs $100 an hour, but if you buy twelve, you can get them for $90. If you buy twenty-four, we will give them to you for $70 each.

"Kind of pricey," she gasped as she leaned over, still breathing heavily from the workout.

"Pricey for who? For you? I saw you pull up in that white Range Rover."

Kendall made eye contact with Rashad. She knew that people had the tendency to think you were loaded when you drove an expensive car, but hey wasn't that the purpose of the nice things?

"You saw me drive up?"

"Yes."

"It's going back."

"Stop it."

"No really, I'm selling it, but what does that have to do with the gym sessions?"

"Nothing. The price is the same for everybody, but since you are cute as hell…"

"I stank right now. What are you talking about, boy?" She then realized that she was comfortable with him and was no longer keeping it professional herself. "You were saying… since I'm cute."

"How's sixty dollars a session?"

"Is that the cute discount?"

He beamed at her, and then she wondered what Rashad would be like in bed. She'd heard that personal trainers would fuck the shit out you, but most of them were broke, and she believed it. What man had that much time to dedicate his body unless that was all he was doing in his life?

"Yeah, so your cute discount is sixty dollars a session."

"You just don't know how to be professional, do you?"

"You don't want the discount?"

"I do." She smiled.

He licked his sensuous lips and said, "You just have that effect on me. I can't explain it."

She laughed.

"So what's your story?" he asked.

"What do you mean?"

"I mean what's your story Miss Range Rover. I don't see a ring on your finger."

"Why would I have ring on at the gym?"

"Good point, but some women keep their ring on the whole time. Especially when they are training with a male trainer. Hell, some husbands don't let their wives train with men. If I was married, I'd probably be that type of husband." He laughed. "Are you married, do you have a boyfriend, or are you one of those strong independent women that don't need a man for shit?"

The trainer named Brian came over, interrupting Rashad's spiel. "Hey, I have to go home for a moment. Can you train my 2 o'clock for me?"

"No problem, bro."

Brian apologized to Kendall for interjecting, then disappeared. After he was gone, Rashad asked, "Are you going to tell me your story or not?"

She swallowed audibly, then said, "I have no idea what you mean."

"Are you involved with someone?"

"What?"

"I'm just asking a question, man. It's called trying to get to know you."

"I'm separated from my son's father."

"Trying to get that revenge body, huh?"

"I'm hitting the gym for myself."

He laughed.

She frowned.

"What is wrong with dude? No way I'd let somebody like you go."

"Thanks. I guess," Kendall said.

"Shorty, you try to be hard, but I can tell you a nice person."

She raised her eyebrows. "I could be a psycho."

"You ain't lying. It's the one that look like they got their shit together be the ones that slash your tires and shit."

"I can tell you ain't nothing but a ho."

His mouth flew up, then he smiled, revealing dimples. "I ain't nothing but a ho, huh?"

"Am I right?"

He licked his lips and said, "I used to be. Those days are over now."

"What changed you?"

"Prison."

"You've been to prison?" She cleared her throat.

"Is that a problem for you?"

"I ain't say that. You just don't look like the kind of man that has done hard time before." She then wondered if pretty boy Rashad had taken it in the ass.

He sat on the bench and took a swig of water. "What kind of man do I look like?"

"An ex-jock. Kind of square." Kendall shrugged.

"Did you just call me a cornball?"

"I didn't say you were a cornball. I never thought that at all."

"Look, I grew up without shit, and I wanted some fast money, so I took a chance and got popped."

"Only a year. Did you snitch?" Kendall asked.

He laughed again, shaking his head. "Good lawyer, I got caught with three pounds of weed and some pills. My case is online. You can look it up just google Rashad Michaels."

"Looks like you are doing good for yourself?"

"You consider working at a gym good for myself?" He avoided eye contact.

"So you trying to get me signed up, and you about to quit?"

"I'm not about to quit right this moment."

"What are you going to do?"

"I don't know yet. Maybe build houses with my uncle. Real estate, or maybe get my own gym." After a few seconds of silence, he asked, "Can I call you?"

She scanned the gym, not wanting to give him her number, especially if they were going to be working out together. "I don't think it's a good idea."

"Are you still sleeping with your ex?"

" Excuse me? I'm not sleeping with anyone." She rolled her eyes at him.

"You know, you're cute when you do that."

"But anyways," she skated around the comment, "I need to head to the locker room to take a shower."

He smiled and watched her ass as she sashayed into the locker room, and she looked back at him before she entered. He was still watching.

CHAPTER 6

They sat at a booth at a local bar called Micks. Tuesday night, margaritas were five dollars, and they were pretty damned good.

"I met this dude named Rashad the other day at the gym. He's a personal trainer there."

"Rashad the personal trainer, huh? Sounds like the name of a certified ho."

Kendall laughed, "That's what I told him."

"What did he say?"

"Said he used to hustle now he's working at the gym, but he's cute though," Kendall admitted.

"Whatever Rashad. You ain't fooling nobody. You are using that job to get all the ass. Boy, you ain't got no money."

"That body and that smile is to die for, and chile he has a beard."

"I bet. Most personal trainers are hoes, and that, my friend, is a fact."

"I wonder why."

"They lead with their body. They don't have nothing else to offer except dick and a nice body. You better stay away from Rashad the personal trainer. He'll have yo ass sprung," Chrissy warned.

Kendall laughed, "That's what I said."

"So, what is Rashad the personal trainer's story. Does he have a woman?"

"I didn't ask."

"You didn't ask, and he didn't volunteer the information either."

"You like him don't you?"

"No."

Chrissy knew Kendall too well. She knew that her friend liked him or at least was entertaining the possibility of liking him. Why else would she bring him up?

"I don't like him." She avoided Chrissy's eyes. "But I have to admit, he did keep my mind off Dre for a moment."

Chrissy held her margarita against her mouth. "Well you need a distraction. Rashad might not be the one, but at least you can get some dick because I can tell you right now, most personal trainers are fuckboys, but you knew that already."

"You think I need sex?"

"You need to be broke off."

"I ain't just giving some random dude from the gym some ass."

"You brought the man up." Chrissy shrugged then sipped her drink.

Kendall sipped her drink before realizing that maybe Chrissy was right.

"Hey, you don't have to marry the man."

"I don't know nothing about this man except he's been to prison and he had a daughter that died."

"What do you need to know about him to fuck him? Just protect your coochie and protect your heart because I'm gonna tell you right now, he's getting a lot of ass."

"It's simple as that, huh?"

"I'm saying nice body, has a job. A beard. What else do you want? Let me tell you before you slip off into this fantasy world. There ain't a whole lot to pick from out here."

"Right now, I just want to focus on raising my son."

"Right now."

* * * * *

Kendall was dressed in black Nike workout gear, ready for her third workout with Rashad. She was about to exit the front door, and Dre was standing at the front door about to enter.

"Can I come in?"

She sighed "What do you want?"

"Kendall, we have a child together. We can't avoid each other for the rest of our lives. We can't pretend we don't have history. Plus we need to work together for Christian's benefit."

She stepped aside for him to enter.

Kendall blurted, "Look, I can't talk long I have to get to the gym."

"The gym?" He raised his eyebrows at her.

"I'm trying to get in shape."

"The gym ain't going nowhere. Who you trying to impress anyways?"

"Why is it your concern?" She stared at her phone. She had fifteen minutes to make it to the gym. "What do you want, Dre? I have a personal training session."

"Getting back on the market, huh?"

She sighed, "I don't have time for this bullshit. What do you want Andre?" She really didn't want to see him. Every time she thought of him or saw his face, all she could think about was Catherine Smith telling her that she needed to get in line. She wanted to tell Dre to get the fuck out of her place—better yet get the fuck out of her life—but he owned the goddamned place.

"I want to talk."

"About what?"

"My son."

"Christian will be here at four o'clock. He's with Miss Ortiz."

"I want to take him with me to spend some time with him."

"I don't want Christian around that woman."

"What woman?"

"Cat. Catherine. Whatever the fuck your little pet name for her is." She checked the time again, but this time she looked at her smart watch.

Silence.

"Did you send her over here to talk to me?" She asked.

His left eyebrow rose. "What the hell are you talking about?"

"Don't act like you don't know your little precious Catherine came over here one day last week. Saying shit like I'm stopping y'all from moving forward."

He grimaced. "Oh my god, are you serious?"

"Why would I lie to you, Andre? Especially about that."

Dre stared at Kendall. Kendall had never been a liar.

"What did she want?"

"I guess to let me know that you were hers."

"I'll handle it."

"Talk to her because if she ever brings her little white ass over here again, I swear I'm going to beat the brakes off her."

"When can I see Christian?"

She ignored him and looked at her phone again. "I'm late for my appointment."

* * * * *

When Kendall arrived at the gym, she approached the front desk and asked for Rashad.

"He's not here today," a thin, freckled-face, redheaded kid said.

"What do you mean he's not here today? He's supposed to be training me."

"I was told that something came up." A blond named Megan interjected, and her and the redhead exchanged glanced as if they were hiding something. Kendall wondered if Rashad had been fired, which would have been just like Rashad; he was unprofessional as hell. Kendall was sure he'd tried to sleep with one of his clients.

"Brian is going to train you. He'll be here in five minutes," the redhead said. "I saw Brian back in the locker room. Do you want me to go get him?"

Kendall was reluctant. She didn't want Brian to train her, but what else was she to do? Unprofessional Rashad was a no-show.

While Kendall was thinking about it, Brian approached the desk, glanced at his watch, then made eye contact with Kendall. "Shall we begin?"

She nodded and smiled.

He asked her what she was trying to accomplish with her body, and she'd told him the same thing that she had told Rashad. That she wanted to tone up her legs and butt.

"What did Rashad have you doing?"

69

Kendall rattled off the list, "Squats, lunges, leg press, lots of weights."

"Ok, cool, well, we're going to mix it up a bit. Going to do plyos and an ab workout."

"What are plyos?"

He smiled "Quite simply jumping."

"Oh, I don't do that," Kendall said.

Brian looked perplexed.

"Yeah, all that jumping and stuff makes my heart beat really fast," she quickly explained.

"Your heart rate is going up, and that's a good thing."

"How is that good?"

"It means that you are burning fat, and that's always good."

"I can't catch my breath though."

He laughed, "I tell you what. If it gets to be too much, we'll do something else."

"Okay."

They worked out for about fifteen minutes, and she decided that she liked Brian's approach. He wasn't as fun as Rashad, but then again, Rashad was flirting trying to get some ass. They did jump squats and box jumps. He had her work with the utility rope to the point where she was drenched in sweat when they were done.

She thanked him for the workout, dashed to the locker room, and showered. When she came out, she saw Rashad standing behind the front desk wearing a blue window pane suit with a pink dress shirt and a blue and white tie with black cap-toed oxford shoes. He looked amazing. She'd always been weak for a man in a suit. She waved and made her way to the door. He called her name, and she stopped and waited on him. Something was bothering him.

"I'm sorry I wasn't able to train you."

"It's okay. I got a good workout in with Brian, and life happens."

"Yeah, life happens," he echoed.

She gave him a once over, and said, "You look very nice today. What's the occasion?"

"I have something to tell you."

Oh God. she thought. Here was the part where he told her that he was going back to prison or that he had to go to court for parole violation.

"What's wrong?"

"I wasn't honest with you."

"Honest about what?"

"I'm not really a trainer. Well I'm certified, but I don't train unless we're short of trainers."

She sighed heavily, "I don't get it."

"I'm the owner of the gym."

"You own the gym?"

"Yes."

"Are you being serious right now?"

"Very serious."

He tugged his beard and licked his lips. "I'm attracted to you Kendall. I—"

"Now this really doesn't make any sense," she interjected.

"And I wanted you to like me for me, but when I saw the Range, I thought 'here is another materialistic chick that ain't got shit to do but workout in the middle of the day,' but when I got to know you, I don't think that at all about you. You really cool."

"I'm offended."

"Why?"

"You just prejudged me."

"I know."

"Why?"

"My ex was like I just described. She broke my heart, and I didn't want you to break my heart."

"Wait a minute." Kendall stopped him. "Who said I was into you?"

"I did."

"What makes you think I'm into you Rashad?"

"Tell me I'm lying. If you can look at me with a straight face and tell me that you don't like me, I'll give you a free gym membership for the next two years."

Silence, then she blurted, "I might like you just a little bit." Then, she busted out in laughter. "So you thought I would be another one of your gym groupies?"

"The gym is just one of my businesses. I have dry cleaners. Collection agencies. Check cashing facilities. Dump trucks."

"Busy man," she commented.

"Yeah, this is why I'm in the suit. Today I was bidding on this job, and I didn't get it. A contract for my trucking business. They said I didn't have enough trucks to do the job. If I would have gotten that job, I would have been set for a while. This was a multi-million dollar contract."

"I'm sorry you didn't get it." Though she was not a gold digger, she was damn sure glad he wasn't a personal trainer.

"I know this must be weird, but will you let me take you out?"

"Do you think that is a good idea?"

"I do. I'm not training you anymore. I'm not going to be around the gym too much. I might come in the afternoon or the first thing in the morning to get me a good workout in, but that's about it."

"So you're not training me?"

"I'm not a trainer, baby."

She laughed. The extent niggas will go through to get laid, she thought.

"Look, I'm not a gold digger, but I'm no cheap date either, and you know I have a son, so we will have to plan it. No last minute shit."

"I understand completely."

"Call me." Kendall rattled off her number and beamed at him.

CHAPTER 7

The next morning, Kendall received a text from Rashad wanting to know if they could meet later that night; he even offered to pay the baby sitter. Kendall called her mom and asked if Christian could stay the night. Her mother responded "My grandbaby is welcome anytime, but that stankin' ass dog need to go somewhere else." Kendall dropped Frank off at the Pet Hotel, and they decided to meet at Lazeez Mediterranean Grill at eight clock. Kendall was ten minutes late, and she found Rashad sitting up front waiting on her when she arrived. He had been kind of irritated that she was late, but she looked breathtaking, wearing a pair of black Vans, yoga pants, and retro statement frames. She didn't look sexy, but rather cool as fuck. He loved the fact that she could switch it up. He'd seen her wearing Athleisure and sometimes smart casual to the gym, and sometimes she would dress up. He smiled, thinking she looked dope.

He stood and hugged her. He desired her, and this made her feel sensational. After they were seated, he'd ordered the lamb, and she followed suit since he'd raved how good the lamb was. She had a glass of Reisling, and they both had ice water. Though she'd eaten at most of the nicer restaurants in Charlotte, she'd never been to Lazeez. She was actually glad that she'd never been there with Dre because her mind would have been on the time they'd gone instead of focused on the man in front of her. She took in the ambiance, while his eyes were on her. The waitress soon returned with piping hot plates. She removed her glasses and placed them on the table.

"So what are you going to tell me about yourself except that you are letting your Range Rover go back and you are separated from your man?"

"Well, I'm selling it."

"My bad," he said and dabbed his mouth with the napkin.

"What do you want to know?"

"Let's talk about your baby's father."

"Must we talk about him?"

"Deadbeat, huh?"

"Do I look like I would date deadbeat?" She rolled her eyes.

"You looked disgusted when I brought him up."

"Because he doesn't matter unless he matters to you. What matters is that Kendall is here with Rashad," she smiled.

He smiled back. "We don't have to talk about him."

"What do you want to know about him?"

"Anything you feel like telling me."

She bit into her lamb. "This is good." She held the water glass up to her mouth.

"I told you."

"His name is Andre, we call him Dre, and he's not my favorite person in the world right now."

Rashad nodded. "I feel that way about my baby mama."

Kendall choked on her water. "Baby mama?"

"Though my baby died, I still refer to my ex as my baby mama sometimes."

"I see."

"But you don't have to talk about him if you don't want to."

Kendall bit into the lamb again. "Look you've already put it out there. We can talk about him."

"Why don't y'all get along?"

"I helped him build a small fortune." She looked away, and she teared up, thinking about all the time she spent helping him.

Rashad grabbed her hand and held it, then stroked it with his thumb.

"It's hard."

They made eye contact. "I know. You don't have to talk about him."

She continued, "Now he's with another woman. Living his best life. He robbed me of my dreams. I had dreams too, you know? Now I have a kid. I feel like I've wasted so much time."

"Whoa."

"Exactly."

"What business were you guys into?"

"Commercial real estate," Kendall lied; she knew it would be much easier than saying that she was in the drug business. Though she hadn't known Rashad long, she felt like she could tell him anything, but some things were better left unsaid.

"So why do you think he left?"

"I don't know." She took a swig from her Reisling. "Maybe because she helped him; her family is in real estate. Then maybe it's because she's white. I can't answer that question."

"She's white?"

"Yes."

"How does that make you feel?"

"She could be green for all I care. The result is the same. He cheated, and we're not together," Kendall lied again. Being that Catherine was white made the situation sting more. It was like saying that she wasn't good enough or pretty enough.

"So, Kendall, you're just a housewife, who takes care of the household and your son?"

"Not even that. I had a nanny, and we have housekeepers that come in twice a week."

"So wait a minute, you had a nanny, and you didn't work. You didn't go to school or anything?"

Kendall sighed. "I know. I had gotten complacent. You know how they say, it's hard to get motivated when you have money. So here I was living a great life home with the most amazing, sweetest little boy in the world. My husband that I'd been with since I was practically a child. I was just relaxing, man. There was no point in doing anything, life was great until..."

"Until what?"

"Until Catherine." She cut her eyes at him. "Have you been listening to me?"

"So what happened?"

"I don't know," Kendall shrugged. "I just think we fell into a routine like most couples do. There was no more fun. No more excitement. I thought I'd be with him forever."

"The relationship fizzled."

"What do you mean?"

"It takes a lot to be in a relationship with someone. It's very easy to take someone you assume will be there for granted."

"Yeah, I guess."

"Did y'all do it often?"

"Do it?" She asked.

"You know."

Kendall rolled her eyes. "Do you mean did he fuck me often?"

Rashad nodded.

"Why didn't you just say that? You sounded like a twelve-year-old."

"I didn't know if you would be offended if I just blurted it out."

"I'm real."

"Well, did y'all do it often?"

She took another swig of Reisling. "I will answer that in a minute, but first, tell me why you asked that."

"I know sometimes, when there is a child around, you can't attend to each other's needs."

"So relationships to you, sir, is all about sex?"

"No, not at all, but it's a big part of it."

"Yeah we fucked—maybe not as much as before Christian—but I think he was satisfied in that department, but you know, I have needs too."

"Did he meet them?"

"Most of the time."

Rashad raised his eyebrow. "Most of the time?"

"Yeah, Dre is a selfish lover."

"But you put up with him because he has money."

"I put up with him because I loved him," Kendall corrected him.

"You fell in love with a different person. He's not the same, and neither are you."

"I supposed you're right. But why do you think he cheated?"

"I don't know. Maybe the relationship has run its course."

"Me either."

"So now that he's gone you don't have a job right?"

"I don't have a job. I'm looking for work right now. I put my life on hold watching this man build his dream. Now he supports me, but I don't know how long that will last. I don't want it to last, honestly. I want to support myself."

"Look you keep saying how you helped him. You need to quit dwelling on what he did and own up to some of this shit yourself. You are an adult. He didn't force you to do anything. I'm trying to understand how you helped him."

"I got things in my name. I fathered his child."

"So you really didn't help him at all?"

Kendall raised her eyebrows. "Excuse me?"

"I'm just being realistic, Kendall. You really wasn't a asset. You were disposable."

"Why are you talking to me like that?"

"Because somebody should have been told you that."

She dropped her fork on the plate and stared at him.

He said. "Look, I like you, but I know what Dre was going through. My ex sat around the house dreaming about modeling and having social media fame, basically not doing a goddamned thing."

"You left her?"

"She left me."

Kendall raised her eyebrows "What is your point?"

"My point is you have to bring value or it's easy to let go of something or someone."

"What happened to real love," Kendall pouted. "My grandmother never worked."

"Those days are over."

"What can you do?" Rashad asked.

"I didn't go to college."

Rashad thought to himself maybe he'd been wrong about Kendall. Maybe she was a pretty girl that didn't want to do anything with her life.

"What are your dreams?"

She laughed, "So you on your Dr. Phil shit?"

"We're just having a conversation."

"Yeah, I'm just kidding." Kendall laughed and then realized that he may have taken her seriously.

He asked, "What do you want to do that you haven't told anyone else? I know there is something you want to do."

"You gotta promise not to laugh."

"First, you have to tell me what you want to do. If you tell me a dream of yours, I'll tell you what I want to do."

"I can't swim. I'm terrified of water, and I want to get over that. One of my properties is on the lake, and I don't go out in the water too much. When I do, I have my life jacket on, and sometimes my friends will jump in the water, but I don't."

"So, you are thirty-one years old, and you want to conquer your fear of the water?"

"Yes. This is what I want to do. This is what I am going to do. I don't think I'll be Michael Phelps or no shit like that, but I will learn to swim, you can believe that." After a few minutes, she asked, "Why do you want to know what I want to do?"

"I'm interested in you. I like you, and you are at a point in your life where you don't know what's next."

"True."

"So, are you going to tell me or not?"

"I want to be a stylist. You know, a fashion stylist." She said twirling her hair, she was really nervous about saying this. No one knew this about her except Chrissy and now Rashad.

"You want fame," he commented.

"Not at all. I want work. Work from regular people. They don't have to be famous."

"Why don't you do it then?"

"I don't have time." She said lying.

"What? You have plenty of time."

She blushed, he'd called her on her bullshit. "What if I don't know what I'm doing? I know I can dress myself, and I think I know style, but dealing with people is very different."

"You sound afraid." He insisted while making intense eye contact.

"Maybe I am a little afraid." She turned from his gaze.

"What if I help?"

"How?"

"You put your business plan together. Get your business license, incorporate yourself. I will pay you a salary as long as you are working at least forty hours a week in your business."

"Look, I'll do it, but why would you help me do that?"

"I like you, Kendall. You seem genuine, and I don't see that many people like you every day. And that guy that let you go is an idiot."

She smiled. Though she felt that Dre had lost for letting her go, she had to wonder if Rashad had a motive besides pussy. He'd made it obvious that he'd like to fuck her, but she wondered if there was something else to this.

"Look, you caught me off guard with this."

"Why?" He reached across the table and took her hand in his.

"I don't know you."

"Don't worry about that. I want to help you, but of course the money would come with some stipulations."

She sighed, sipped some more Reisling, and thought, *Here comes the bullshit*, the part where he wanted her to be some weird sex slave.

"Stipulations?" Kendall's eyes narrowed.

"I just want to make sure you are actually working toward your goal."

"And how will you know that?"

"You'll tell me how much time you are working, doing research building your website, making how-to videos. Whatever you can think of that will help your business."

"How much work will I have to do?"

"It's up to you."

"I can start working two hours a day!" Kendall cheered.

"Two hours a day?" He laughed. "You're not serious. Seems like you're looking for a hobby; you're not looking to be successful."

"Huh?"

"Perhaps you need to look to do something else. If you can only dedicate two hours to it. That's not enough."

"Well, it's going take some time to be able to work all day."

"Why?"

"My attention span."

"Stay off social media."

"I'm hardly on social media."

"What's the problem?"

"The problem is you want me to go from not working at all to working all day."

"I understand. I'll give you a month, then I need you to be able to work for at least six hours a day."

"Doing what?"

"Styling people."

"I have no clients."

"Start by styling people for free."

"You know, I've always thought about styling single moms in the workforce for free."

"Okay, do that."

"But even then, I'll need some money. Not a lot, but a lot of them don't have anything, so I'll need to go thrifting."

"I'll give you a budget. I just want you working toward your goal."

"Six hours. Whew. That's a lot."

"You want to be a stylist, or you want to talk about being a stylist?"

"You sound like every bit of advice I've ever heard."

"I don't know shit about style, but I know if you want something, you need to put the time in it."

"You're right." She finished her Reisling.

"Don't be disposable out here."

"You're right," she repeated.

* * * * *

Rashad was dressed in black compression pants, ready for a quick workout in the building gym when he received a call from the concierge to inform him of a visitor, Layla Nelson—his baby mama and the woman that he'd been involved with for about three tumultuous years. He'd actually helped her finance her boutique. He leased her a space in the mall. Then, he'd gotten her pregnant, and she'd birthed a baby girl named Mya. Two years later, Mya died of pneumonia. After they buried her, the plans were to try again to start a family.

He'd thought they were in a good space then one day he was in the workout room in their house punching the heavy bag, when she came in and told him that she wasn't happy and that she was moving to Houston.

He stopped punching the bag and caught his breath. "What do you mean that you're not happy? I give you everything, I'm financing your boutique in the mall. You driving a new Tesla, and you have my credit cards."

She flung her hair back over shoulder and said, "I know, and I appreciate everything that you have done for me, babe, but I just think there is more opportunity for girls like me in a bigger city." She then passed him the 3-karat engagement ring.

He stared at her like she was crazy! "Girls like you?"

"You know, pretty girls."

Layla spent time at an orphanage and was adopted at the age of 9. She believed that she was adopted because she was beautiful—because her parents told her this every day—but she was insecure about the fact that she'd never known her real parents. She knew she was pretty, and when she realized that men would help her because she was pretty, she used it to her advantage.

"What is it you want to do?"

"I want to model."

"You're too old to be a model."

"But how old do I look?"

"Thirty."

"No the fuck I don't." She was fuming, though she was actually twenty-nine at the time, she didn't want to look twenty-nine.

"I thought you wanted to start a family?"

She shook her head. "I got to work on my career. I have been thinking a lot, and I want to be a brand ambassador, a social media influencer."

"Huh," he laughed. "What the hell is a brand ambassador, and what the fuck is a social media influencer? That shit is Fake News."

She frowned. "Yeah, you know model for brands. Promote their products and get paid for doing it."

"You can stay here and do that."

"I could, but I'll never get anywhere. This country mentality will hold me back."

They'd argued for the next few days, and in the end, he told her to get the fuck out of his house, which she did. She moved to Houston, and they unfollowed each other on social media. He didn't hear from her for almost a year when she texted him and then opened the communication lines again. They even followed each other on social media again.

He'd saw that she had a few procedures since the last time he saw her, and now she looked a hot mess—a botched rhinoplasty and rock-hard breast implants. She'd sent him a picture a few months ago with her and a few of her friends from Texas, visiting the Dominican Republic. He didn't recognize her. He even asked 'Are these girls?' thinking there was a slight possibility that they may have men pretending to be women. He knew you had to be careful nowadays; these transsexuals were getting better and better.

Layla: Yes why did you ask????

Rashad: I don't know. I thought they may have been sex dolls, I'd seen a few of them on IG today.

Layla: It's me and a few of my friends.

Rashad: You??????????

Layla: I'm wearing the yellow sundress.

Rashad: Wow.

Layla: You don't like?

Rashad waited five minutes before he responded to the text. He gathered his thoughts. How was he supposed to tell her that new nose looked awful? He didn't want to hurt her feelings. He'd once loved her, and he still had love for her. He was staring at the pictures trying to decide if she'd lightened her skin. The truth was he hadn't even recognized her. She was still attractive, but much less than before.

He finally responded. "You look still look great." A lie.

He stood and dashed to the door. Layla stood at his door at 8am looking like she'd just left the club, her face heavily made up and dressed in a red dress that clung to her body. Rashad stood there and wondered where the fuck was she going this time of morning. Even he had to admit she looked less hideous in person. She coyly asked, "Are you going to invite me in?"

He stepped back and nodded. "Please come in."

She leapt into his arms, and he held onto her for a while. Though he hated to admit it, he'd missed her crazy ass.

When he released her, they just stared at each other awkwardly for a moment before Rashad asked, "So what brings you here, and where are you going this time of morning all dressed up?"

"I wanted to look good for you, Zaddy."

Rashad swallowed hard. "Who is Daddy?"

"I said Zaddy," she laughed.

"Zaddy?"

"Please tell me you've heard of the term 'Zaddy,'" she giggled. "I missed you Rashad." She sat on the love chair without asking.

"Would you like water?"

"Do you have coffee?"

"There is a Keurig in the kitchen."

She stood and walked into the kitchen as Rashad watched her. Her ass was still on point. For a moment, he imagined himself fucking her doggy-style. But he had to remind himself that she had an agenda. Now he just had to figure out what the agenda was.

"Where are the K-cups?" she yelled back to him.

"There is a box on top of the fridge."

She removed the box from the top of the fridge. "You don't have Starbucks? What the hell is this shit?"

"That's all I have." He laughed. "Same old, Layla."

"I've decided to come back home."

He raised his eyebrow. "Lil' old Charlotte, huh?"

"Stop it." she said, sipping her freshly-made coffee.

"You're the one that said that Charlotte was too small for you."

"I missed Charlotte, and I missed you. You were good to me, and I didn't appreciate you. I know you haven't moved on yet, and I was just wondering if we can pick up where we left off. Look, I've changed," she begged.

"Yes, you have." Rashad said it before he'd realized what he'd said.

She sat her coffee down and questioned, "What the fuck is that supposed to mean?"

"I was just saying that you look different."

"Better?"

"I thought you looked great before. You're still a very pretty girl."

She smiled. "I'm glad you still think I'm pretty."

"There is more to life than being cute and getting a lot of likes on social media, though."

"I know that, and I've grown up a lot, and I dated a couple of guys when I lived in Houston, but they all just wanted one thing. They didn't want anything serious, and I'm at the point of my life where I want to settle down with the man I'm going to grow old with."

"And that man is me?"

"You don't miss me, Rashad?"

He laughed, thinking of the nerve of this bitch to disappear and run off after Mya died and she miscarried another baby and now she was back talking about she wanting to settle down. But, he had to admit that he had missed her and had thought about her a lot. She knew him, his flaws and his secrets. But he liked Kendall.

"Why are you laughing?"

"The whole situation is laughable. First, you just assume that I don't have a girlfriend. Assume that you can just pop back in my life after being gone for two years."

She stood and tip-toed around the condo. He remembered the marathon sex sessions they used to have, and he missed that, but he didn't want to think about it. Good sex had a way of making you feel like you're in love.

"This is a really nice place." she commented.

"Thank you."

"Still doing well for yourself..."

"I try. Its hard work, you know, but it is what it is."

"You know, I don't know what you have going on." She paused and then picked up her coffee. "I'm proud of you."

"Thank you."

"And I'm not going to sit here and think that an attractive man with all kinds of businesses would stay single for long. "

"I am single, but I'm dating someone."

"Lucky girl."

"I'm the one that's lucky. She's special."

"I was saying I'm proud of you, and I'm not going to force a man to be with me that don't want to be with me. I'm not that desperate, but can you do me a favor?"

"What?"

"I found this nice place out by Northlake Mall. It's not expensive, only 2200 dollars a month. I was wondering if you could pay my rent for a year," she said as if it was the easiest thing in the world to do."

"You're kidding, right?"

"I know your secrets, Rashad."

Rashad raised his eyebrow. "What does that mean?"

"You don't think our friend out in L.A. would like to know that you stole a hundred kilos from him to get on your feet?"

His nostrils flared. He breathed slowly as he thought back to the day his connect, named Lowdown because he was from South Central, Los Angeles, had shipped a hundred kilos of coke by freight, and he'd showed up to the company, retrieved the product like he'd done so many times before. A guy named Turtle, who worked for the freight company and had also been a high school classmate of Rashad, approached him to let him know that the feds were there, they were rummaging through a large shipment of coke that had originated from Los Angeles, but the shipment was someone else's; Turtle assured him not to worry. He'd given Turtle a thousand dollars to take some pics of the feds going through the freight. Rashad told Lowdown that the coke had been confiscated by the feds. Sent him the newspaper article and legitimate paperwork, that revealed that it had been an eighty-two kilo bust, but Rashad just convinced him that that the crooked cops had stolen the other eighteen kilos. He sold the 100 kilos and profited two million; that allowed him to open the gym, the dry cleaners, and the trucking business. That was enough money to allow him to go legit.

"So you're blackmailing me?"

"It's not blackmail. I need help."

"Then why did you even bring that up? It sure sounds like blackmail to me."

"Look, I would never let Lowdown know what happened. I was just reminding you that I was down with you."

"You need seventeen thousand dollars."

"Twenty-five. I'm going to need some new furniture," she added.

"Call me tomorrow."

* * * * *

Layla had been staying downtown in her friend India's townhouse until her apartment was ready. They'd been friends before Layla had left for Houston after meeting on a video set for a local R&B singer. They sat at a bar inside the Ritz Carlton.

Layla asked, "Do you have any men you can introduce me to?"

"I know the perfect guy, but he's young."

Layla laughed. "I don't do young guys."

"He's a rapper."

"A rapper? Oh, hell no."

"Don't act like you you've never dated a rapper before. You know I follow you on the 'Gram."

"I have dated rappers, and that's why I'm in this situation I'm in now. I prefer an older man. Like way old. Like forty-five minimum."

"Rashad is not old."

"I'm looking for someone willing to help me."

"You're looking for a sugar daddy," India corrected.

"Hell yeah, you know you want the man with the bag too."

"Of course I do, but I ain't about to be dating an old ass white man with shriveled up balls, either."

"Who said he had to be white?"

"Look, do you want me to hook you up with someone or not?"

"Yeah, but not some young ass rapper."

"He's about to sign a major deal. He's the hottest thing in the street right now."

"What's his name? Maybe I've heard of him."

"Drive-by."

"What the fuck?" Layla laughed. "Please tell me you're lying. This man's name is not Drive-by."

India laughed, "It's just a name."

"You got a picture? Is he on IG?"

India nodded, pulled up his Instagram account, and presented it to Layla, who examined the pictures.

"He's skinnier than I usually like them, but I think he's cute."

"Girl, he's about to be rich."

"That's him in the picture with the Rafe."

"The Wraith, you mean," Layla corrected. "Is it his?"

"Probably somebody else's, but he does have a Range."

Layla passed the phone back to India. "Everybody has a Range."

"Look, you don't have to fall in love with the him. You can just hang out with him."

Layla shrugged. "I don't know."

"Let me call him."

"Don't call that man."

India ignored her and dialed the number. It rang twice before he answered.

"Hello."

"Stacy."

"Don't call me Stacy."

"Boy I've known you since your name was Stacy. I'm not going to be calling your ass no Drive-by."

He hung the phone up.

She called back "Drive-by?"

"That's more like it, sis."

"I can't believe you made me call you Drive-by." She laughed.

"Look, sis, that's the way it is now. Don't be offended."

"Hey, I got somebody that I want you to meet."

"How she look? Do she have a fat ass?"

"You know how my girlfriends look. Do you think I would set you up with someone ugly?"

"Hey, I just asked a question, sis."

"I will send you a picture."

"Do that. Look I gotta go, but send the pic."

She ended the call.

Layla looked on expectedly and asked, "What did he say?"

"He wants a pic."

Layla sorted through her pics before finding one of her standing on a balcony in Puerto Rico, wearing a purple thong. She taken it while on vacation with an NBA player she'd dated. She forwarded the pic to India, who then sent it to Drive-by. A minute later, he called right back.

India answered, "That was fast."

"Sis, that is not a real person."

"Yes, that's a real person."

"She is fine as fuck."

"I told you, all my girlfriends are fine. "

"I see."

"She's a little older than you.

"How old is she, sis?"

"Oh, she's thirty."

"Oh, that's not that old. I like cougars anyway."

"Thirty-year-olds are not cougars."

Layla frowned. "Now that is the exact reason I don't fuck with young boys. They have a young mentality. And that motherfucker better not call me a cougar again."

India laughed before getting back on the phone. "Hey let's get some food and hang out tonight," India suggested.

"Aight. I'll bring my boy K with me."

"Is he cute?" India asked.

"Look, you know I don't know if a nigga is cute or not. I ain't gay."

India scoffed. "Send me a pic of K."

"Okay bet."

India ended the call.

"So," Layla asked, "What did he say?"

"We're going to meet them tonight."

"Where? I'm not going to some bullshit restaurant."

"What about Ruth's Chris?" India suggested.

"Yuck. I hate chain restaurants."

"Ain't we bougie?"

"I'm just saying. If we have to go to a chain, let's go to McCormick and Schmick's."

CHAPTER 8

India and Layla arrived at the restaurant around 9 o'clock, thirty minutes late, and Drive-by was not happy about it. He'd been calling India for the past thirty minutes.

When India and Layla approached the table, Drive-by's frown turned into a grin when he put eyes on the black backless dress and the heels that made that ass look exquisite. Drive-by, who was wearing a pair of corduroys and a suede motorcycle jacket, stood and approached Layla.

She noticed that he had a bottom row of gold teeth and smelled like a combination of Creed Aventus and OG Kush. She was turned off a bit, but what else would a twenty-something-year-old rapper smell like? He hugged her and then pulled her chair out. His eyes were on her ass until she was seated.

Kevin, known as K was a thickly built, light-skinned guy with a bald head. He looked to be at least thirty. He pulled the chair out for India, and when they were all seated, K asked, "What took y'all so long?"

"We're girls. You know that girls take forever."

"Is that right?"

The waitress approached the table, and the girls ordered two Lemon Drops.

Drive-by was texting on his cellphone, and Layla said, "I must be boring you."

He smiled revealing his gold teeth. "You can't be serious. I think I'm in love."

"With the person you are texting."

"No, I'm in love with you, shawty"

"Can you not call me that?" Layla asked.

"What's your name again?"

"Layla."

"And yours? And don't tell me Drive-by. I'm not calling you that."

"Stacy."

The waitress placed the lemon drops in front of the girls.

"Stacy," Layla asked. "Why don't you have a girlfriend?"

India interrupted, "So she gets to call you Stacy, and I gotta call you Drive-by?"

Drive-by laughed, "You don't look like Layla look."

"What?"

"Well, you know you've always been big sis," he started, then he cut his eyes at Layla. "Look at her. She looks amazing, and she smells even better than she looks."

Layla grinned at the flattery.

Drive-by grabbed her hand and sniffed it. "What the hell is that scent? What are you wearing?"

"Fucking Fabulous."

"I know you're fucking fabulous, but what are you wearing, baby girl?"

Layla and India laughed. "No that's the name of the fragrance."

K said, "Wait a minute, the name of the fragrance is fucking fabulous?"

The women nodded in unison, then Layla explained, "Yeah, Tom Ford makes it."

"I've never heard of it."

The waitress was back again and asked for their orders. They all ordered, Drive-by and Layla ordering the same thing—Grilled Salmon with rice pilaf.

And when the waitress left, K said to India, "I see you ordered off the "Fucking" side of the menu."

"Excuse me?"

"That was damn near a hundred dollars worth of food. Either you fucking or you paying for your own shit."

India narrowed her eyes and grimaced. Drive-by laughed and said, "K, chill. bruh."

"Chill my ass, I was just telling her that she is being greedy." K shrugged.

India said, "Lame ass nigga, I can pay for my own shit."

Drive-by said, "I got you Sis."

When the food was delivered, K and India checked their social media accounts while Layla and Drive-by were getting acquainted.

"So why don't you have a girl?"

"Who says I don't have a girl?" Layla raised her eyebrows. "So you do have a girl," she stated.

He laughed. "I'm just playing with you, Ma."

Layla didn't like this young ass boy calling her Ma. Something about that irked her; it sounded almost incestuous.

"I don't have a girl. You want to be my girl?"

"Just like that? I'm not that easy—you have to wine me and dine me."

"I know. I'm willing to put in the work if we can get along. I mean, I'm physically attracted, but how is your attitude?"

She was getting annoyed at this little boy asking her about her attitude; she was not that desperate. "This might not work."

"You don't know that."

"Look, I know what I like."

"You don't think I'm cute?"

"I didn't say that, but it ain't all about looks."

"So is it the age difference?"

"Maybe."

"I've dated cougars before."

"Bruh, do *not* call me *a* cougar!"

"My bad. I'm just saying I've dated older women."

"Why can't you just say that?"

"Hey, I'm a young boy. I'm still learning, but I would like you to be my teacher. The question is, are you willing to be a good teacher?"

"Tame this, young boy." She winked.

After the meal, they stepped into the parking lot. India made her way to her car, without so much as saying goodbye to K. *Fuck that petty ass nigga,* she thought. Drive-by took Layla by the hand and led her to a light blue Wraith.

As they leaned against the hood of the car, he stated, "You like my car?"

"It's nice." she agreed.

The young boy grinned. To her, he was clearly a man that was not used to finer things.

"If you be nice to me I'll let you drive it. You ever been in a Rafe before?"

"You know it's called a Wraith, right?"

"I know that, but the hood calls it Rafe. I guess you ridden in one before."

"Yes."

He frowned. "You have?"

"My ex had one."

"What the fuck did he do?"

"He was in the NBA."

"Who does he play for?"

"He plays for the Rockets."

"Who is he?"

"Look, that's not important. Just know that I've dated men with money, but I'm feeling you," she lied; she needed to stroke the young boy's ego.

"And I'm feeling you. Can I call you?"

"Yeah."

"What's your number?" He pulled out his phone and she gave him her number, which made him ask if she was from Houston.

"No, but I used to live there."

He twirled her around. He wanted to get one more look at her in the black dress. That ass looked delicious. He wanted to fuck her, and she could sense that he wanted her. She liked feeling desired.

"So are you on the 'Gram?"

"I am."

"What's your name?"

"Slow down, partner. Let's get to know each other," she said. She knew that most men would see a pic or a story and create a whole scenario in their head about what she was doing and who she was fucking. She wanted to make sure Stacy was mature enough to handle her lifestyle.

He smiled, revealing the bottom row of gold teeth. "I'm sorry for calling you a cougar earlier."

"It's okay."

He leaned into her to kiss her, but she turned her head. "Whoa, there will be plenty of time for that."

He got off the hood of the car and held her hand as he walked her to India's car and she stood in front of the passenger door waiting for him to open the door for her. They stood there in silence for a second before he finally picked up on the hint and opened the door. She hopped inside and he leaned in to attempt a kiss, but again, she stopped him.

"There will be plenty of time for that."

India was on her phone, still scrolling through her timeline on Instagram, then she looked up at her brother. "You like my girl, huh?"

"I love her."

"I told you."

"Yeah, you did."

"Treat her right."

"You know I got that, sis."

* * * * *

Kendall stood in the mirror getting dressed, preparing herself to meet Rashad. Kendall wore distressed boyfriend jeans, a blazer, and pumps, with a black clutch. She wore very little makeup, and she felt and looked amazing. The doorbell rung, and Kendall opened the door to find Dre and Catherine standing before her. Kendall's heart skipped a beat; though she knew that they were a couple, seeing them together made her angry, but she was not about to let them see her sweat. She invited them in. "Would you guys like something to drink?"

"No thank you." Catherine said.

"You look really nice tonight Kendall," Catherine commented. "I love that bag and those shoes."

Kendall was wearing the Jimmy Choos that Catherine had worn the first time they'd met. She was hoping that the bitch hadn't thought she'd inspired her.

"Andre bought them for me." She paused. "Did he buy yours too?"

Silence.

"You going on a date?" Dre asked.

"Did you come here to discuss my personal life, or is there another reason for your visit?"

"Looks like she moved on." Catherine said.

Kendall had to admit Catherine looked great too, but she wasn't going to tell her that. "Why are y'all here?"

"I wanna see Christian."

"Just have a seat; he will be here shortly. He's with Miss Ortiz."

"Can I take him with me?"

"No."

"Why?"

"Dre, don't play stupid. You know I don't know Catherine yet."

Catherine cut in, "Oh my god, you act like I'm a criminal or something."

"Maybe you are. Maybe you just haven't been caught."

"You're more of a criminal than me." Catherine sniped.

"Please, you two don't start the bullshit. We are going to have to learn to get along."

Catherine stood and paced.

Kendall lips curled. She cracked her knuckles. She wanted to fuck this bitch up, but she was going on a date. She cut her eyes at Catherine, who was still pacing. "Who stands and starts walking around in another woman's house? Will you please sit down. You are making me nervous."

"Andre, let's get out of here." Catherine pouted. "It's obvious that this woman is still in love with you."

"Oh, please," Kendall said.

Dre and Kendall exchanged glances.

"The best thing that could have happened is that you took this man away from me." She paused, then continued, "I realized he wasn't the man that God wanted me to have."

The doorbell rang seconds later, and Christian burst through the door as Frank trailed him. When Christian spotted his dad, he sprinted into his arms. "Daddy I missed you. Are you back from work?"

"Daddy is back from work."

Catherine beamed, and her cheeks glowed at the scene of the dog and the little boy. Catherine said, "Hello Christian, I've heard so much about you."

Christian examined Catherine as Frank continued to bark.

"Who are you?" Christian asked as he stared upward toward the strange woman.

"Her name is Catherine, and she is Daddy's friend."

"Is she Mommy's friend too?"

Oh hell no, Kendall thought, but opted for shaking her head no.

"She's just Daddy's friend for now?"

Kendall made eye contact with Miss. Ortiz. "I'll be back in a couple of hours. Take care of Christian for me, and if you need anything, you know how to reach me by my cell."

"Of course." Miss Ortiz nodded.

* * * * *

Kendall and Rashad met at a Thai place called Basil restaurant downtown. The waitress led them to a table in the back of the restaurant, and once they were seated, they ordered their food.

She said, "For someone that is in shape and believes in working out, you sure love to eat out a lot."

He laughed, "Hey, I believe in enjoying myself. No one knows when their last day is coming."

"I understand."

"I eat healthy ninety percent of the time, but hey I like macaroni and cheese just like any other black person."

Kendall agreed, "I love macaroni and cheese; that's why this whole fitness thing might not be for me. I'm a girl who likes to eat."

"I feel ya. I understand. I like you just the way you are, trust me." He paused then laughed.

She blushed, revealing her dimples, then asked, "So, Rashad, what is your vice, sir?"

"I don't understand." He looked confused, but he was more startled; she'd caught him off guard with the question.

"You know what a vice is, right?"

"Of course."

"Name something that you like to do that you shouldn't be doing."

"I like to drink on the weekends, and I like cigars."

She raised her eyebrows. "That's it?"

He laughed, "What did you expect me to say? Well, I used to look at porn as a teenager, and I used to smoke weed."

"Really?"

"Never thought I would kick that habit. I loved it."

"What happened?" She held the glass up to her mouth as she watched him. She loved his conversation. He was one of the most interesting men that she'd ever met. He'd sold drugs and did a stint in prison. He was physically fit but he loved to eat. He didn't want a woman that lived in the gym, and he encouraged her to pursue her dreams. Nobody had ever encouraged her to do anything. Whenever she'd come to Dre with an idea for a business or to talk about her desire to be a stylist, he would just brush it off as hobbies, but Rashad encouraged her. She liked that. She thought Dre was her soulmate, but perhaps the idea of a soulmate was a myth.

The waitress returned with the food.

He sliced the duck for the both of them.

"Did you work on your business?"

"No."

He laughed, and she was annoyed by his laughter.

The steam from the Pad Thai assaulted her face. She sipped on some water while she waited for it to cool. "There was nothing stopping me from working. I certainly could have written the business plan."

"Why didn't you?"

"It's hard for me to work on something that I'm not getting paid for. I don't know if I will ever get paid for my work." she laughed.

"I told you I'd pay you like a job."

"I thought you were joking."

He ate a piece of duck. "Do I look like I'm kidding?"

"No."

"You want to be famous?"

"God, no."

"Well, you know if you style someone famous then there is a chance that you will get famous."

Kendall sighed, "I hope I'm never famous."

"Why not?"

"I think fame is one of the worst things that could happen to a person."

"Why do you say that?"

"Because your life is no longer yours. It belongs to everyone to criticize you. And I have a son; I don't want him living in the spotlight."

"Are you on social media?"

"Yes. I have forty-five Facebook friends that I know, I have thirty Instagram friends, my accounts are private, and all of these are people I know personally. And I think that is the worst kind of fame for a woman to have.

He raised his eyebrow as he thought about Layla the attention whore. She'd posted a picture in a red thong this morning.

Kendall's Pad Thai had cooled and she spun the noodles onto her fork. "Enough about me. What's been going on with you, Mr. Businessman?"

"I had a visitor today."

"Your period?"

"You got jokes." He laughed. "That was a good one."

"You know, men have periods too. There are days when men can act like bitches."

"I'm sure, but I'm not on my period." He chuckled. "You're quick witted. I like that."

She ate a fork full of Pad Thai and raised her left eyebrow. She didn't want to talk with her mouth full and waited on him to continue.

"Yeah, my ex. I haven't seen this woman in almost two years, and she shows up at my place."

Kendall dabbed her mouth with her napkin. "What did she want?"

He laughed and sipped sparkling water before continuing. "She thought that we should get back together because she said she missed me and all that shit."

"So how long were you two together?"

"Four long years."

"You liked her, didn't you?"

"I liked her a lot, she's had a rough life. She's gorgeous, but she's had a lot of work done. She'd looked much better before honestly."

"Work?"

"You know, like plastic surgery."

"Oh, I don't fuck with that, but to each its own." Kendall was quiet for a few moments before saying, "You said that she's had a rough life."

"Yeah."

"So you felt that it was your job to save her. You like to save women, Rashad?"

He shook his head. "Not at all."

"I think you like being a hero to women. A lot of guys are like that."

"Maybe." He shrugged. "I've never thought about that, but perhaps that's a flaw of mine."

"You like projects. People you can fix."

"Interesting that you would say that."

"What happens when you think I'm fixed? Do you kick me to the curb?"

"Oh no, it's not like that."

"But you want to help me—pay me to work on my business—and you don't even know me."

"I just see potential in you."

"I think that's a flaw in a lot of men. They look for women they can help or fix. You're not responsible for me, Rashad, and you're not responsible for your ex."

He sighed and then ran his fingers through beard. "I was young and stupid, and I wanted a 'bad bitch' but that was all she bought to the table. I don't want to take her back."

"Was it a bad breakup?"

He thought for a moment. "No it actually wasn't a bad breakup, but it was sudden."

She twirled her Pad Thai again and ate a forkful then she drank from his water before realizing it.

They both laughed. "I'm sorry." She said.

"It's okay unless you have mouth herpes."

She shot him a side eye, then smiled when she realized it was a joke. "So the girlfriend is back in town."

"Ex," he stated shortly. He was chewing on a duck drumstick, then took a swig of the sparkling water.

"There's a crazy woman out there that's going to want to fight me over her man."

"No, it's nothing like that, believe me. I told her that it wasn't going to work out. I told her it was over."

"She really has some good timing."

"What do you mean?"

"Women can sense when a man is moving on or about to move on."

"I think you might be right about this one. Because I swear I'd been dating but nothing serious, then I meet you—a woman I really like—and this chick shows up out of the blue."

"You make it sound like she was living somewhere else."

He nodded. "She just returned from living in Houston."

"So are you going to get back with her?"

He dropped his fork onto his plate stared into her almond shaped eyes. "You don't have that to worry about."

She laughed, "Who said I was worried?"

He laughed, too. "Cocky!"

"Confident. There is a difference. Even if you got back with her, I don't need a man to complete me. Would I like a man? I'm a relationship type of girl at this stage of my life, for sure, but do I need a man to complete me right now? No."

Rashad paid the young attendant at the valet station for both his and Kendall's cars. They brought his car out first, a two-door sapphire blue Bentley coup, and she laughed; this was the first time she'd seen his car, but she had thought about how he raved about her Range Rover that day in the gym.

"Why are you laughing?"

"How you made me seem like I had the most amazing car in the world, driving a Range Rover, and here you are driving a Bentley."

The young attendant stood and held the door. Rashad approached him and passed him a five-dollar bill and told him that he could close the door because he was waiting with Kendall.

The attendant thanked Rashad and closed the door as instructed before sprinting to the parking lot to retrieve Kendall's vehicle."

Kendall shivered in the night air. When Rashad noticed, he wrapped his arms around her.

"Thank you."

"You're welcome."

It felt really good to be touched by a man. This simple gesture was the first time in months that she'd felt desired.

The attendant pulled Kendall's car up to the curb. Rashad escorted Kendall to her car, then passed the attendant another five. She kissed him on the cheek. She'd had a good time with him.

He smiled. He'd had a great time, too. She watched him until he walked to the car. He hopped into his automobile and sped off. Seconds later, he called her from the car and talked to her until she pulled into her garage.

"I'll talk to you later. If my son is up and he hears your voice, he's going to think that you're his daddy."

He laughed, unperturbed by this information. "When am I going to get to meet your son?"

"I don't know if that is going to happen. Slow down, but I certainly hope you meet him soon."

"Didn't you say that your ex brought his girlfriend to meet your son tonight?"

"True." She nodded though he couldn't see her.

"So why is it different for him?"

"You want to meet my son?"

"Look, I'm not here for games or to play with you. I want this to lead to something, and your son is a part of you. I want to meet him."

"Let me think about it."

"Okay. Goodnight, my love."

"Goodnight."

CHAPTER 9

When Kendall entered the house, Miss.Ortiz was sitting on the couch watching Queen of the South on Netflix, and she accidentally startled the nanny. She stood and stretched before saying "Mrs. Walker, I didn't realize you were home."

Kendall didn't really like her referring to her as "Mrs." especially since her ass was older than her. "Is Christian in bed?"

"Mr Walker. took him."

"His father did what?"

"Yes, I called you six times, and I texted you."

"I didn't get any calls."

Kendall removed the phone. There were no calls, but there were two text messages. Miss. Ortiz was being truthful. She frowned.

"Your phone went straight to voicemail."

Kendall remembered powering her phone down at dinner.

"Why did you let him take him?"

"He's the father. I'm the nanny."

Kendall dialed Dre's number, and demanded, "Bring Christian home now!"

"He's spending the night with me."

"Bring my son home right now, or I'm calling the police and telling them you kidnapped him."

He laughed. "Bitch, you sound crazy. How can I kidnap my own son? Who's going to believe that shit?"

"Dre, I'm going to give you one hour to bring Christian home, and if he's not home in an hour, I'm calling the police. It's real simple, Andre."

"Whatever." He ended the call.

Kendall's nostrils flared as she paced back and forth.

"I'm sorry," Miss. Ortiz said.

"My son is not with me. Get the fuck out of my house."

Miss. Ortiz eased toward the door, and Kendall stopped her from leaving. "Look I'm sorry I'm just upset right now." She dug into her purse and passed Miss. Ortiz a hundred dollar bill.

Miss. Ortiz looked at the money, surprised. "Mrs. Walker, you only owe me forty dollars. Actually, I wasn't expecting anything since Mr. Walker took Christian. I should have been home by now, but I fell asleep watching my favorite TV show."

"Take the money. I'm very sorry, I shouldn't have yelled at you."

Miss. Ortiz thanked Kendall then left the house in a hurry.

An hour passed, and Dre still had not returned Christian. Kendall hated Andre right now but she didn't think that she should call the police on the man. She didn't believe in it. She called Rashad to get his advice.

"Hey."

"Did I wake you?"

"No."

The call did wake him, but if there was a possibility that he could get some ass, he wanted to be fully attentive. He sat up on the bed and hit the switch on the light above the night stand.

"Is there something wrong?"

"Yes. My son is not here."

"What do you mean he's not there? Where is he? Did you call the police?"

"Dre took him from the nanny without my permission."

"Oh, thank god. I was concerned." Rashad was a little concerned, but his voice displayed more concern than was actually the truth.

"I need your help, Rashad."

"My help? I'm not getting in the middle of shit between you and your kid's father."

"That's not what I need." she laughed. "I wouldn't ask you to do anything like that."

"I'm listening."

"Actually I don't need your help. I just need some advice."

"Advice?"

"I'm just wondering if I should call the police on Dre."

Rashad laughed, and it agitated her.

He stopped laughing when he realized she was annoyed.

"Babe, how are you going to call the police on the man for taking his own child?"

Had he called her babe? She closed her eyes and shivered. She felt good hearing him call her that but she had a real issue, and he was laughing about it.

"I'm his mother."

"I know."

"I have custody of my child."

"Have the courts given you custody?"

"We haven't been to court yet."

"Let it play out. I'm sure he will return him tomorrow."

Rashad was right, and Kendall knew it, but she continued to whine.

"I don't want that woman around my son."

"So it's not about your son, but about that *woman* being around your son?"

"What's wrong with that?"

"Nothing... I guess."

"You feel alone, don't you?"

"A little."

"I can come over." He paused. He didn't want to come across as being all about sex.

She laughed, "What makes you think that I want you to come over?"

"You sound like you could use a little company."

"Maybe."

"You're into game playing."

Kendall asked, "What do you think is going to happen if you come over?"

"I don't know. I don't care. What I do know is I hear a friend in need of a little of support right now."

She thought about what he'd said. She could use some company, and she wanted to fuck him, but she didn't want him to think she was easy. "I'll text you my address."

She hung up the phone. Tonight was the perfect time for him to visit since Christian was with Andre. But she'd keep him at a distance; he'd sleep on the sofa. She would not be a ho. She slipped into a t-shirt and a pair of running shorts, her ass cheeks spilling from the sides.

Rashad arrived thirty minutes after she'd texted the address, but she knew he would be on time. He wanted to get laid, and that was not going to happen tonight, but she would have fun teasing him a little. His eyes were drawn to the tight bootie shorts, then to the vaulted ceilings, when she caught him staring.

She embraced him and said, "Thanks for coming over."

A silly ass grin was plastered on his face. "I figured you needed a hug."

"You have to understand, my baby is all I have right now and now that he's gone, I'm alone."

He nodded. "I understand."

"Would you like a drink?"

"Maybe later."

She noticed a chestnut brown colored weekender draped over his massive shoulders.

"Let me take that for you." She asked.

He passed her the bag, and she stuck it in the coat closet. He watched her ass cheeks as she maneuvered around. She turned and caught him staring again, and they exchanged smiles. She then disappeared into the kitchen and poured a glass of Moscato. when she returned, she noticed the handgun print underneath his black t-shirt.

She sipped the wine. "You're planning to kill someone?"

"No."

She lowered her eyes to the gun again, then stole a look at his package, then took a quick sip of wine.

"Oh no, I just brought this just in case."

"There won't be any drama here."

"He's paying for this place, right?"

"Yes, right now he is."

"So trust me when I tell you, he will have an issue if he knew I was here."

"Have a seat."

He sat on the sofa. She sat on the armchair opposite him.

"Is this my bed?" He laughed.

"Good guess."

"This sofa is kind of small for a big dude like me." He winked.

"You seem resourceful, I'm sure you will make it work."

"I have slept on worse."

She paused, sipped her wine, then stole another glance at his package.

"You are really going to make me sleep on this thing?"

She laughed. "You came here for pussy, didn't you?" She gulped down the rest of the wine. "And here I am thinking that you came over here to help a friend out. To comfort me."

He removed his shoes. "I can make it on the couch I guess."

She walked back into the kitchen to refill her wine glass, switching her ass a little as she walked. She knew he was watching.

Seconds later, she'd returned with the wine. Maybe she'd get drunk and fuck him and blame it on the wine. She took her position back on the armchair and stared at his package. She wanted him to notice her looking.

"Honestly, I felt you didn't need to be alone. I remember when I broke up with Layla, I didn't have a kid to comfort me, so there was no one but me."

"So you understand why I want Christian here."

He nodded. "He gives you something to live for."

"He's my best friend. He says he's my best friend, but he says his Daddy is his best friend too. I know I can't come between a father and his son. I know I can't teach a man to be a man."

"So his name is Christian, right?"

"That's his name."

"Do you love him?"

"Of course I love my son."

"Do you love Dre?"

"I love him. If I told you I didn't you'd know I'd be lying. I love that boy. I hate that I love him, but I know it was not meant to be. I realized I didn't know him at all. Anybody that could just pick up and leave like that, I don't need him." She sipped the wine again.

"Come. Come over here and sit beside me." He patted the sofa beside him to indicate where he wanted her to sit.

"You promise not to feel me up?"

He licked his lips and asked, "Do I look like I would do something like that?"

She eased toward him. His eyes settled on her camel toe. When she sat beside him, he massaged her thighs.

She felt moisture between them, then she imagined him stroking her from behind. She knew he was a good fuck; he was in shape, and she'd bet he could go on forever.

"You know you liked that," he said slyly.

"Liked what?"

"My hand on your thighs."

"Of course I did."

She picked his hand up and led it to her kitty before pushing it away.

"What did you do that for?"

"I'm a tease."

"I see." He laughed. "I'm glad I got your mind off Dre."

"I ain't thinking about that boy. Tell you the truth, it was about Christian. I wanted my best friend to be home with me."

He laughed. "Who is really your best friend?"

"A girl named Chrissy."

"Chrissy seems like a best friend type of name. Seems like all chicks have a friend named Chrissy."

She sat the wine glass on the table, then leaned into him, and their lips met. She inhaled his cologne. So masculine. She was glad he was there. He placed her hand on the package that she'd imagined inside of her. He was thick, just like she knew it was. She unbuckled his pants and wrestled that penis from his fitted boxer briefs. She stroked it a few times, and he leaned back and closed his eyes, the way guys do when they are ready for head.

She just kept stroking. She wanted to fuck him. She wanted to hop up on his dick and ride that big motherfucker, but what would he think? Would this be the last night she saw him? Did he have a condom? And if he bought a condom that meant that he'd planned to fuck her. He'd think she was easy. She'd been with Dre for a very long time, and she'd never fucked a guy other than Dre, except one time.

He stood and she was eye level with his package. He tried to guide it to her mouth, but her mouth remained closed.

He frowned. "Moving too fast?"

"Just a little."

"Have another glass of wine to loosen up."

She stood and walked toward her bedroom, switching her ass, her little shorts giving her a wedgie. She glanced over her shoulder. His penis was pulsating and he was trying not to think about what had just happened. Seconds later, she emerged with bedding for him. She handed it to him, then pecked him on the lips, saying, "There will be plenty of time for this if you are worthy."

He laughed and stuffed his penis back in boxers. "I can't believe you just did me like this."

"Sleep tight."

* * * * *

At six a.m., he woke up to pee, walking in the direction of the bathroom, but it wasn't there. Where was his phone? Where was his nightstand? He remembered that he'd spent the night at Kendall's place. He walked to her bedroom door and tapped on it. She opened the door dressed in blue silk pajamas and yapping into the phone to her best friend.

"Can you tell me where the bathroom is? I have to pee, then I want to take a shower."

"Hold on, Chrissy." She turned to him and said, "There's a shower across the hall and clean towels in the closet. Remember, I put your overnight bag in the coat closet." She avoided his morning kiss with the excuse of morning breath.

"How'd you sleep?" She asked.

"Uncomfortable. How was I supposed to sleep with a stiff penis?"

Chrissy laughed through the phone.

"Did you tell your best friend that's how you did me?"

"Of course not. She just knows me."

"And now I know you."

"You do."

"Tease."

"Whatever." He laughed then disappeared into the bathroom to shower. The doorbell rang, then the door opened. Christian yelled, "Mommy, where are you?" When she'd heard Frank barking, she realized that Dre had brought Christian home.

"Chrissy, Dre is here. Let me call you back later." She hung the phone up and began to panic. Rashad was in the shower. Now she regretted ordering Dre to bring Christian home, but it was too late. "Mommy where are you? I missed you."

She could hear the shower running. There is nothing to be afraid of. Dre was paying for this place, and he'd let it be known. What would he say if he found another nigga taking a shower? He'd assume the worst because that's what men did. There was no way he would believe that they didn't have sex. Damn the fact that he was fucking Catherine Smith. She remembered that Rashad had a gun. Did he take it with him in the shower? The last thing she wanted was her son to witness his father get gunned down in cold blood. She met Christian in the living room, wearing a robe and shower cap, hugged him, and petted the dog. She kissed Christian again and asked, "Did you miss Mommy?"

"Yes, and I missed Steven Universe."

Dre said, "What the hell is Steven Universe? He kept saying something about that."

Kendall shot Dre an annoyed look and rolled her eyes. "Shame on you. Steven Universe is a cartoon he likes to watch but I might stop him watching it because it has gay characters."

"I don't want my son watching no shit like that."

"Hey, there are gays in the real world."

"So you let him watch shit like that?"

Kendall was annoyed as fuck and snapped, "Didn't I just say I might stop him from watching it?"

"Oh, you seem a little too gay friendly for me."

"I just think he's too young for me to be explaining it to him right now. But anyway..." She turned back to Christian. "I think you might have missed those cartoons more than me. " She glanced at Dre and muttered, "Thank you for bringing him back."

"What did you think I was going to do, keep him?"

"Did you feed the dog?"

"Not today."

"Did you feed Christian?"

"He wants cereal. I didn't have any, so I thought you could give him some."

How could this man who had millions of dollars not go to the store and get a box of cereal? This is why he's not fit to have custody, she thought. He didn't have basic common sense when it came to children.

The shower stopped. Dre didn't notice.

"I gotta pee," Christian whined before releasing Frank's leash then beelined in the direction to the bathroom. Kendall cut him off then and guided him to the half bathroom in the living room.

She said, "Thanks for bringing him back again," and prayed Dre would get the hint and take his ass back to his little white princess.

Then, the buzzing of an electric razor came from the bathroom.

Dre turned his gaze toward the bathroom and asked, "Is somebody here?"

There was a long silence. She knew that he knew somebody was in there. What kind of goddamned question was that? He heard the heard the electric razor humming just like she'd heard it. There was no need to lie.

"I didn't know you were bringing Christian home this early."

"Who is in there?"

"My friend."

"Guy or girl?"

"Guy."

Dre smirked, "You have some really big balls to have a man in the place I pay for. You know that's what set OJ the fuck off, right?"

"So are you threatening to kill me, Andre?"

"I'm just saying."

"You have your girlfriend that you are going to marry."

"I'm the one that is paying for every goddamned thing in here. You think I'm paying for this shit so you can lay up and get fucked on my dime in my house on mattresses that I paid for? You must be out your goddamned mind."

Rashad yelled, "Kendall, bring me a towel!"

Christian darted from the bathroom and held his hands up to show her. "Mommy I washed my hands."

Kendall kneeled, kissed her son, and said, "Good boy."

"Christian, you are coming with me." Dre spat.

"But I want cereal." the boy whined.

"I'll buy you some cereal."

"Are you serious right now?" Kendall said.

"I don't want my son around some strange nigga."

Dre held Christian's hand as they walked toward the door, and Frank followed.

Rashad called for the towel again. Kendall headed to the hall closet near the bedroom, and Dre shut the door forcefully. She gave Rashad the towel, and ten minutes later Rashad was dry and dressed, walking into the living room. Kendall was sitting in the same spot on the sofa where she teased him the night before.

"Is there something bothering you?"

"Nothing to concern yourself with."

"Tell me, what's wrong?"

"It's Dre."

"Your son?"

"No, my son's name is Christian; his father is Dre. I keep telling you this." Kendall was annoyed because she was almost certain she'd mentioned their names a half dozen times. But why would this man remember their names? Particularly Dre. He didn't give a fuck about him.

"Did something happen to Dre?"

"No."

"Please don't tell me he let something happen to your Christian?"

"No, Christian is fine." She grabbed a Kleenex from a lavender box on the end table. "Dre brought Christian home while you were in the shower." She sniffled a bit, then continued, "He heard you shaving."

"I'm sorry—"

She cut him off. "It's okay."

"So what did he say?"

"That he didn't want his son around some nigga that he didn't know, but first he accused me of laying up here fucking somebody in a home that he paid for."

"You can't be serious right now, but I knew this was how he was going to react."

Rashad stood, and his nostrils flared. Kendall didn't deserve to be treated like Dre was treating her, but he knew how men thought. Men always wanted women to be faithful to them, while they ran around cheating. It was a double standard for sure.

"Dre is an ass."

"If I don't get my son back, I'm going to call the police."

"You're going to get your son back. Don't worry about that."

"Don't worry about my son? Are you fucking crazy?"

"Your son is with his father." Rashad said, as he thought to himself perhaps this Kendall chick was crazy as fuck. Maybe he shouldn't have gotten himself involved with her, as if it wasn't bad enough that his ex was back. He disappeared back into the bathroom and returned, carrying his weekender. He leaned into her and pecked her forehead with his lips. "If you need me for anything, please call me. I'm here to help."

"Thank you."

He walked to the door, and before he reached the door, she called to him. He stopped and turned, and they made eye contact.

"Thanks for the offer to help and thanks for coming over, that meant a lot, I didn't mean to be a bitch."

"I know you didn't."

* * * * *

Layla was impressed when she stepped into Drive-by's condo; it was decorated scarcely, with an expensive leather sofa and a luxurious Italian dining room set, but the home was cold, like a man had decorated it—there were no textures, and it lacked character. He'd led her to a rooftop deck and offered her a drink.

She said, "I'll take an orange Lacroix."

He looked confused. "What the fuck is that?"

"Just sparkling water." She sat at a large wooden table.

"I don't have any of that."

"Well, I'm good, then."

"You mind if I smoke?"

She looked at him confused. "Smoke what? Cigarettes?"

"No I don't do cigarettes." He laughed. "I mean do you mind if I roll a blunt?"

She didn't want to leave his house smelling like weed. "Can you do it when I leave?"

He sat down in the chair across from her. Today, her hair was up, revealing more of her face.

"You look beautiful as always."

She smiled. "You look very handsome today, sir."

"I'm surprised that you came by to hang out with me."

"Is that what we're doing?"

He smiled, and she noticed that the grill, that had been in his mouth before, was gone. His teeth were brownish, and she was turned off a bit.

"You know what? I want a drink."

"I don't have that Lacroix bullshit." he teased.

"Just give me some Ciroc. Peach Ciroc if you have it."

"Ciroc and what?"

"Peach Ciroc straight up."

He stood and stepped inside, and she watched his skinny frame and thought *damn this was one thin ass boy.* She couldn't quite call him a man because he was still very much a boy. Just a boy with money. Soon to be a rich ass boy. He returned with the Ciroc, passed it to her, and a strong marijuana smell lingered in the air. He sat back down.

She downed the Ciroc.

He was sitting on the sofa dumping weed into Backwoods.

"I had a little bit of weed. Is that a problem for you?"

"Not at all. Have you ever thought about using vapes to smoke?"

"Why would I do some shit like that?"

"For one thing, it doesn't smell, so you won't be smelling like weed."

"Does me smelling like weed bother you?"

"No, but you're a musician."

"What does me being a musician have to do with anything?"

"You're about to be famous, man, you have an image. I'm sure you'll have meetings and things, and you don't want to go up in meetings smelling like weed."

"I don't see where you are going with this."

"Do you think Jay-Z goes places smelling like weed?"

"Jay-Z is old as fuck, I'm not even half his age."

"Jay-Z was about his business from day one. Do you want to be trendy, or do you want to be about your business and be a billionaire one day?"

He sipped the Hennessy he brought out for himself. "Can we change the subject?"

She stood, strolled to the edge of the rooftop, and peered out into the Charlotte sky. He eased behind her and wrapped his arms around her. She didn't move. She felt his tool throbbing against her ass cheeks, and for a moment, she wondered what the young boy would be like in bed. When she turned to face him, he leaned into her and kissed her. She returned the kiss, but she tasted the kush on his tongue. She stepped back.

He frowned. "What's wrong, shawty?"

"Please don't call me shawty, ma, cougar, none of that shit, Stacy."

"I thought you were feeling me."

"I am." She walked back to the table and sat down.

He went back inside and returned with the bottle of Ciroc, then poured more liquor into her glass.

She laughed. "You're planning to get me drunk?"

"No."

He sat down.

She sipped her liquor and said, "Stacy, let's cut the bullshit. How can we help each other?"

Scratching his temple, he stated, "I don't understand."

"There is an age difference."

"What does that mean? Haven't you ever been with someone that's not your age?"

"Yes, usually older."

"And what happens then?"

"He supports my lifestyle."

"Are you trying to turn me into a sugar daddy? I'm not old enough for that. Want me to be your sugar boy?" He laughed.

"Cut it out."

"I'm a man."

His mouth was slightly open, and she was disgusted again by his corn-colored teeth, she couldn't believe that she'd kissed him. "What do you want from me?"

"I want to chill with you."

"See Stacy, that's the difference between me and those little young girls that you go out with. I don't just chill. I want a relationship. I want to travel, I want to be with someone that wants to buy land together. I don't want to be fucking around with no man that just wants to fuck me."

"You got needs. And so do I."

"What are you saying, Stacy?"

He laughed. "I'm not here to pay for pussy. I haven't ever paid for pussy, and I ain't about to start now. I got thousands of bitches that will fuck me. I hope you know that."

"So is that what I am to you? A bitch?" She laughed. "I bet you're telling your friends that you had a date with your old bitch, right?"

"Not at all."

They exchanged smiles then seductively, he said, "I love that perfume. What is it called again?"

"Fucking Fabulous."

"That shit makes me want to do something to you."

"Something like what?"

"I want to bend you over that balcony and fuck you like I just got out of the pen."

She liked the young boy's candidness, but there would be no fucking today.

"So, Stacy, I have a proposition for you."

He frowned.

"And it's not offering sexual favors for money. I'm a lady not a whore." She said, though she'd fucked for money on more than one occasion. When she was in Houston, she'd regularly blow this sixty-eight-year-old Jewish man for her $2,700 a month rent, but the young boy didn't need to know all of that.

"I want to be your consultant. I can turn you on to accountants, I can advise on travel, make hotel accommodations, and even be your personal shopper, give you a style makeover and make you an appointment with my dentist. Let's get you a set of veneers."

He frowned. "What's wrong with my teeth?"

"Nothing, but I noticed the other day, you had gold fronts."

"Yeah."

"That's so 2008. Notice all the rappers, 50 cent, Gucci Mane, TI, they've all invested in their smiles."

"So you think I have bad teeth." It was more of a statement then a question.

"No, I think you have good teeth. We just to need to highlight them more."

"Why can't we just whiten them?" He said, then made the mistake of blurting out, "I can't believe I'm letting some old bitch make me feel insecure."

The words "old bitch" angered the fuck out of Layla. She stood and ran through the doors that led into the condo and he followed her, screaming. "Wait, wait, wait!"

She turned and faced him, realizing that she wasn't the slightest bit attracted to his scrawny ass. But she assumed he must have had a big package. Skinny dudes generally had big dicks.

"What?"

"I want you to help me."

"Look if you call me old—or a cougar—one more fucking time, I swear to God, I'm done with your ass."

"Look, I'm sorry."

"Are you sure you want my help?"

"My goal is to be the biggest rapper in the world, and if you can help me, I would appreciate it."

She shot him a fake smile, then sat down on a brown leather sofa. "My first order of business is to decorate this apartment; whoever decorated it has no taste whatsoever."

He chuckled, "You don't like my place either."

"It is impressive, but like I said, whoever decorated it has no taste."

"What are your fees?"

"We'll work something out."

"What about me and you?"

"What about us?"

"Am I too young for you?"

She smiled and invited him over with her middle finger. He made his way to her and stood in front of her. She pulled him into her, and they kissed. She grabbed the young boy's package. It was very impressive. She stroked it for a moment, but she would not give him any tonight. He'd have to wait.

CHAPTER 10

Jeremy Long was a tall, biracial man with a chiseled face and a man-bun with a sleeve tattoo of a tiger. He had been told that his father had been Nigerian, and his mother was trailer trash who had a fetish for black men. His stepfather was a black man named Hank, who had done prison time with Rashad's uncle, Lenny. Jeremy and Rashad had met each other when they were eight years old in the third grade, when Uncle Lenny and Hank smoked weed together, and Uncle Lenny would bring Rashad to play with Jeremy. They had become best friends. Though Rashad had retired from the drug trade, Jeremy still hustled cocaine and heroin. Jeremy and Rashad sat across from each other in Rashad's living room, and Rashad filled him in on Dre showing up at Kendall's while he was in the bathroom.

Jeremy plucked almonds from a wooden bowl and sipped from can of Coke Zero. "Bruh, that could have been ugly. Words could have easily been exchanged, and you could have popped his ass."

"I know."

"What was she thinking? What the fuck were you thinking?" Jeremy took a swig of soda.

"I mean if some chick calls you over in the middle of the night..."

Jeremy laughed, "You were thinking about dat ass though."

"Yes, that ass."

They laughed.

"So how was it?"

"How was what?"

"Dat ass tho, nigga! What you think I'm talking about?"

"I don't know."

"What do you mean you don't know?"

"Just what I said."

Jeremy laughed his ass off. "So you drove over there in the middle of the night and spent the night, and you didn't even get it."

"No."

"Bruh," he laughed, tossing more almonds into his mouth. "Don't tell me you slept beside that ho with a throbbing dick."

"I slept on the couch."

Jeremy laughed so hard, water spilled from his eyes. "She played you, bruh." He paused. "On second thought, maybe she didn't play you. I know I would have rather not been in the bed with her if I wasn't going to hit. I would have volunteered to sleep on the couch. Nah, I would have left that ho. She was playing games."

"I know, right?"

"You like her?"

"I do."

"You were never like me."

"What do you mean?"

"You do better in relationships. I hate relationships."

Jeremy had been with sixteen women during the last three years. He'd been in one long-term relationship, and that relationship lasted three years with his son's mother before she'd found him in bed with her best friend.

"Speaking of relationships, guess who is back?"

"Who?"

"Layla."

Jeremy took a swig of water. "Stop playing."

"I'm not."

"What the fuck does she want? I guess she couldn't land an athlete or a rapper, now her ass came running back to you."

Rashad laughed, but he knew Jeremy was right.

"You gonna take her back?"

"Nah."

There was an awkward silence. Though Rashad had made up his mind that he wasn't going to take Layla back, he'd always love Layla. They'd been through a lot together.

Security of the building called and said Layla was there. Rashad told them to send her up.

"Damn." Rashad swore. "She must have heard us talking about her."

"Damn homie. I can see Layla walking around here now like she own this motherfucka."

"Whatever."

Jeremy stood strolled into the kitchen and tossed the almond bowl into the sink before returning to his seat. Layla entered the apartment wearing purple yoga pants and a vintage Hendrix t-shirt. She kissed Rashad on the cheek before her eyes lingered on Jeremy's man bun, trying to decide if she liked it. "Jeremy," she said.

Jeremy turned and faked a smile. She was hella cool, but she wasn't right for Rashad.

Layla ran to Jeremy and embraced him.

"What brings you here?"

"Getting older, and my roots are here. You know. I wanted to be around people I know."

"Interesting. I really didn't see a girl like you coming back to Charlotte."

"What is that supposed to mean?"

"You're a New York or LA type of girl."

"Getting older. Jeremy."

"Good to see you again."

"I follow you on the 'Gram."

"You do?" Jeremy didn't realize she followed him. Hell, he'd barely checked Instagram.

"Yeah" she laughed. "Why haven't you followed me back?"

"What's your name there?"

"ThatdimepieceLayla."

"I'll follow you." He said, then he gave Rashad a pound before heading out of the door.

When the door closed, Layla entered the living room, Rashad trailing her. She sat in the spot that Jeremy had had been in.

"What brings you here now?"

She crossed her legs. "I'm about to sign the lease for the apartment. The one I was telling you about near Northlake. I need the money."

"Why do you need to pay it all up front?"

Layla looked at him like he was stupid. "Now please don't tell me you're going to play games with me. You said that you were going to give me the money. Now is not the time for stupid ass questions. Are you going to give me the money or not?"

He frowned. "I just wanted to know where the money was going."

"I have to pay the money up front because my credit is ruined okay? I had a G-Wagon repossessed while I was in Houston."

Rashad remembered seeing her post a black G-Wagon wrapped in a red bow on Instagram. "Was it the one on Instagram?"

"Yes. What is that supposed to mean?"

"I was under the impression that somebody else bought it for you."

"Things aren't always what they seem on the Gram; you know that."

"I'm seeing that, but it seemed like a gift."

"Well, it was kinda a gift..."

"Kinda a gift?" He raised his eyebrow.

"A guy made the down payment on it, so it was kind of a gift." She said. "So can you give me the money, or are you going to bullshit me?"

He disappeared into the kitchen, then returned with a checkbook.

She frowned. "What the hell are you doing?"

"I'm writing you a check."

"Gimme cash. My account is overdrawn."

He sighed, "You're making my life really complicated right now."

She stood and made her way over to him and plopped down on her knees in front of him. Her hand traveled his thigh before taking possession of his penis. He took hold of her wrist and held her.

She looked up at him. Her eyes hazel—contacts, he'd figured—were sexy as hell. "I don't want to make your life complicated. I'm here to make it better."

He stared at her beautiful face, her full lips, and her erect nipples about to explode through the t-shirt. With her free hand, she removed his hand from her wrist.

"Let me please you, Daddy."

She then took possession of his manhood, stroking it until it stood erect, and she admired its stiffness and thickness. She smiled and then made eye contact. He smiled at her and thought to himself that Layla was still one sexy motherfucka. He lowered his pants more, then scooted to the edge of the sofa and forged his penis further into her mouth, caressing the back of her head and brushing her hair. He stood, and his pants slid down by his ankles. He looked down at her as she continued to massage and slobber on his manhood. He felt powerful. Like a king. A champion. He was enjoying himself, then he thought about how much he liked being around Kendall. She was a good woman, and he'd felt guilty about getting head from his ex, but he justified it in his mind. He wasn't in a relationship with Kendall. Dre was still coming over, while paying for her home. How did he know that she wasn't still sleeping with Dre, too? All of this ran through his mind while he enjoyed spectacular oral sex.

She stood, easing out of her yoga pants. She wore a black high waisted bikini panty that struggled to contain her ass. The bikini came down and was now looped around her ankles. She leaned into him and forced her tongue into his mouth. His hand now on her neck, traveling down her back, he removed the sports bra, and those perky tits stared at him. He turned her around, her back now facing him, and she kneeled to the sofa. Her elbows rested on the sofa. He moved the coffee table with his foot.

He thought about a condom. The last time they'd had sex was two years ago. She could have an STD now, and he knew he didn't want to get her pregnant.

"What are you waiting on, Rashad?" She pouted. "I want you right now."

He throbbed. He needed to cum right now. He'd been feeling this way ever since Kendall had teased him. He plunged inside her walls. He then yanked her hair, and she screamed "Zaddy!"

He kept stroking.

"Zaddy, treat me like the slut that I am. I deserve to be punished. I've not been a good girl."

They collapsed onto the sofa, his tool inside her. She lay on her side as he spooned her, yanked her hair, and turned her to face him as he shoved his tongue in her mouth.

"Manhandle me, Zaddy." They untangled themselves and she lay on the couch. He climbed on top and entered her again. "I missed you so much."

He'd missed her too but didn't want admit it.

"Did you miss me, Zaddy?"

"I did." He admitted. There was no way he was going to say no.

She smiled then held him tight, her mint green nails plunging into his lower back. "Cum for me."

He kept stroking. Sweat beads trickled into his pupils. His eyes now bloodshot, he tried hard to cum, but he couldn't. He wondering if this hoe was trying to trap him, trying to get a free ride. She wasn't stupid; Layla knew his businesses were doing well and he had more money now than he'd ever had before. But he knew being famous was more important than babies to her and having babies would slow a girl like Layla down.

"Cum for me, Zaddy. What's wrong? You don't like me?"

She bit his ear and pushed her tongue inside it; this always aroused him before.

He exploded inside and panted, trying his best to catch his breath. There were several quick breaths, then more panting. She laughed, then she attempted to forge her tongue into his ear again. He pushed her away. She attempted to possess his semi-hard penis and kneeled, opening her mouth again. She wanted him to put his manhood back into her mouth. She wanted to go for round two. He walked away with his dick swinging, and she frowned.

"What's wrong?" She asked as she trailed him into his bedroom.

He didn't respond.

"Do you mind if I take a shower?" She asked.

He pointed through the wall. "The guest bathroom is that way."

They locked eyes. He was the first to break contact and turn away from her.

"Is there something wrong?" She asked.

"We shouldn't have done that."

"You wanted it."

"You seduced me."

"So I peer pressured you into taking pussy. Are you gay now nigga? The Rashad that I once knew and loved, loved pussy."

"I'm just saying. We're not getting back together. I shouldn't have went down that road with you. I ain't blaming nobody. I'm just saying that we shouldn't have done it."

"You're acting like a motherfuckin lame."

"What?"

"Yeah, you're acting lame as fuck."

"How?"

"Can I have my money please?"

"Your money?"

"The money you'd promised me."

"When you come out of the shower, I'll have it all together for you. The rent in advance."

"What about the furniture?"

"I'll have it all."

* * * * *

Dre and Catherine had fallen asleep on the bed watching a Will Smith movie on Netflix. At eight o'clock, Alexa sounded to wake Dre up. He hopped up before looking for his phone; it was time to pick up Christian from his mother's house. He stood from the bed before scooping his pants from the floor. Seconds later, Catherine woke, stretching and yawning, then she sat up on the bed. "Where are you going babe?"

"I have to go pick up Christian from my mom's house."

She swallowed then cringed. "Okay."

"Hey, is there something wrong?" She shook her head no and offered a slight smile.

"I asked is there something wrong, Catherine?"

"And I said no." She stood and walked toward the bathroom, his eyes on her naked ass.

"Cat."

She stopped, turned, and faced him.

"What is bothering you?"

She sighed then dropped her head. "I was just hoping we could have some time by ourselves."

"Christian has been with my mom for the past two days. Look, I'll go get him now, and I'll take him back to Kendall in the morning, but know that my son is a part of me. I told you I had a child from day one."

"It wasn't exactly day one, but whatever."

"Are you having regrets?"

"No," she lied, looking away from him.

"Look, Catherine, if you don't want me to be with my son, I'll pack my shit and go."

She narrowed her eyes. "Pack your shit and go? This is your place not mine."

"I don't give a damn about this place. If my son is not welcome, I'm leaving."

"Dre why don't you ask me to leave? This is your place." she repeated.

Silence.

Catherine realized she was completely naked and grabbed a red towel hanging on the bathroom door to cover up.

"Are you breaking up with me Andre?"

"If you don't accept my son. Fuck it, Catherine."

"Of course, I accept your son. I love him. But I was just saying that this is all new to me."

"Are you sure you can accept him?"

"Yes, of course I can accept him. Like I said, I love Christian."

"Good."

* * * *

Kendall was lying on the sofa eating popcorn, watching Queen Sugar. She'd called Dre twenty-four times, still no answer. She'd made up her mind that if she hadn't heard from him by the end of the night, she would have no choice but to call the police. She wanted her son home with her where he belonged. At 8:45 pm Dre, Christian and Frank burst into the house and Christian hurried into his mother's arms. She kissed him. "I missed you baby."

"I missed you too," Christian repeated.

She glared at Dre then kissed Christian's forehead. "Have you eaten, baby?"

"Daddy took me to McDonald's." Then the toddler looked at Dre and said. "I'm sorry Daddy, I forgot that you said not to tell anyone that we went to McDonald's."

Kendall took the chance to inspect his clothes. "What in the world are you wearing boy." Christian was wearing overalls that were way too short with a yellow t-shirt, black church socks and Chuck Taylor Converse.

"Daddy dressed me."

"And it looks like it. You got my son looking like a peasant." Kendall laughed at the ridiculous outfit that Dre had put together for Christian. "Take Frank into the bedroom and play with your games or watch Adventure Time, while I talk to your daddy."

"What's Adventure Time?" Dre asked, clueless.

Kendall laughed. "You know nothing about raising a toddler."

"Hey, I just don't know all these TV shows."

"Because I'm the one that spends most of the time with Christian." After Christian had disappeared, Kendall said, "I'm glad you brought him back."

"Of course I was going to bring him back." He scanned the room, searching for a hint of the nigga that had been there the last time they'd spoken. There was nothing; she'd cleaned the place up neatly. Kendall always kept the place neat, one of the things he still liked about her.

"You want to talk about what happened?" He plopped down on the armchair.

"What is it to talk about?" She sat up on the sofa and then paused the TV show.

"Talk."

"Who was he?"

"Just a guy."

"Just a guy, my ass. You don't bring just a guy to your house. Who is this motherfucker, Ken?"

She studied his face. The nerve of this motherfucker questioning her about a man when it was clear that he was planning on moving on with his life with this Catherine woman.

He was staring, breathing hard, waiting on her to answer.

"Want to tell me how you met him?"

She avoided his gaze. "Not really."

"Why not?"

She resumed eye contact with him. "If you must know, he was my personal trainer."

"You fucking a broke ass personal trainer?"

"First of all, I ain't fucking nobody. Secondly, he owns the gym, but what difference does it make who I sleep with? You're with someone else, so don't try to control my life because you can't."

"You can do what you want to do, just don't bring nobody to this house, and I don't want the motherfucker around my son."

"You took Christian, so I invited him over. You shouldn't have taken my son without my permission."

"Our son, you mean," he corrected her.

"Of course."

"So I can't spend time with Christian?"

"I never said that."

"So, you and this personal trainer," he paused. "Is it serious?"

"He's not a trainer."

"You're the one that said he was a trainer."

"I said he was my trainer, but he owns the gym."

"So is he a trainer or not a trainer?"

"He was my trainer, but he owns the gym."

He leaned forward, his elbows resting on his knees. They locked eyes. He repeated the question. "Is it serious?"

"I just met the man. How could it be serious?"

"Well you brought him over and fucked him."

"I didn't fuck him."

"Why was he here?"

"I was lonely." She turned from his gaze, then flung her hair over her shoulder. "I guess I was lonely."

"Where did he sleep?"

"Look, I don't have to answer all these questions. All I know is I've never lied to you." She walked past him, and he grabbed her hand to make her face him.

"I made a mistake. I'm sorry about Catherine. I'm sorry you had to find out the way you did. I didn't want to hurt you. And you're right; you've never lied to me." His eyes were sincere.

She couldn't believe that he'd just opened up to her like that. What had gotten into him?

"Catherine."

"What about her?"

"I don't know if she's for me."

"What do you mean?"

"When I came over this morning and you had your friend over here, it made me realize that I don't want to live without you. I want to be with my family."

She laughed. "So you think it's that easy?"

"No, I know it's not that easy; I'm just telling you what I want."

"Why should I care about what the fuck you want?"

"Look at me." He ordered. "Are you telling me that you don't love me? You don't love what we have? You want to throw all that away?"

"I love you, but I can't put myself through this bullshit again. I thought I knew you, but turns out I didn't know you at all."

"That shouldn't have happened." Dre stood, smoothing his hair with his fingers. "I don't want to lose you Ken. It shouldn't have happened. I knew right from wrong; I knew I was risking a lot. I can't take it back, but I'm here to tell you I want my family back. I don't want some strange ass man raising my kid. I want to be in the house with you and Christian."

"Damn right, it shouldn't have happened, but it happened, and now that it has happened, you are mad because I went on with my life."

An awkward pause fell between them before Kendall continued.

"What did you expect me to do, Andre?" She laughed. "I'll tell you what you expected me to do. You wanted me to sit and cry my head off because you left me. You thought just because you're paying the bills that I wouldn't have a life."

"I didn't think that. You're a beautiful woman. I knew that you were going to find someone sooner or later. But I ain't going to lie—I thought It would be later. You moved fast." He laughed, and it annoyed her.

"I went out on a date. I mean if you call that moving on, okay, but I don't think I moved on at all."

"This date that you had, wound up spending the night."

"Because he spent the night, you assume we must have fucked. Do you think he would be showering in the guest bedroom shower if we would have fucked? That man would have used the bedroom shower. We have a huge walk in shower with three shower heads remember? If he had slept in bed with me, do you really think I would have made him use a separate shower?"

"I thought about that later."

"And if you would have looked at the sofa, you would have seen his bedding. But you didn't look. You didn't care about all of that. You'd made up in your mind that I was a ho. Though you'd fucked Catherine and was planning to marry her, according to that little birthday card. But I was the ho."

"I didn't."

"You feel intimidated. Why don't you just admit it, Andre? You don't want me, but you don't want anyone else to have me."

"Maybe you're right."

"So you don't want to be with me?"

"I do want to be with you."

"You just admitted that you just don't want anyone else to have me."

"I didn't mean it like that. What I meant was I don't want to see you with someone else."

"Dre, I want my son to be with his father, and if this is something that you really want, fight for your family."

"Can I spend the night?"

"I don't know. Can you spend the night? Will your fiancée let you spend the night?"

He laughed. "I'm my own man, and you're my wife."

Christian burst into the room with Frank bounding behind him. "Mommy, I want a juicy juice.

Before Kendall could say anything, Dre announced, "Daddy is spending the night."

CHAPTER 11

The next day, Kendall and Rashad met up for lunch at a Mediterranean restaurant in Midtown. It was Kendall's first time there. After they were seated, he complimented her outfit; she was stunning. Kendall was wearing a floral print dress and sandals, and her hair was up in a bun, exposing her exceptional cheekbones.

"You look Ethiopian. Has anyone ever told you this?"

"All the time."

"You look really pretty today."

"Thank you." she smiled.

Rashad's mind drifted to Layla and the very fulfilling sex he'd had with her. He knew that he shouldn't have done it, but despite Kendall's issues, he liked her a lot. He noticed that she wasn't smiling.

"What's wrong?" He asked.

She sipped on ice water. "I have something to tell you."

"You're getting back with your baby's father."

She smiled, "Yeah. How'd you know?"

"What? Are you serious?" He laughed, but he'd felt betrayed though he'd just slept with his ex. He was disappointed that there would be no Kendall and Rashad. He had envisioned them living together, along with baby Christian, but now, none of that was going to be possible.

A young man around twenty delivered the salad, lamb, and potatoes.

"I'm sorry, Rashad."

"It's okay."

"No it's not okay. I was feeling you, and I can tell you were feeling me too."

"I was, but I'll be okay. I like the way you handled this. The fact that you were honest says a lot about you. I guess our timing was just kind of off."

Kendall bit into her salad. "It was hard for me to ask you to meet up with me, so I could tell you this, but it was the right thing to do."

He nodded then sliced his lamb, half-heartedly.

"You're going to try to work it out, huh?"

She nodded. "For my son."

"What about you, Kendall? Do you think you can be happy with Dre?"

She'd thought about that a few days ago, and the last time she'd been truly happy was before she was pregnant with Christian. Of course her son had made her happy, but the last time she'd felt alive was before he was born. She used to go out dancing with her friends and was in great shape then without extra exercise. Her life had become routine, and Dre's life had become routine; she supposed that's why he'd stepped out. She'd never talked to him about it, but it made sense to her.

Rashad bit into his lamb, then asked, "So you ever think that the only reason he wants to get back with you is because he doesn't want to see you with me?"

"That's what I told him."

"How did he respond?"

"He said something about he didn't want to be without me."

"So has he moved back in?"

"He's never *really* moved out."

"I see."

"Are you okay, Rashad?"

His eyes now crimson, he winced. "I'm okay."

"We can still be friends?"

"Can we?"

"I don't see anything wrong with the occasional text."

"But is that really being friends?"

"I guess you're right."

"Does he know that you're meeting up with me?"

"No. He doesn't need to know." She looked at his plate and realized he hadn't touched his food. "Did I ruin your appetite?"

"Maybe." He forced a smile.

"I'm sorry."

He shrugged and said, "Shit happens."

"Good way of looking at it."

"Hey, I have something to tell you myself to ease my pain."

"Now you have me feeling bad." She sipped her water. "I'm really sorry Rashad, you didn't deserve this."

"Why is it the good guys that always get hurt?" He winced, then his chin trembled. "I'm joking. I'm a grown man, and I'm not really good guy. I slept with my ex the other day, so I feel you."

She forced a laugh. "You slept with your ex?"

"Does that bother you?"

She didn't know why, but she was jealous.

"Did y'all sleep together before you came to my house or after?"

"Does it make a difference?"

"It makes no difference." She ate a spoonful of potatoes. "Wow."

"It's not like that. I don't like her; it was just sex."

"Look, you are single. I suppose you can do whatever you want. I just didn't think you were like that."

"It happened."

"Sex doesn't just happen, but no need to explain shit to me."

"I thought I'd be honest with you, since we're being honest."

"Right, but you could have kept it to yourself." She ate another spoonful of potatoes then sipped her water.

"I'm not a cheater when I'm in a committed relationship."

"I guess we'll never find that out. Will we? Rashad, you're a great man. What you do with your ex is none of my business. I guess you can say the timing was off with us."

"I guess." He toyed with his food then averted his eyes from her, not really knowing what to make of all of this. He adored Kendall and didn't want to let her go, but she had a history with Dre, and he knew that it was just a matter of time before they faded from each other's memories. They finished their meals in silence. He escorted her to her car, opened the door, and she sat inside as he stared at her.

He started, "I have a question…"

"What is it?"

"Do you think we could have made it?"

"Timing was wrong."

"Really wrong."

He thought she looked so pretty sitting in the Range Rover. The floral color of her printed dress made her seem so girly.

"But do you think we would have made it?"

"I do. I like you Rashad, and this is very hard."

"If it wasn't for him, we'd be together."

"If it wasn't for them." She smiled. "Remember you just slept with your ex."

"I guess this is goodbye."

"Yes."

"Can I have another hug?"

* * * * *

Inside the locker room of a luxury spa, Chrissy and Kendall sat on a shiny mahogany bench, draped in white robes. This had been the first time they'd seen each other since Kendall decided that she was going back to Dre. Chrissy shielded her toes under the flap of the slippers, when Kendall noticed and asked "What the hell are you doing?"

"My feet look horrible. I didn't get a chance to get a pedi last week."

"But you're at the spa."

"I haven't had time for all of that."

"Show me them feet," Kendall laughed. "What are you going to do when she massages your feet?"

"I'm not letting her touch my feet."

Kendall laughed her ass off. "You should get them done instead of a massage. That's what I would do."

"You're the one paying." Chrissy noted.

"Get the pedi and then the massage. I got you girl."

"Thanks." Chrissy said. "Seriously, I'm happy that you and Dre are back together."

"Thank you."

"You don't sound like you feel like it's the best thing to do."

"I don't."

"Why not?"

She turned and faced Chrissy, who was still concealing her ugly ass toenails.

"I'm not sure Dre is the man for me anymore."

"Why do you say that?"

"We've outgrown each other."

"Trainer Bae have anything to do with it?"

"No."

Chrissy nudged her. "Are you sure?"

Kendall shrugged. "He might have something to do with it."

A spa attendant wearing khakis and a light blue polo shirt gently opened the door, handed them a glass of Chardonnay each, then vanished.

Kendall sipped her wine, then said. "I'm happy for Christian's sake, but I have to admit it doesn't feel right."

"Have you two forgiven each other?"

Kendall looked away from Chrissy. "Of course we've forgiven each other, why else would we even be together? I mean..."

Chrissy stretched out and exposed her toes briefly. They both laughed, and then Chrissy secured those toes under the rubber flap.

"What I'm asking is did you two say 'I'm sorry' to one another?"

"No we didn't say it. It was just kind of understood." Kendall took another sip.

The attendant returned again to the room and apologized to them for double booking and offered them a twenty-five dollar voucher and said their massage would start in fifteen minutes. When she was gone, Chrissy said. "All I'm saying is that you need to talk about what happened. Don't just pretend that it didn't happen."

"Do you really think we should discuss that?"

"Hell yeah." Kendall was her bestie and had always been the prettiest and the smartest, but she didn't have the experience that Chrissy had. After all, she'd spent most of her adult life with Dre.

Kendall sipped her wine. She knew that Chrissy was right. She couldn't go on pretending like they didn't have problems.

"You're right."

"I know I'm right, and now is the time to be working on getting a backup plan just in case things don't go right."

"I know. I've been thinking about that too."

"What am I going to do?"

"I don't know. Get you a job first, maybe wait tables or something. Get some money coming in. So just in case the nigga starts tripping you'll be okay. I got a friend she bartends down at the Ritz Carlton, and she makes two hundred dollars a night in tips. I know that's not what you are used to, but it's pretty good money for us commoners."

"Bartender?" She laughed. "I don't know shit about bartending."

"How hard can mixing drinks be? You've mixed a lot of drinks over the years. I know that for a fact."

They giggled, then Kendall said, "Very true. But you make it sound like I was a drunk."

The attendant entered the room to let them know it was time to be seen.

* * * * *

Layla met Rashad at Cowfish, a restaurant on the South End, wearing a red, backless dress that clung to her body, and she turned the heads of guys and girls when they entered the restaurant. They sat near the window that offered a perfect view of the city.

It had been about a week since they'd had sex; he had seen her only that one time and it felt awkward. They peered at each other while glancing atop the menu, neither of them not really knowing what to say.

Finally, Rashad broke the ice. "I was surprised that you invited me to dinner."

"It's the least I could do; you've been so kind to me."

The waitress appeared, and she ordered the sesame salmon with a glass of Merlot. He had ordered the Indian tuna burger.

"What did you want to talk about?" He asked.

"About us."

"What about us?"

"I want my life and my ring back."

He raised an eyebrow. "Really?"

"You're the man that I'm supposed to be with."

"You think so?"

"I was thinking about that the whole time after I left. But you never told me how you felt when I left for Houston. You never asked me to come back. I never heard from you. You never liked any of my pics on social media. It was like I didn't exist to you."

"So likes mean what?" He laughed.

"I don't know. What do likes mean?"

"I just can't believe grown adults get so caught up on whether someone likes their pics or not. I like you in real life, isn't that enough?"

He sighed. She was bringing up old memories that he'd once suppressed. "I don't want to talk about this."

"You never want to talk, Rashad, and that was the problem. You're not a communicator."

"That was the problem?" He repeated. "All I know is that you showed up one day saying that you were moving. There was no time to communicate. You told me what you were going to do, and you did it."

"And you didn't try to stop me."

"I asked you not to go."

"And that was it."

He sighed. "What do you really want to talk about? I see no reason to bring up the past."

The waitress placed another glass of wine in front of her.

She sipped her wine and said, "Rashad I'm not dwelling on the past; I just want to know how you felt."

He narrowed his eyes. "Why is that important?"

"To see if it's worth pursuing a relationship with you."

"It's not," he said a little too sharply.

"What about the other night?"

"We shouldn't have done it."

"I could tell that you wanted me."

He shrugged.

"I was just a fuck," she scoffed, then finished off her glass of Merlot.

"With our history, you could never be just a fuck."

"You wanted me. I know you did." She sounded desperate.

"I did and you wanted me and that was that."

"Where do we go from here? What the fuck do we have? Do you see me in your future?"

Rashad placed his dinner fork on the plate. "Where do you want it to go?"

Their eyes met momentarily.

"I'm sorry about what happened in the past, but I can't help it. I know you have someone else, but I love you Rashad, and I want to be here with you. I want to have your baby."

Rashad shook his head. "And I'm 'posed to believe that bullshit."

"Why wouldn't you?"

He laughed, and it annoyed her. She stood and was about to make a dash out of the door, when he stood and demanded that she sit down.

She took a seat, tears cascading down her cheeks.

"You left me when I needed you the most. You left me to chase some bullshit ass modeling fame, while I wanted a family."

"I wanted to give you a family, but after Mya died, and I got pregnant then miscarried, I was so high all the time off Zannies. And I wasn't happy here, so I had to get away to get back to being me."

"What about me? All you are thinking about is what you were going through. What do you think about what I was going through and how I felt after burying a dead baby that had my nose and your eyes? Mya was dainty like you and stubborn like me. Did you remember how she used to like to lay on my chest? I watched the videos of her taking her first steps every day for a year until I couldn't watch it no more."

"I know." She dabbed her eyes with the napkin. "Of course I remember my baby. You think I didn't love her? I loved her very much, you will never understand the bond between a mother and a child."

"How do I know you won't leave again?" He asked.

They locked eyes, and she said. "I'm here to stay."

"I'm through playing. I'm not getting any younger. I want a real woman."

"What about your little girlfriend?"

"What girlfriend?"

"You said you had one the other day."

He shrugged. "She is trying to work it out with her ex."

Layla smiled as if that was the best news she'd heard in a while. "And me and you should try to work it out. Can't you see this is supposed to happen?"

"I just don't want to live with regrets."

"Take a chance or you'll never know."

CHAPTER 12

Christian pointed to the Ferris wheel, then jammed the raspberry cotton candy into his tiny mouth. They waited in line for the bumper cars at the amusement park. Christian didn't meet the size requirements for most rides, but that didn't stop him from asking about all of the rides from the paddleboats to the airplane rides and wanting to go to the haunted house. He wanted to play all games. Dre had won him a giant elephant by throwing a football through a hole. Dre and Kendall were tired and were beginning to think that this was maybe a bad idea. Kendall also didn't like that the park had her hair now smelling like cigarette smoke and fried fish. But they labored through the day for Christian's sake. The most memorable moment came when they sat down to enjoy caramel candy apples, and the boy looked at his mother and then back at his father, grinning, as he held the stuffed elephant that Dre had won.

"Why are you smiling, baby?" Kendall asked.

"We're a family," he said.

Kendall and Dre were both silent.

Christian sipped his Coke and said, "I love my family."

Kendall teared up at her son's proclamation of love. She leaned and kissed him. "And your family loves you too, baby."

Kendall cut her eyes at Dre. "How does that make you feel?"

"I know I made the right decision."

Kendall was happy to hear him say that, but she couldn't stop thinking about how he had betrayed her. Later that night as they lay in bed, he slid up against her and caressed her butt like he used to do, and she tingled and turned to him. She was aroused; she was always aroused when he touched her there.

She faced him and asked, "And what are you trying to do sir?"

"Nothing." He smiled.

She massaged his tool. "Excited, huh?" She smiled revealing dimples.

"You make me that way."

"Good to know I can still turn you on."

"I have a question that has been bothering me."

She let go of his penis and asked, "What is it?"

"Did you do it with him?"

"Do it with him? You sound like you are in the third grade, Andre. Did I fuck Rashad you mean?"

"Rashad?"

"That's his name."

"Did you fuck Rashad?"

"I already told you I never fucked Rashad. Why is that so hard for you to believe? Have I ever lied to you, Andre?"

She'd never lied to him, but he wondered what the fuck the man was doing in his house in the first place.

"I never slept with that man."

Their eyes met.

"I believe you," he said after a moment.

"Why didn't you believe me the first time? You sure know how to piss me off."

"Why?"

"Because you can go out and destroy what the fuck we have built. Obliterate my trust, break up our family, have a full on relationship with that white girl, and now you have the fucking nerve to question if I've slept with Rashad."

Dre sighed. He didn't want to hear about what he'd done. He didn't want to relive the past, but he had brought them to this point in the conversation by asking about Rashad.

"Dre if we don't trust each other, we are better off apart. Without trust, what do we have?"

"I know." He turned from her gaze.

"Look at me, Andre," she ordered.

Dre faced her again, but he avoided looking her in the eye.

"Andre, do you trust me?"

"Of course."

"Good." She said, trying her best to be positive.

"What about me?"

She narrowed her eyes.

"Do you trust me, Kendall?"

Silence.

That positive shit was about to go out of the window. She didn't trust him, and she couldn't believe that he asked her that.

Dre waited for Kendall to answer, but when she took too long, he asked a follow up question. "You don't trust me do you?"

"I don't." She couldn't pretend like she trusted him. She'd trusted him before, but she couldn't fake it now.

"Why not?"

She closed her eyes then sighed. Was this motherfucker serious right now? Wasn't it him who had stepped out on her? How could she trust him? Not only was he fucking some white bitch but he'd plan to divorce her for the white girl at that.

"It's just too much for me to talk about right now."

"We're having a serious conversation right now."

"How can I trust you right now? You deceived me, but I think that trust can be earned again. And I'm willing to work at it with you. You're the man that I've loved forever, and I want to work at it."

"I see." He winced.

"Do you really?"

"I'm not slow, Kendall, I understand. I made a mistake and I'm trying to work on myself. Nobody is perfect, you know."

"I know."

"If you know that, what's the problem?"

"The problem is you had a secret life with a girlfriend that you were about to marry. I thought I knew you, but after that I wasn't so sure."

"So it's going to take time to regain the trust?"

"Yes."

"Okay," He reached for her thigh, but she swatted his hand.

"What's wrong?"

"What do you think? You ruined the mood, motherfucker."

* * * * *

Layla and India posed for a photoshoot on the rooftop of India's luxury apartment. A famous photographer named Vlad, a thin balding Russian who had worked top mags like GQ and Vanity Fair, shot them.

Rashad and Jeremy watched as the girls posed, and Vlad guided them through the shoot.

Jeremy said, "I thought this was posed' to be a fitness photo shoot."

"It is."

"Looks like its a photo shoot for hoes selling ass, bruh, this is what they do on Instagram nowadays."

"You would know better than me."

Jeremy took a drag from the vape pen. "I'm telling you nowadays you can get a million followers for having an ass that you worked for or bought in Columbia," Jeremy laughed.

"I know."

"So how much you pay for this photoshoot?"

"Twenty thousand dollars." Rashad said simply.

"Twenty thousand dollars? Are you out of your goddamned mind? You pay a motherfucker twenty thousand dollars for some shit I could have done with my iPhone."

Rashad laughed. Jeremy was right.

"So you and Layla are back together."

"No."

"This ho takes off to Houston right after Mya dies. Then, she pops back up and now you dropping twenty stacks for a photoshoot. I guess you got money to blow."

"It's not that simple."

Jeremy shook his head. At that moment it became clear to him that Rashad still loved Layla. Jeremy felt guilty for calling her a ho, but what the fuck else could he call her?

"Talk to me brother make me understand. I don't care. I mean, whatever you want to do I support you."

"Understand what?"

"Why you doing this, bruh?"

"Remember the woman I told you about a few weeks ago?"

"The one that let you come over and you slept on the couch?"

"Yeah, her."

"What about her?"

"That shit didn't work out."

"You think?" He laughed, still thinking about the story of Rashad sleeping on the couch.

"So you need to get back with Layla?" Jeremy asked.

"I don't want to talk about it right now." he huffed.

"If this is who you want to be with, then I support it."

Layla and India wandered over to them, and Layla introduced India.

Jeremy extended his hand. "Nice to meet you India."

Layla laughed, "I've already told her about you and that's all you got to say? Nice to meet you? What is wrong with you? She's stunning! I would fuck her."

Jeremy stared at her fake breasts and her shiny, Columbian chiclet teeth. India was nothing special to him—just another bitch trying to come up from a man's dime.

"She told me all about you." India gushed.

Jeremy smiled. "What did she say?"

"Said you knew how to treat a beautiful woman."

Jeremy laughed, "You're too rich for my taste."

"What is that supposed to mean?"

"I can't afford you."

Vlad the photographer scurried over, waving his hand. "Ladies! Time to get back to work."

India smirked, then she and Layla trotted back to the edge of the rooftop.

"I'll catch up with you tomorrow sometime, bruh. I'm going home to read to my son, then jerk off while thinking about that hoe. Save myself twenty or thirty thousand dollars. A nut is motherfucking nut, right?" Jeremy laughed.

"I'll hit you up tomorrow." Rashad said.

* * * * *

Later that evening on Rashad's balcony. Rashad, Layla, and India were drinking wine and appreciating the skyline.

"What's up with Jeremy?" India asked.

"What do you mean?" Rashad asked.

"He was acting kind of funny." Layla asked.

Layla spilled wine as she rolled her hips to Rihanna's "Wild Thoughts." "Jeremy acted rude as fuck. What was his problem? I mean he barely spoke. We used to be cool before I left. I noticed the other day that he was acting kind of weird, then, too."

Future's "Mask Off" came on, and Layla sat on India's lap, India's hand resting within Layla's thighs.

"I was just trying to be cordial. Layla said he was cool. I thought he was cute, but he was acting like a typical light-skinned nigga. I usually don't fuck with them, but I thought he was kind of rugged with his tiger sleeve tattoo. So I was like fuck it, if my girl say he's cool, I'll holla at him, but he acted like I wanted something from him. Rashad, I hope your other friends ain't like that."

Layla sprang from her lap then sat down beside Rashad. "I just get a weird vibe from him." She said.

"He was wondering why y'all needed a twenty thousand dollar photoshoot."

India spat her wine out. "Are you being fucking serious right now?"

"That's what he wanted to know." Rashad said.

"What a cornball." She turned to Layla. "You tried to set me up with him."

"Wait a minute, that's my brother." Rashad said.

"He's not your brother." Layla said.

"We're closer than brothers." He paused. "Look, I wondered the same thing. What exactly is that going to accomplish?"

"Look, babe." She unbuckled his belt, then put her hands inside his boxers to wrestle his limp penis free.

"Tell me, what is this going to accomplish." Rashad asked.

"Vlad has shot Vogue, British GQ, and Harpers Bazaar—all the major magazines. He is world renowned, so to get him for twenty thousand was a steal. When people see that we shot with him, it will give us credibility, and we're not like the other ten million bitches on social media. Instant celebrity. My followers will shoot up because Vlad has about four million followers. He's going to post eight of the pictures on his IG, and he shared the shoot on his Snapchat."

"I get ya."

Layla stroked his penis until he stopped her. He wasn't in the mood.

"So what are you trying to do again?"

"I'm a brand ambassador. I want to get paid by brands and get sponsors for my fitness brand and be the face for some of these fitness companies."

Rashad raised his eyebrows "I don't know what that is. but okay."

"But you own a gym."

"A real gym. Not some fake Instagram bullshit."

"I'm offended."

"I didn't mean it like that, but it just seems nowadays, everybody is a personal trainer. Everybody is a model. Everybody is a singer. Everybody is a rapper. Everybody is a writer. What's wrong with someone saying I paint for living?"

"My friend is a painter. He sells a lot of his paintings on IG." India said.

Rashad frowned. "I'm talking about a regular motherfucker that paints houses for a living."

India said, "Did we offend you?"

"No I'm just saying some of this shit is unrealistic. It's fake fame. Beyonce is famous, not a chick with silicone ass."

"You seem upset."

"No, I just don't want you to waste your time pursuing something that may not materialize."

"Then we can parlay that into a YouTube channel and get paid by YouTube."

"These are career goals for thirty year old women?"

"No it's just something I want to do now while I'm young before I become a mom again."

"You're not that young."

"I'm not old, either."

"I guess you're right when you got forty-two-year-old women on Instagram stripping."

"You sound like your boy," India commented then turned to Layla. "You know the hater, Jeremiah."

"Jeremy." Layla corrected.

"Whatever the fuck his name is. I'll just call his ass 'The Hater,'" India huffed.

"Was he really hating?"

"If the motherfucker wasn't wishing me good, he was hating."

"He just doesn't want me to get used." Rashad defended his friend.

"You think I'll use you?"

"I didn't say that."

"You want me to give your money back?"

"I value time over money."

"You can say that again." India interjected.

Rashad's penis was limp again. Layla stroked the dark shaft and the pink head, the color of strawberry ice cream. It was beautiful to her. She took him into her mouth, arousing India.

Layla's tongue circled the tip before looking up at him and smiling. "You taste like pineapples."

He knew there was truth to this; he'd had pineapple the day before.

"I want a taste." India asked.

"Can India taste, too?" Layla asked.

Rashad didn't respond instead reclined looking toward the brilliant red sky clasping his hands together as India and Layla shared his seed.

CHAPTER 13

Christian was about to force a fingernail clipper into the power outlet before Kendall snatched it from his hand and startled him, then popped him twice on the wrist. The toddler hollered, "I want my Daddy."

Kendall felt guilty, watching the tears streaming down his chubby face. It caused her great pain to see Christian crying. She leaned into him as he held the hand that stung from the whipping. Frank trotted out from the bedroom, tail wagging and began to bark as Christian cried. Kendall said, "Mommy is sorry."

"But Mommy hurt Christian."

"Mommy loves you."

"No."

"I do love you." Kendall pointed to the socket. "See son, this socket is bad, and it will hurt you if you put something inside of it."

"Mommy hurt me."

"It will shock you."

"Shock me?" He stopped crying, but Frank barked and scurried around in circles on the Moroccan carpet.

"Shut the fuck up!" Kendall yelled at the dog.

"Mommy is being mean." Christian began to cry again.

"Mommy is not mean."

Dre burst through the door.

The toddler immediately tattled. "Daddy, Mommy is being mean."

"Mommy is not being mean."

Christian approached Dre with outreached hands. Dre scooped him up. Dre studied Kendall's face and laughed. He realized that she'd been having a rough day. Kendall's lips curled, and she swallowed hard.

Frank started barking again before Kendall yanked his collar, led him into the guest bedroom, and slammed the door behind her.

"Mommy whipped me," Christian whined.

"Tell him why I hit you."

"She hit me because she was being mean, and she said a bad word to Frank!" he cried.

Kendall shook her head at her son telling half-truths just like his daddy.

Dre laughed. "What happened? His hand is bruised."

"Yeah I popped him because he was about to stick something inside the wall socket."

Dre narrowed his eyes. "But the house is child proof."

"Yes, but not every house that he goes to is child proof. I just wanted to let him know that it is not alright."

Dre sat him down at a chair in the kitchen and said, "Don't play around the socket."

"I'll get shocked."

"You know this?"

"Mommy told me that, then she started being mean."

"Before I told Frank to shut the fuck up." Kendall slipped in, and Christian shouted.

"Mommy said a bad word!"

Dre laughed his ass off.

"She hurt my hand." Christian presented his hand to his father who had already seen the bruise. "It hurts, Daddy."

"Boy ain't nobody hurt you. It's just a little bruise; it's going to go away. I used to get way worse than that."

Kendall approached Christian and asked. "Let me see your hand son?"

Christian stuck out his hand. Kendall examined the bruise before saying, "Mommy is going to kiss it for you so it will feel better."

He smiled.

She kissed the bruise on Christian's hand. "Mommy sorry."

"I forgive you. Mommy."

"Mommy loves you."

"I love you too, Mommy."

"Now go to your room and play with Frank. Let me and Mommy talk," Dre ordered Christian.

"Frank is not in my room. He is in the guest room."

Dre laughed because you had to be so specific with toddlers. "Go into the guest room then to play with Frank while Mommy and I talk."

After Christian disappeared, Dre leaned into Kendall and kissed her. "One of those days, huh?"

She shook her head. "Watching a toddler is not easy."

"So what's up?"

"I just wanted to let you know that I appreciate you."

She smiled; she was still trying her best not to look at him and think of Catherine, the birthday card, and the plan to leave her.

"We need a vacation. Don't you agree?" Dre said.

"A vacation?"

"Yeah, me, you, Christian, and Frank."

"Can we leave Christian and Frank?" Where are we going?"

"Maldives."

"You know, that is my dream vacation. You know that's where I wanted to go on my..."

"Honeymoon, go ahead and say it."

"I don't want to say it because it looks like it isn't going to ever happen."

"Don't be so negative."

She smiled again. "How can I be negative when we're going to the Maldives?"

"Exactly."

"This is wonderful. I can't wait to tell Chrissy."

"Why don't you invite her? Tell her to bring a guy and let's make this a couple's trip?"

"You would do that?"

"Of course I would, but I know you've slandered my name with Chrissy."

"Dre, don't go there."

"You're right."

"Can you take Christian to get something to eat?"

"Yeah."

"Can you take Frank too?"

He laughed, "You really don't like him do you?"

"I love him, he just barks too much."

They laughed their asses off.

* * * * *

Chrissy and Kendall sat on Chrissy's deck, grilling hamburgers and steaks.

Cato was frying some fish in a wash pot the way his granddaddy had taught him. The fish tasted damn good that way, and he liked to have his fish with beer.

Chrissy and Kendall sipped white wine with fried fish, and he'd teased them that they were "clatchet"—classy ratchet girls—eating fried fish with mustard on it and sipping wine. To him that just didn't mix.

Kendall told them about the offer Dre made to fly them to the Maldives.

Chrissy extracted bones from her fish and fanned mosquitoes away from her at the same time. She faced Kendall and asked, "I don't mean to sound like a dummy, but where the hell are the Maldives?"

Cato said, "Everybody knows where the Maldives are."

A harsh look appeared on Chrissy's face. Was Cato trying to say he was smarter, more cultured than her? She'd graduated from community college, not him.

"Where the fuck are the Maldives?" Chrissy asked.

"They are right near the Fiji Islands." Kendall explained.

"Yeah, she's right." Cato agreed.

"Too bad you ain't going with us." Chrissy snapped.

Cato reached into the cooler, grabbed him a Bud Light, and popped the top. "I might go one day."

"You were just complaining about your baby mama wanting you to take your son to Myrtle Beach, talmbout ain't nobody got no money for that. I know damn well you ain't going nowhere near the Maldives."

"And you ain't either."

"See, that's where you are wrong. Didn't you just hear Kendall say that they invited me? It's a couple's trip."

"Couple? U ain't got no man. Who you taking? Slim? If he wanted you, you'd already be with him."

"Fuck you and fuck Slim."

Cato turned to Kendall. "Can I go?"

"You got a passport?"

"No, but I can get one; I'm caught up on my child support."

Kendall laughed, "Look I'm sure if I ask Dre, he'll say that you can go."

"He's going to pay for it right? Cause I ain't got no money like that."

"I thought you were a hustler."

"Small time." he mumbled.

Kendall and Chrissy laughed.

"I'm sure Dre will pay for it."

"Good, I ain't seen that nigga in a long ass time. I'm glad y'all worked it out, can't let a little cheating get in between a good relationship. I'm sure the nigga ain't mean to do it, and I ain't trying to be funny, but you ain't going to find another Dre out here in these streets."

Kendall clenched her teeth. It took everything in her power not to curse Cato's ass out.

Chrissy said, "Will you shut the fuck up, Cato? Ain't nobody asked your ass shit."

Cato grabbed another piece of fried croaker and doused hot sauce on it.

Kendall sat her plate on the table.

"I was just saying I'm glad Kendall and Dre worked out. If anybody belong together, it's them two."

"Yeah especially since you think there is a chance that we are going to take you to the Maldives."

Cato sat his fish plate on the table, approached Kendall, and placed his arm around her neck in an awkward side-hug. "Kendall, you aight, right? Everything is okay, right?"

"Kendall looked Chrissy in the eye. "I know you're right." she said but she sounded unsure.

* * * * *

A month had passed since Carlos had spoken to Dre at the barbershop. He'd called him six times, but Dre never picked up the phone. TaTa the barber remembered that Dre had once bragged that he'd had a townhome downtown on the corner of Fifth and Poplar, so Carlos drove downtown, that's when he noticed Dre's car, the Maserati that he had sat inside in the barbershop parking lot. He knocked on the door of the home that the car was parked in front of. He knocked again before realizing there was a bell. He rang the bell, but there was still no answer. He was walking away from the home when the door opened to an old white lady, holding a small handgun.

He held up his hands and laughed, "Hey, I don't want any problems ma'am."

"What do you want?"

"I'm looking for the owner of this car." He pointed to Dre's car.

"He lives in the townhouse to the left of me."

"Thanks."

The old woman watched Carlos until he climbed the stairs and rang the bell of the next townhome.

The door opened, and Carlos stepped back. Standing in front of him was one of the most beautiful white women that he'd ever seen. She had a short, boyish blonde haircut, dancing blue eyes, and pouty pink lips.

The woman asked. "What can I do for you?"

"I'm looking for Dre."

"And what is your name?"

"I'm Carlos. I'm an old friend."

She invited him in. He didn't look dangerous; besides, they had a top-notch security system, and Dre was there to defend her.

"Carlos?" She raised her eyebrows. "Can I get you something to drink?"

"No thanks, but what did you say your name was?"

"I didn't say. My name is Catherine, my friends call me Cat."

Catherine pointed to a leather chair next to the front door. "Make yourself comfortable. I'll go get Andre."

Carlos watched Catherine walk away. She didn't have a big ass, but there was enough. Not really thick enough for him, but there was definitely sex appeal, and he would sure fuck the life out of skinny ass Catherine if he had the opportunity.

Moments later, she returned with Dre with a fake ass smile plastered on his face. Carlos knew it was fake.

Dre approached Carlos and gave him a pound, though he was trying to figure out where he lived in his mind.

"I see you met my lady."

"Yeah, she's very beautiful. How in the hell did a nigga like you get her?" He paused then cut his eyes at Catherine. "My apologies, ma'am, for cursing."

"It's okay." She smiled, showing off those sparking white teeth. "Thanks for the compliment. How do you and Andre know each other?"

Carlos said. "We're from the same neighborhood. Dre is a few years younger than me, so I'm kind of like his O.G. you feel me?"

"O.G.? I've heard that term in songs," Catherine said, amusing Carlos because clearly the white bitch was confused as fuck at his street lingo. "Like older brother?"

"Yeah I was like the older brother Dre never had."

Dre turned to Catherine, "Can you let me and Carlos have a moment, please?"

"Yeah."

Catherine walked through some double doors, and Carlos unapologetically watched her ass until she was out of sight, then turned to Dre.

"Nice little life you got here with your white woman, nigga."

"Look I was going to call you, I swear to God. I was going to call you today."

"Why the fuck every time I call you, I go straight to voicemail or you don't answer?"

"Let's go outside and talk."

Carlos stood, then followed Dre outside, and they stood on the porch. The old white bitch with the gun had also come outside and was looking over at them suspiciously.

"Let's take a walk," Dre suggested.

"Lead the way. This is your fancy ass neighborhood not mine."

As they walked, Dre explained that his money was tied up in real estate investments and he'd taken a huge loss on a load of coke. They continued to walk until they stopped at a dog park and a young Indian man wearing glasses with a beagle approached Dre. "Hey, where is the dog today?"

"He's with my son. I only have the dog when my son is here."

The man stared down at his dog. "I think Princess was beginning to fall in love with Frank. I noticed every time we're at the park, she's looking around for him."

Dre laughed. "My son will be here this weekend, so maybe they'll get to see each other."

The young man laughed. "Maybe. You have a good day."

"You too."

Carlos said, "Damn this neighborhood is full of do-gooders."

"Carlos you were a fucking kingpin. You were used to living in nice neighborhoods."

"Yeah, I was a kingpin, now I'm broke as fuck now, bruh."

"What happened to the money I was giving you?"

"I don't have to tell you what the fuck I was doing with my money, but since you must know, I have six kids. I was fighting my legal case before

Obama stepped in. I have a mother and family in Puerto Rico that's broke as fuck, too."

"I see."

"Dre, I need my goddamned money, and I need it soon."

"I understand."

"Do you?"

"Yes." They walked and made small talk until they reached the townhouse, Dre turned to Carlos. "Why don't you just contact Juan and get some product since you're broke?"

"I've been in touch with him. He wants to see proof that Obama really cut my time. I gave him the paperwork. He's getting his attorneys to look at it, but that's besides the motherfuckin' point. We had a deal, and now I need my money. Is that understood?"

"I got you."

"I'm not playing no more fucking games with you, Dre."

"Look, I got you."

CHAPTER 14

Raphael Ortega was a twenty-five-year-old openly gay man from Honduras, who boasted best skin and perfect teeth. Raphael was an esthetician, and Layla had enlisted him to help with Stacy's makeover. Raphael and Layla arrived at Stacy's apartment at 6:15. Stacy frowned after the obviously flaming gay Raphael entered his place. "Stacy, this is Raphael. Raphael, this is Stacy."

The men shook hands without making eye contact. Raphael detested men like Stacy, alpha, macho men who always had to project an air of masculinity.

"Why is Raphael here? No offense homeboy."

"Now why would I be offended?" Raphael said knowing damn well Stacy wanted his flaming ass to get the fuck out his house.

"He's here to give you a facial."

"A what?"

"A facial," Layla repeated.

"That's for girls and for…" He glanced at Raphael.

"Fags," Raphael finished for him.

"Yeah."

"You have got to get over this attitude." Layla scoffed. "There is nothing wrong with a man taking care of himself. By the way, I signed you up for a clothing subscription box, so be on the lookout for it."

"I can deal with the clothing upgrade, but I don't know about this facial thing. I've never had a facial before."

"And it shows," Raphael commented.

Stacy rolled his eyes at Raphael. "Next thing, you're going to have me dressing like this dude." Stacy said as he glanced at Raphael's tight distressed jeans that were suffocating his balls.

"It's just a facial."

"Looks like you've never in your life been exfoliated either," Raphael said.

"What is that?"

"Oh my god," Raphael said.

"Trust me, you're going to like the results." Layla said.

"So a facial is like when they rub cream all over your face?"

"Yeah I'm going to cream all over your face," Raphael joked.

Stacy said, "Now you see that's why I don't like being friendly to motherfuckas like him. They always try to go there with straight niggas."

"You ain't even my type." Raphael said, before cutting his eye at Layla. "One more homophobic statement, and I'm out of here."

Layla said softly, "Stacy, I'm going to need you to calm down."

"You want me to calm down, and this nigga said he was going to cream all over my face!"

"It was a joke."

"Where is your powder room?" Raphael said.

"The bathroom is in the back to the right," Stacy directed.

"I'm going to get set up. I'm going to need you to come back in five minutes."

"You're going to be there with me, right?" He looked at Layla.

"I will, but I'm going to have to go in a minute."

"There is no way I'm going to be here alone with this fucking fairy."

"You don't trust yourself?" Layla laughed. "Look, I have to run to the bank and make a deposit. I'll be right back."

"Okay." He passed her his key fob so she could enter without stopping at the desk and bothering the concierge.

Layla left midway through the facial.

Stacy and Raphael sat in silence before Raphael broke it.

Raphael said, "I'm a human being, you know."

"I know you are."

"Why were you being such an asshole? I was asked to do a job. I'm here to do a job and that's it. I didn't come to try to hit on you, Stacy," he huffed. "I just don't understand men like you."

"Look, I'm sorry."

"Okay, apology accepted. I think you're really going to like the results of your facial. You actually have pretty good skin; you just needed a good exfoliation. FYI, exfoliation is removal of dead skin."

Stacy laughed, "Good to know. I have a question Raphael."

"Yes, what is it?"

"Were you born that way?"

"You mean gay?"

"Yeah."

"I don't know."

"What do you mean?"

"I have an attraction for girls, but most of the time, I want boys. I think it was because I was molested at three years old."

"Wait a minute, you were molested at three years old? What the fuck kind of sicko would do that?"

"My uncle." Raphael stated plainly.

"Your uncle?"

"And your Dad didn't kill him?"

"No, I didn't tell anybody until I was thirteen, and by that time, my attraction to my uncle was so strong I didn't want anybody to do anything to him, and he was dying of AIDS by then anyway."

"Damn, I'm sorry that happened to you, Raphael," Stacy sniffled.

"Are you crying, Stacy?" Raphael asked.

"Hell no."

"Hardcore gangster rapper crying."

"I wasn't crying."

"I think you were."

"Look, I have a soft spot for children, a'ight?"

"I'm a grown man."

"I know, but I have to wonder if you didn't get molested, if you would be the way you are now."

"I'm okay."

Layla walked in. "I'm glad you guys are talking."

"Raphael is alright." Stacy said.

Raphael smiled. "Yeah, I'm alright for a faggot, right?"

"Hey, you said it. Not me." Stacy laughed.

Fifteen minutes later, they were done, and Stacy stood in the mirror, admiring his glowing skin.

The door opened, and then a woman's voice yelled out, "Stacy!"

Stacy looked at Layla and Raphael and then said, "Oh shit, it's my girlfriend."

"Your girlfriend?" Layla swallowed.

"I'm in the bathroom, babe."

Seconds later a curvy girl with skin the color of chestnuts appeared.

"Raphael and Layla," Stacy turned to Layla to begin an introduction. "This is my girlfriend, Malika."

Malika shook Layla's hand, then Raphael's before looking at Stacy.

"So what's going on?"

"Raphael gave me a facial."

She raised her eyebrows in disbelief. "Raphael gave you a facial?"

Layla said, "Yeah I thought it would be a good idea to give him a facial."

"You did?" Malika said, giving Layla the side eye.

"Yeah, is there a problem?"

"Yes, there is a problem!" She snapped. "A woman that I haven't even met is here with a man I've never met giving my man a facial."

Stacy cut his eyes at Malika. "Layla's my advisor. I thought I told you about her?"

"You know you ain't told me shit about her being your advisor, and what the hell do you need an advisor for?"

Layla cut in. "Excuse me. Me and Raphael are going to leave now."

Raphael stuffed his things into a leather bag and Layla passed Stacy the key fob and they left.

Later that evening, he called Layla.

Before he even said hello, she demanded, "What the fuck was that all about?"

"She was just mad because she saw an attractive female in my house."

"No shit. I thought you didn't have a girlfriend?"

"I never told you that."

"I guess not."

"So does that change what me and you have?"

Layla raised her left eyebrow, though he couldn't see her little quirks. "So what do me and you have?"

"I thought you were feeling me."

Layla laughed, "So you want me to be side bitch to your little girlfriend?"

"I want you to be my manager, not advisor, but I want you to be my manager. I like having you around."

"I do need a job, a more permanent situation. Let me think about it."

"I'll start you off with a hundred thousand dollars, half upfront."

"Look I need the money, but I've never managed an artist before."

"I've never had a manager before, so we'll learn together."

"What about your little girlfriend? I don't think she likes me."

"Don't worry about her. I can handle her. Why don't you just come over in a little bit, and I'll give you your first check."

* * * * *

Stacy was dressed in grey Chino's, a white shirt, and a black Moto jacket, and he was wearing a scent that Layla recognized but couldn't put her finger on. It was very sensual, and it made her want to yank the young boy's clothes off. He invited her in. They sat on the sofa, and he presented her with a contract that his attorney had drawn up that had entitled her to

8% percent of his bookings and other engagements, but there would be no money from his music. She frowned after learning that.

"Look, I did a little studying, and I know I'm supposed to be entitled to ten percent."

He laughed. "You're not a real manager. This is a position I created for you because I like you."

"What?"

"I know you need a job, and I like your sexy ass being around."

"Good," she said, "because I can't really dedicate that much time to being a road manager. I can travel with you sometimes, but I can't be on the road."

He looked confused. "Why not?"

"Hey I have a man, and I can't be on the road with you."

"You have a man? What the fuck?"

"And you have a woman."

"Okay, I just didn't know."

"And I didn't know. You didn't tell me about her, and I didn't tell you about him."

"Fair." He stood, and his scent lingered.

"What the fuck are you wearing?"

"What?" She'd caught him off guard.

"The scent."

"I'm not telling you." He smiled, teasing her.

"There is something different about you." she stated.

"I got my teeth whitened."

"Yes, you were against it."

"I was. To tell you the truth, you made me feel a little insecure about myself, but then I realized that you upgraded me for the best."

"Isn't that what a cougar is supposed to do?" Layla questioned.

"Tell me about your man."

"I don't want to talk about him right now."

"Cool."

He sat down beside her and then placed his hand on her thigh. She didn't know why, but she was getting aroused by the young boy. Then, she thought about his annoying little girlfriend and if she busted in and caught them. That turned her on even more.

She reached over and gently touched his chest. He stood and scooted out of his jeans, and she stood and removed her dress. She'd gone commando, and this obviously excited him; she could see his dick print becoming more and more visible. She rubbed his penis through his boxer briefs that he quickly dropped. His package was as polarizing as she'd thought it would be, long and skinny with a huge head. She dropped to her knees and took him inside her mouth, all the way to the back of her throat. She slurped away before gagging a little. He was just too big for her. He sat on the sofa as she continued showing him her oral abilities before she could feel him swell inside her mouth, and she stopped.

He frowned. "What did you stop for?"

"I want you inside me."

"I'm twenty-two, baby. I can cum and still get back up in seconds."

She laughed. She knew it was true. She went back to work, and he held onto the back of her head. She liked how aggressive he was. He erupted into her pretty little mouth. She opened her mouth, flashing the mouth full of cum before swallowing it, then smiling. She knew this turned most men on. She stood, then he stood,his dick was semi-erect. Hard enough to push himself inside her, and after she bent over the sofa, he did just that. After entering her, he placed his hands around her tiny little waist and fucked her doggy-style.

She screamed, "Talk to me, Daddy!"

"This is what you've been wanting all along, right?"

"Yes!"

"You like getting fucked by a thug, don't you?"

"I love it!"

He pulled her hair and smacked her ass.

She ordered, "Choke me, nigga!"

He grabbed her neck and smiled to himself, thinking the old bitch had tried to play hard to get but now he was pounding her pussy just like he knew it would happen. They all wanted to fuck the hottest young rapper in the game.

The door opened, and Malika entered with a brown grocery bag from Trader's Joes.

Layla tried to disengage from Stacy, but he held unto her tightly.

"Don't worry."

"What the fuck you mean don't worry?" She was trying her best to scurry away. Malika dropped the groceries, entered the living room. Layla was still trying her best to break free from Stacy's grip, but he was too strong for her. "Would you let me go?" she asked.

Malika brushed Layla's hair away from her face and smiled. "Relax. It's okay." Malika said, her hand now massaging the base of Layla's neck. Layla and Malika's eyes now held one another's gaze. Malika closed her eyes before leaning forward and taking Layla's mouth with hers.

* * * * *

The next morning, when Layla woke, she found Stacy gone. She made her way into the kitchen to get a glass of water and was startled when she found Malika at the dining room table enjoying scrambled eggs and bacon with a glass of orange juice. What the fuck was she still doing here? She didn't know how she felt about the girl after the incredible threesome. Were they friends? Were they enemies? She'd be naive to think the girl trusted her now that she had witnessed her man making out with her. She cut her eyes at Malika before Malika smiled and greeted her.

"I would have cooked you breakfast, but you just seem like the kind of girl that doesn't eat pork. Maybe no meat at all."

"Well I'm a pescatarian."

"A what?"

"I eat fish."

"Oh? What do you call it again?"

Layla smiled and repeated herself, thinking Oh my god this is one dumb bitch, its 2018 and she's never heard the word Pescatarian.

Malika sipped her orange juice. "Have a seat, please."

Layla sat across from Malika on a cushioned bench, replacing hard chairs.

"Sure you don't want any eggs? These cheese eggs are banging."

"I'm good," Layla declined, "but thank you for offering. Where is Stacy?"

"He's going to the studio."

"At this time of morning? It's not even 8am?"

Malika looked at her phone. "That boy lives at the studio, at least 60 hours a week."

"I guess that's why he's a big star."

"I guess." Malika finished off the OJ, still maintaining eye contact.

"How do you feel about that?"

Malika shrugged. "I guess I'm okay with it. I mean what can I do? It's part of being a rapper's girlfriend."

"Yeah I suppose."

Malika smiled, then Layla realized that she was quite a pretty girl. She had a few blemishes but had nice full lips, a perfect little nose and could have been a catalog model if she wasn't so curvy.

"Last night was unbelievable." Malika gushed.

"Yeah, I was surprised about that." Layla paused.

"You were surprised about what? Surprised that I was so cool about it?"

"Well, yeah."

"I mean what can I do? I want to satisfy my man, but I had fun." Malika stood, strolled to the fridge, and got more orange juice. In her blue runner's shorts, Layla noticed she had nice sprinter's legs.

Malika poured another glass of juice, then sat back down. "I imagine you must have had a lot of threesomes in your day."

Now what the fuck did this bitch mean about her day? It was still her day.

"I've had one other threesome, but I don't just go around sleeping with couples." Layla explained.

"I didn't mean it like that. I mean I just thought that you were probably a lot more experienced than us, being that you're thirty-five and all." Malika shrugged.

"Thirty-five?"

"How old are you?"

"I'm thirty!" Layla cried.

"Oh, I could have sworn Stacy said you were thirty-five, maybe he didn't. I don't know where I could have gotten that from." Malika sipped her juice.

Layla fumed. She knew damn well that nobody told Malika she was thirty-five, but she wouldn't let her see that she was upset.

"You look amazing though."

"For a thirty-five-year-old woman?"

"No, for an older woman."

"Do you have a problem with me?"

"No, I don't."

"Good. Look, I'm going to take a shower and leave if that's fine with you."

"Of course."

Layla walked toward the bedroom before Malika called out "Layla!"

Layla turned to faced her. "Yeah?"

Malika guzzled the rest of her orange juice. "He will never be yours."

Rashad gasped then clamped his eyes shut when Layla presented him with twenty-five thousand dollars.

He grimmaced "What is this for?"

"I wanted to pay you back."

"Where'd you get this kind of money?"

"After the photoshoot, my following went up to over a million. A few brands asked me to promote products, and I got a couple of hosting gigs."

"And you made over twenty five thousand dollars? Damn I need to do that myself."

She laughed. "I know what I am doing. I'm going to be a star, just watch."

He frowned.

"What's wrong?"

"I've been down this road with you before."

"This time it's different. I'm just trying to get my followers up."

"You have over a million followers on Instagram. How many more do you need?"

"That is just one platform. I want a million on YouTube, I want millions on Facebook and Snapchat. More followers means more checks."

He scoffed, "Are you serious?"

"You see something wrong with that?"

"This is supposed to be the aspirations of a grown ass woman? But what about a family? I like your ambition and all, but I want to start a family. I don't want to be some old ass man chasing a two-year-old."

She laughed. "Who says I can't raise kids and balance social media fame?"

Rashad eyes tightened; Layla really thought she was Beyoncé because she had a million followers.

"Tell Jeremy that I gave you your twenty thousand dollars back."

"I will."

"And you know what else? I'm going to give you the money back for the apartment, too."

"Oh really?" He raised his eyebrows.

"You think I'm some deadbeat ass freeloader?"

"No."

"Jeremy is acting like I'm a opportunist."

"You think so?"

"I'm talking about how he was treating my girl. I was just trying to look out for him."

"You have to realize that he's been my best friend since the third grade. He is like my brother, and he's going to look out for me. He doesn't believe that you love me."

"What?" She laughed, eased away from him, then faced him and studied his face. When she didn't hear him laughing too, she stopped and asked, "Are you serious?"

"I am."

"I love you. I told you that. Do you really think I would be back here if I didn't love you? And don't say it's about the money because I've given you back every penny except for the money that I used to move."

Rashad calmly explained, "You asked what was his problem, and I told you what his problem was."

"Fuck him! What do you think, Rashad?"

"What do you mean what do I think?"

"Do you think I love you?"

Silence.

"I think you loved me before, but I don't know about now."

She paced around the room, tears materializing in her eyes. He avoided looking in her direction; instead; he studied the check and noticed that it was post-dated for tomorrow, but that wasn't a big deal.

"Trust and love are always earned." he said.

"I know all of that bullshit. You sound like a goddamned Hallmark card. This is real life." she huffed. "There must be some way I can prove to you that I love you."

"Have my baby?"

"Your baby?"

"Yes, I've been wanting a baby ever since Mya died. This is the way that you can prove your love to me."

"Besides that."

He stared at her without blinking. "Before you left, we should have started our family. You knew I wanted a family with you. You said you wanted a family with me. But seems like all you care about is having a bunch of goddamned followers."

She was quiet. She didn't want a kid right now. She had plans to expand her fitness and fashion brands and to start her clothing line.

"You just said a second ago that you could do both."

"I can."

"Well, prove it."

"Lemme think about it, Rashad."

"What is there to think about?"

"It's a lot to think about."

"You asked me what I wanted, and I told you."

"Give me six months to a year then we can get married and have a baby."

He smiled.

* * * * *

Kendall had texted and called Dre for the last two hours but couldn't reach him. She'd put Christian to bed, and Chrissy came over. They sat at the kitchen table, playing cards and sipping wine. Kendall stood before punching in Dre's number again. The call went to voicemail, again.

"You see this is the kind of bullshit I'm talking about Chrissy. This is why I said it wasn't right. I shouldn't have never took him back. See? You let niggas off, and they go right back to doing the things you forgave them for."

"Why?"

"Men with money think rules don't apply to them."

"I think—"

Kendall cut Chrissy off. "They think they can do what they want to do because there is always some desperate chick out there that wants their bills paid and will let them run all over them."

"Did you check her Instagram?"

"Whose Instagram?"

"Catherine Smith's."

"No, I didn't think to check her Instagram."

"Why not?"

"Why should I?"

"To see if your assumptions are right."

"I know I'm right." Kendall crossed her arms stubbornly.

Kendall paced some more, then stopped and picked up the wine glass, sipped it, then refilled Chrissy's glass and began pacing again.

Chrissy said, "Sit down, please. All this walking is making me nervous."

Kendall sat down. "I don't need to check her Instagram. My gut is telling me that he is with her. I'm right because its already in my mind. I don't need to go stalking her social media."

Dre burst through the door and smiled when he saw Chrissy. He approached her and hugged her. "I'm ready to go to the Maldives. What about you?"

"I'm ready to turn up. I was ready the day after Kendall told me that I was going."

Dre laughed then glanced in Kendall's direction. "Hey, babe."

Kendall sat stoic.

Chrissy stood and finished her wine. "Look, it was good seeing you Dre, but I gotta be going home."

"You can stay the night, you don't need a DUI."

"Right." Kendall said.

"Are you sure?" Chrissy said.

"There is no way I'm letting you drive home after you've been drinking." Dre said.

"I'll take an Uber."

"Okay take the Uber, and I'll bring your car to you in the morning," Kendall planned aloud.

Chrissy summoned her an Uber with her phone, and Dre beelined to the shower as Kendall and Chrissy awaited the Uber.

Dre showered for seven minutes and had toweled off and was applying coconut oil to his chest when Kendall burst into the room. He made contact, but continued to moisturize himself.

Dre smiled some more. "Did you call Chrissy to make sure she made it home okay?"

"She texted me and said she'd made it home."

"That was fast."

"Yeah I thought so, too."

Dre stood, and Kendall's eyes dropped to his semi erect chocolate tool that was still exposed. He walked over to the dresser and removed a pair of black Calvin Klein boxer briefs and a white V neck t-shirt then slipped into them.

"What were you and Chrissy doing up this time of night?"

"Dre, cut the bullshit, you need to tell me where the fuck you are coming from."

"Eric's house."

"I don't believe it."

"That's your problem not mine."

"So it's my problem?" She sighed. "So this is how we work on a relationship by saying that's your problem not mine? What the fuck, Dre? Do you want to be with your family or not?"

"What was so important?"

"I called you because you told your son that you were going to read to him. Did you forget that Andre?"

Dre yawned. "Let's talk in the morning. I'm tired."

"Yeah, so you can think of the lies that you are going to tell," Kendall snapped.

"Lies?"

"Lies about where you were."

"I already told you where I was."

Kendall smirked. "I'm supposed to believe you?"

He nodded.

"Okay. So why didn't you answer the phone?" She presented him with her phone displaying the screen "I called you multiple times and I texted you."

"I lost my phone."

"You don't expect me to believe that."

Dre looked sincere, but Kendall was trying to see through that act. "Ken, we were watching the game and the cable went out, so we went to Wingstop, got some wings and finished watching the game."

"Why didn't you come here and watch the game?"

"I know you don't like some of my friends."

"Bullshit."

"It's the truth, Ken."

"And you stayed out 'til three in morning?"

"I didn't know I had a curfew."

"You have a goddamned family, Dre," Kendall cried. A trail of tears rolled down Kendall cheeks.

Dre took hold of her waist and pulled her into him, his hands now gripping her ass. "Ken, I love you."

She pushed him away. Her phone pinged with a Facebook message. "Ken, this is Morgan, Eric's wife. Tell Dre he left his phone over here. I can bring it by in the morning or he can pick it up when I get off work."

"Ken, you have to believe me."

"I believe you. Mike's wife just pinged me. Your phone is at her house."

"Mike? You mean Eric?"

"Yeah, whatever."

* * * *

The next day, Kendall called Rashad and said that she wanted to see him. He texted her his address, and fifteen minutes later she met him at his place. He was dressed in black and white Vans, white denim, and a white oxford, looking very sophisticated. He hugged her and then offered her a drink. They sat next to each other at the bar.

She complimented, "You look very dapper today."

"Thank you."

"You can really dress."

"You think so?"

"Yes, for a man that I presume is not gay."

He chuckled. "Well-dressed equals gay?"

"I don't know." she giggled, then she glanced at his sneakers."

"Is wearing no socks feminine to you?"

"Why did you ask?"

"You were staring at my feet."

She nodded. "Very daring. There is no way that Dre would dress like you."

"So how is his fashion sense?"

"I like it, he wears a lot of athletic gear, even with suits, but I will say he can dress. I love men that can dress." Kendall sighed.

"So that's all that matters is that you like it?"

"I've been trying to get him to take chances. I think that will be one of my challenges when I become a stylist."

"What?"

"Getting black men to take chances."

Rashad shrugged. "I think being confident in who you are is the key."

"Bingo. That's what I always say!"

"So, can I be a client?"

"You don't need me."

He stood and walked to the other side of the room to the liquor cabinet. She watched his curved ass in those fitted jeans as he poured her a shot of Patron then passed her the drink. "You came here to talk about fashion?"

"No."

He sat back down and gulped down his shot in one drink.

"Are you going to give me a tour of your place?"

He raised his eyebrow. "Yes, but first tell me what's on your mind."

"I missed you."

"Really?"

"Yes, really."

"You want to tell me what's going on?"

She stood and turned away from him.

"What's wrong?" He asked.

She faced him. A tear slid down her jaw.

He stood then embraced her, and she burst into tears.

"What's wrong, babe?" She liked that he called her babe; the simple word made her feel secure.

She broke free from his grip then said, "Look it's just not right."

"What's not right?"

"Me and Dre. It just doesn't feel right anymore, and we're in a really weird space. I don't know how to explain it."

"Weird space?" He shrugged; there wasn't much he could do with that information. "Please tell me what's going on."

"He's cheating again."

"What makes you think that? Wait, one sec." Rashad entered into the kitchen, poured another shot of liquor, returned, sat down, and looked her in the eye. "Now tell me: What makes you think that he's cheating?"

"Women's intuition."

Rashad laughed, "So you don't have any proof?"

"Yes... No. What difference does it make?"

"It makes a lot of difference. You can't just go around making accusations."

"You sound like him."

"You'll never trust him again, will you?"

"I don't think I can. He's not like you."

"What do you mean?"

"He's immature. You don't seem like the kind of man that would break up his family over side pussy."

"I was a personal trainer and an ex-dope boy."

Kendall scoffed, "What is that supposed to mean?"

"I'm not some youth pastor."

Then she remembered how flirtatious he had been when he'd trained her. How he didn't know how to be professional. How her first assessment of him was that he was a man that got a lot of ass on the side. How she thought he didn't know how to be faithful. She wondered what made her change her opinion about him. She liked him. At that moment, she wished she could be with Rashad instead of Dre.

"So I guess no man is faithful. You all cheat is that what you're saying?"

"I'm just saying don't put me on a pedestal, but if I was with you, I think I could be a hundred percent faithful."

"You think?"

"I'm a grown ass man. I don't play around no more."

"Anymore." she corrected.

He shrugged. "I was a fuckboy once."

She laughed at the notion of how men just routinely ran around on faithful women until they felt like it was time to settle down.

"Look, I don't have time to hear about your player days. Tell me about them some other time."

"Oh damn." He laughed. "You told me."

"Look, Rashad I came here to fuck you, but I know that your little girlfriend is back."

"What about Dre?"

"What about him?" she challenged.

"Look, I don't give a fuck about the nigga—I don't know him. But you just told me a few weeks ago you were trying to make it work. I ain't trying to break up your home."

She stood. "Thanks, for being there for me, I just needed someone to vent to and I'm glad you listened."

"Anytime."

She walked toward the door, her high heels clacking against the hardwood floor. Just before she reached the door, he called out to her. "Ken!"

She turned and faced him. "Ken?"

"Yeah, I thought that would be short for Kendall."

"That's what my friends call me."

"I'm your friend, right?"

She smiled. "You are."

"Did you mean what you said earlier?"

She swallowed. "I said a lot of shit today."

"Yeah, but did you mean what you said, that you missed me?"

"You didn't believe me?"

"I was just asking."

"Yeah." She turned away from him again. Her definition in her back and her tiny ass waist was sexy as fuck. He liked the fact that her ass was still nice and plump. He preferred his women's asses slightly jiggly, and he hated to admit a little cellulite turned him on as well. She opened the door.

"Do I get a hug before you leave?"

She stopped, then smiled. He hopped from the bar and approached her. As he hugged her, his hand made its way down to her ass. He gripped it, and she didn't move it. He slammed the door shut, and they kissed, her hands on his chest and his hands on the small of her back. She felt like a little girl inside his arm. He would protect her from the world.

He picked her up and took three steps before they collapsed onto the sofa. He removed his t-shirt exposing his barrel-chest and ripped abs. He stood, dropped his pants, and his massive dick print revealed itself through the slate boxers he had on. She smiled, anticipating his enormous tool. She removed her pullover then her bra. Her tits were miniature and perky. Her stomach was mostly flat, but there was a tiny bulge, result of her pregnancy maybe. Now was not the time to analyze her body. His penis throbbed, and he wanted nothing more than to be inside her.

Her high waisted fuchsia colored bikini contrasted her skin. She slid out of them right away and revealed her hairless kitty. He sat on the sofa and dragged her over to him, his semi-hard dick swinging between his knees. She seemed bashful almost virgin-like as he faced her kitty. Her hanging clitoris excited him. He pushed her to her back, and thoughts of Christian and Dre flooded her mind. She was slutty. This was the first time in a while that she'd even thought about sleeping with someone other than Dre, but he'd pushed her to this moment. He was the cheater, not her. She closed her eyes, blocked everything out then exhaled. Her heart pounded.

He whispered, "Relax."

His voice calmed her. She closed her eyes. He pried open her legs and pushed his index finger inside.

Rashad repeated, "Please, relax."

She unlocked her legs a bit, he buried his face into her love cave, his tongue toying with her love-box.

She relaxed, her nails sinking into his shoulders, while she panted.

He pushed inside of her further.

She moaned, "Right there. Right there, babe." The way she'd just called him babe felt natural.

"You like it?" He asked, pissing her off. Why was he talking and not working his goddamned tongue instead of chatting and making her feel guilty?

"You like it." He repeated.

Shut the fuck up and work, she thought. She seized the back his head and pushed him back in the position she wanted it in. His tongue felt so good. He was right on the spot where she needed him to be, the spot where he'd been before he'd stopped to ask that stupid ass question and she held on to his head.

Her nails gouged deeper into his back, making his tool more rigid. His tongue plunged further in her and, she squirmed, holding onto to the back of his head. "Please stop."

He scooted back to look at her and asked, "What's wrong?"

She laughed. "Nothing's wrong. You just feel so good, I want you inside of me."

He stood and she glanced at his long black slinking penis.

She tilted her head back, her hair now resting on her shoulder, and wondered if he fucked as good as his oral abilities. She bit her bottom lip and waited. He slid between her thighs. She scrawled her nails across his back, breaking one in the process. He was inside of her unprotected. *What if this man had a venereal disease?* she thought. *What if she got pregnant?* She hadn't taken birth control in years. Another baby was the last thing that she needed, her life in shambles. Despite the negative thoughts, She had to admit he'd felt motherfucking amazing, She felt so feminine against his rock hard athletic body. She nuzzled his neck and he ordered, "Bite my neck."

She did as she was told, marking her territory. Letting his ex know that she'd been there aroused her. She had never been one to fuck another woman's man, but here she was, and she felt great about it.

Her tongue swished inside his earlobe.

"You feel amazing." he moaned.

She squirmed as he invaded her love hole. She held onto the arm of the sofa murmuring and biting her lip. He felt so amazing inside her, she wished they could last forever. She wished that she could stay with him. She could get rid of Dre, he could get rid of his ex, and she, Rashad, and Christian could be a family. She envisioned Christian's tiny little face saying "We're a family." Guilt overcame her for a second, then Rashad grabbed her hair and then pushed himself further inside her.

"I love the way you feel."

She placed her hands over his mouth, hushing him. She didn't like talking during sex, but then thought maybe she should allow him to talk, so she wouldn't think of Dre or Christian.

He kept stroking, scars of passion decorating his neck.

He leaned forward and whispered into her ear. "Why don't you just leave him and move in with me?"

"I can't."

"Why not?" He panted.

She closed her eyes and hoped that he'd quit asking stupid ass questions. They were fucking. This was not twenty-one questions.

"Why can't you just move in with me?"

"You have someone, and I kind of have someone."

She placed her hands over his lips. "Shhh." she said, she was trying to focus on the moment she needed an orgasm.

He kept stroking and panting.

She stared at the ceiling clearing her mind of guilt. Focusing on the moment, the moment that she was enjoying. It was something that she'd thought about since the day that she'd met Rashad and so far it was everything that she'd imagined it to be.

He hadn't yet came, and he stroked her for a few more minutes. "What's wrong?" She asked.

"Nothing's wrong."

"Something's wrong. Why ain't you cumming?" She felt insecure. Was he not attracted to her? "Would you please cum?" she begged.

"If you would just be quiet. It's going to be alright."

She licked his ear again. He breathed hard and then exploded. She smiled; this was what she was waiting for.

He stood and entered bathroom. Her eyes locked on his beautiful chocolate body.

She trailed him into the bathroom and ran her fingers through his hair. She wanted to get right into the shower, but she didn't want to get her hair wet. "You have something I can put on my head?"

"Yes, look in the drawer. There are shower caps in there."

She grimaced and wondered what in the hell he had shower caps in his bathroom for.

He noticed the confusion on her face. "I was a bachelor for two years."

She laughed. "So I guess you just took it upon yourself to get shower caps for your women?"

He nodded. "And toothbrushes."

She grabbed the box of shower caps, removed one, and placed it on her head, then asked, "Do you have tampons too?"

"No. What, are you on your period?" He narrowed his eyes as he spun to face her while lathering up.

"It's a joke."

He laughed, then ordered her, "Grab a wash cloth from the shelf above the sink so you can wash my back."

She grabbed a white hand towel then tiptoed into the shower with dual shower heads. She stepped inside and walked past him to the other end of the shower. He turned and faced her as she was adjusting the water, waiting on the cold water to turn hot. He stared at her, the water now coming down hard. She turned her back toward him, and he noticed that she did have stretch marks on her hips. She was not perfect physically, and he loved that. Kendall was a "what you see is what you get" kind of woman. She turned and faced him, and they exchanged smiles.

"What are you afraid of? Get under it." He said.

She whined, "It's cold."

"I love cold water."

"Well, I don't. You can take your cold shower on that end. I'm not taking a cold shower. Boy, are you crazy?"

"A little bit."

The water had warmed up, and she stepped under the shower head then looked in his direction before saying, "Why did it take you so long to come?"

Rashad answered, "I don't know."

She lathered up her chest with body wash then her stomach before asking, "You didn't like it?"

"I did."

"Well, I don't understand why it took you so long."

"You want me to be honest?"

"Yeah, of course."

"I don't see what difference it's going to make; it's not like you're going to fuck me again. I mean, when you leave today, you're going right back home to your man, and I'll be alone."

"You won't be alone; you have your woman."

He removed a bottle of shampoo from the shower caddy then lathered his beard.

"I thought you were going to be honest with me."

Soap trickled into his eyes. "Fuck!"

She laughed at him as he rubbed his eyes.

"That's funny, huh?"

"Damn right it is."

He rubbed the irritated eye and she laughed at his now bloodshot eye.

"It's not funny."

"Your eye is red as fuck. It's really only funny because you said you were going to tell me why it took you so long."

"Well because I asked you a question during sex, and you brushed me off. I guess I was inside my head too much. I wasn't focused, and when you put your tongue in my ear, it was like an alarm went off, and said, 'Rashad, you're fucking a beautiful woman.'"

"Fucking?" She questioned. She didn't like his choice of words.

"Huh?"

"Am I just a fuck?"

"Of course not. I was just saying."

She frowned and turned her back to him.

He walked over to her and put his arms around her, his dick grazing the small of her back.

"Look, babe, what do you want me to say?"

She faced him. "I know I'm being difficult."

"Very."

"Let me ask you a question." She asked.

He put her hands behind her head pulling her shower cap down for her. "Ask whatever you want."

"What did you mean when you asked me?" She said.

"If you are asking if I meant what I said about us being together. I meant every word." Rashad said.

"You know that can't happen though. So were you just saying what you thought I wanted to hear?" She smiled.

"No." He assured her then kissed her on the forehead.

"I wish I'd met you five years earlier."

She leaned into him and kissed him.

CHAPTER 16

Kendall tiptoed into the house at 2:13 am, flicked the light switch, and found Dre sitting at the kitchen table playing chess on his IPad. He looked up from the tablet and greeted her. "Hey!"

"Hi." She said.

Silence.

She whisked past him, opened the fridge, and then grabbed a bottle of water.

She felt guilty, because she was guilty, and they both knew that she had been unfaithful, but he'd betrayed her trust first, so he deserved it.

What would she tell him? Would she lie? She'd hadn't thought about what she would say until now. All of her thoughts were about Rashad and how she wished that they could be together, how they'd bonded, the chemistry that they'd had, and how she was in love with him and couldn't have him.

"Why are you up?" She asked.

"I couldn't sleep."

She took a swig of water. "Why not?"

They locked eyes. "Where have you been, Ken?"

"With Chrissy," Kendall lied.

"Really?"

"Yeah."

He laughed, and she looked at the front door. He knew something that she didn't know. Perhaps he knew she was lying and maybe she'd have to make a run for the front door. Though Dre had never been violent with her, she didn't know why she was thinking this way.

"You were with Chrissy?" he asked again.

"Yes earlier, then I went driving." She took another swig of water then sat at the opposite end of the rustic farmhouse kitchen table.

"You went driving?"

"Yes."

"After you were with Chrissy?"

"Yeah."

"You never were a great liar."

He had been in contact with Chrissy. She knew she should have called Chrissy first to let her know that she would be using her as an alibi.

"Who says I'm lying?"

"I'm saying you're lying."

"So how do you figure I'm lying?"

"Because I know you."

Silence.

"Where were you?" he asked again.

"It's none of your business, just like it was none of my business the other night when you were out and about."

He frowned. "I told you where I was."

"That was a lie, and you know it. You can get those people to say anything for you."

"It could have been a lie but it wasn't." He stood and stared at her, until she stood too, and they were facing each other, their noses almost touching.

"Where is Christian?"

"He fell asleep trying to wait up on Mommy."

"Waiting on me for a change, huh?"

"What is that supposed to mean?"

She laughed. "Christian and I have waited up plenty of nights for you to come play with him or read him a bedtime story."

He sat down again, unlocked the tablet, and resumed his chess game.

"Do you think it's worth it?"

"What?" He looked up from the tablet.

"Me and you. Do you think it's worth it?"

"What do you think?"

"I think without trust we have nothing."

"You don't trust me, Ken?"

"And you obviously don't trust me."

He closed the case on the tablet and explained, "I trust you more than anyone."

"More than Catherine?" she asked.

He nodded. "I trust you more."

"Why did you want her?"

"I can't explain that."

"You can't explain it, huh? But you are accusing me of lying."

"I was just playing. I was showing you how it feels to be accused of doing something that you didn't do."

She smiled. "Is that what you were doing?"

"Yes."

"Why you waiting up on me?"

"Because I was worried about you."

"That makes me feel good."

"And I was horny."

She laughed. "Well, we're going to have to wait till tomorrow, I'm very tired."

He made a sad face.

"I'll make it up to you."

"Promise?"

"I do."

* * * * *

The next night, he slid underneath the covers. Her back was turned to him. Her head wrapped in a bonnet, she was asleep and he massaged her ass. She jumped, woke up, looked at him and laughed.

He said, "You know what you promised."

"I know."

"So you're reneging?"

"I'm tired."

He pouted, then lowered her yellow lace panties below her knees. His manhood was already stiff, and he attempted to push himself inside her.

She frowned at the intrusion despite her promise. "You're going to have get me ready. I'm not wet."

She spread her thighs, and he lowered his head, sandwiching it between her legs. He forged his tongue inside of her, and she squirmed. She closed her eyes, then thought what if he knew that she slept with Rashad. She wondered if she felt differently to him; after all, she'd fucked Rashad only a day ago. When Dre's mouth topped her lower lips, she realized that he didn't know. Dre was never big on oral sex; he rarely performed it. She knew that had he known that Rashad's penis had penetrated her earlier, there would be no way he would have been kissing or pleasuring her. He sucked on the lips while moving his fingers in and around her opening, and she was now aroused. She clasped his waist with her legs. He lifted his head, and she said, "I'm ready."

His tongue wandered from her stomach to her breasts, giving the left tit most of the attention; it was his favorite. She used to tease him about that. He kissed her, pinning her hand down. She'd always loved kissing Dre, but today she went through the motions. Her mind drifted to Rashad and how wonderful he had made her feel. She thought more about when he'd asked her to just leave Dre and she and Christian could be with him.

She was tired of all the foreplay and wanted to get it over with. "Put it inside of me, Andre."

He took possession of his tool and tried to insert it, missing the entrance before she grabbed it and forged it inside of her, herself. He was atop of her, staring down at her, smiling. This annoyed her, but she pretended to be excited, like she desired him, but he actually disgusted her and she didn't love him anymore.

She moaned, "Daddy, you feel so good. I want you to cum inside me. Cum inside me right now."

He kept stroking. She clawed his back like she'd done Rashad the day before.

Dre said. "Is it good to you?"

"You're the best, Daddy."

He stood, and she turned over on her side to allow him spoon her. Dre was known to be inattentive sometimes, but today he seemed to be just going through the motions too, not really caring if she orgasmed. He plunged deep inside of her again, spooning her, and she threw it back at him. Even his loud breathing irritated her, now that she thought about it. Dre was never a good lover to her, perhaps to Catherine he was. Kendall had once loved him and that made his love-making tolerable. Now that she no longer loved him, she hated his sound, scent, and his touch. She shuddered, trembled, and closed her eyes, as she faked multiple orgasms. "Oh, Dre you feel so goddamned good!" She screamed.

Dre grinned. He was the lover of the year in his mind. Seconds later, he exploded inside of her and he lay atop of her, gasping for air. Finally, he dozed. She jumped from the bed to the shower, degraded and disgusted.

* * * * *

"Is that a hickey on your neck, Rashad?"

"A hickey? Naw. No way, how would I get a hickey?"

He didn't think to try to cover it. He had not been in a relationship in so long that he had actually forgotten that he was in a relationship now.

"Looks like some bitch has been sucking on your neck to me," Layla scoffed.

"I can guarantee you that that has not happened."

"Oh really?"

"How would it have gotten there?"

She narrowed her eyes. "Now you know I know what a hickey looks like."

"But who would have put it there?"

"I don't know, maybe Jeremy." she laughed.

"Don't play with me like that."

"What about that chick that you claimed went back to her man?"

He narrowed his eyes at her. "What the fuck are you getting at?"

"Are you getting defensive, Rashad?"

"I just asked you what you were getting at."

"No, you are like 'What the fuck are you getting at?'" She mocked him.

"I'm sorry," he said, "but I guess I got a little upset because first you accuse me of fucking Jeremy, and now you're accusing me of sleeping with an ex."

"I'm just saying you want me to keep it real with you, but you don't want to do the same. Now how is this supposed to work?"

"What do you mean?"

"That is a hickey, and those are fucking claw marks on your back— you've fucked somebody. I know you, Rashad. I know your spots, she probably sucked your neck and stuck her tongue in your ear."

He sat down on the sofa and made eye contact with her.

"Keep it real with me. I know I just came back to town. I'm not stupid, I know there might have been some unresolved feelings with someone—I can deal with that—but what I can't deal with is lying."

There was an awkward silence before he started to explain.

"Her name is Kendall."

"What kind of name is that? Sounds like the name of a dude," she thought aloud, "but anyway, tell me about Kendall."

"What do you want to know?"

"Do you care for her?"

"I do."

"Why ain't you with her then, since you care so much about her?"

"Kendall is the woman that I was telling you about that went back to her man, so you were right."

"Really?" She raised one eyebrow, then she stood and ran her fingers through her hair. Though Layla was a beauty, she was very insecure and she didn't like feeling like she was coming second to any woman.

"Have a seat." he offered.

"I don't want to have a seat."

"Look, you asked me to keep it real, and now when I keep it real, you ain't feeling it."

She paced around the room, avoiding eye contact with him. "You like Kendall?"

"Doesn't matter if I did or not. She has a husband."

"But if she didn't have a husband, you would be with her. So I'm your second choice?"

He stood and inched toward her.

She held a hand up to stop him.

"What?"

"Am I your second choice?"

"How can you be my second choice when you were first? You had my first child."

"You know what I mean," she snapped.

"I think everybody is somebody's second choice, but I think what you want to know is if it was possible to be with her then I would be with her."

"Yes that's exactly what I want to know."

"Yes. The answer is yes because I was with her when you showed back in town, so if it was possible to get with her, we'd be together. That doesn't mean I don't want to work things out with you."

Layla smiled "Good, because I'm moving my shit in tomorrow."

"What about your apartment? The one I just paid up for a year?"

"What about it? I'm moving in, sub leasing it to someone else. We're getting married, and I'm having your baby."

CHAPTER 17

Chrissy poured Kendall a glass of Chardonnay then sat back down in front of her desktop computer and skimmed pictures of the Maldives, closed her eyes, then imagined herself snorkeling in the Indian Ocean.

Kendall asked. "What are you doing?"

"Vacationing in my mind."

"The vacation is two months away. Are you going to keep doing this until the we leave?"

She turned and faced Kendall as she sipped her water. "Why not? This is a vacation of a lifetime. Without Dre's help, I wouldn't ever be able to afford no shit like this. I appreciate him." She stood, disappeared into her bedroom, and returned holding up two high-waisted bikinis, one green one and the other purple. "Look, I already got my swimsuits."

Kendall said. "Now all you got to do is get your fat ass in the gym."

Chrissy laughed, "I'm going to start a boot camp this weekend."

"That ain't going to help you if you are going to eat like a horse."

"Ain't nobody got no money for no personal trainer like you," she huffed and sat her bikinis on the desk.

Kendall picked them up and examined them. "If you're going to get your big ass in these bikinis, you better start doing two-a-days."

"I am doing two-a-days. I went to the Waffle House this morning, and I'm thinking about going again later tonight."

They laughed.

Chrissy said, "Speaking of personal trainers..."

"I didn't speak of a personal trainer you did." Kendall interjected.

Chrissy sat back down in front of her desk and picked up her cell phone to check the time. "When is the last time you heard from Trainer Bae?"

"You're too much. First of all, he's not a trainer. He owns the gym."

"So what's up with you and him?"

"What do you mean?"

"When is the last time you seen him?"

"A few nights ago." Kendall avoided eye contact with Chrissy.

"A few nights ago for what? A late-night body assessment?"

Kendall resumed eye contact with her and then said, "Promise not to say shit to anyone about this."

"Who am I going to tell?"

"You're my bestie."

"I know."

She blurted, "I fucked him."

"What the fuck, Kendall? Are you crazy? What the fuck? I can't believe you done some dumb shit like that. Are you trying to ruin everything with Dre?"

"Am I trying to ruin your dream vacation you mean?"

Chrissy sat back down. "That's fucked up that you would say that."

"Why are you so concerned about who I fuck?"

"I'm thinking about Christian, your family, and how I like seeing y'all together."

Kendall sipped the rest her wine, disappeared into the kitchen to pour another glass, then returned "I understand, but where was that concern when Dre was running around with that white girl? You were the one telling me that I ain't going to find another Dre. So what am I supposed to do? Just sit here and let him run all over me? What about me? I have feelings. I have needs. I like to be held. I like to be told I'm beautiful."

Chrissy nodded slowly. "I know you have needs. We all have needs."

"So why are you coming so hard for me for fucking Trainer Bae? I mean Rashad."

"I'm not, as long as it was a fuck. As long as you don't have feelings for this man. I mean a fuck is a fuck, but when you start having feelings for a man that's when things become crazy."

"Right."

"So it *was* just a fuck, right?" Chrissy hoped aloud.

Silence.

"Oh my god, Kendall, you don't have feelings for this man, do you?"

"I don't know. Maybe I do have feelings for him. Is that so terrible? It's Dre's and your fault."

Chrissy grimaced. "How the fuck is it my fault?"

"It's your fault because you told me to go out there and meet people. You told me to go to the gym. I joined the gym, and I met Rashad."

"So it's my fault," Chrissy said dryly

"Of course it's not your fault. It's Dre's fault. If it wasn't for Dre, I wouldn't be in this situation. He was the one with the secrets, not me."

"Right."

"So you agree with me that I needed some companionship?"

"Look just because he did something doesn't mean that you have to do it. You chose to do this. You chose to fuck Rashad." She paused. "I don't even think this qualifies as just a fuck, because you have feelings for the man."

"Right."

"What are you going to do?"

"I don't know."

* * * * *

The next afternoon after Miss. Ortiz had taken Christian to the park, Kendall's phone buzzed. It was Chrissy.

"Hey girl."

Chrissy sighed but didn't say anything.

"Hey, Chrissy. Are you there? Hello? Hello!" Chrissy didn't respond, and Kendall muttered, "Damn girl must have pocket dialed me."

"I didn't pocket dial you." Chrissy said before Kendall could hang up. Kendall could tell that she was upset; she could hear her friend crying.

"Chrissy, what's wrong? Is everything okay? Did something happen?"

Chrissy sniffled a few times, then she said, "I'm okay."

"What's wrong?"

"I'm wrong."

"What do you mean that you're wrong? What are you talking about?"

"About Dre."

"What are you talking about? What's wrong with Dre?"

"He's with that girl, Catherine. He's still with her."

"What do you mean he's still with her?"

Chrissy broke out in tears. Kendall had never heard her friend cry so hard especially over a man that wasn't even hers.

"Chrissy," Kendall started, "Get yourself together and tell me what you know."

Kendall activated the speaker phone and sat the phone down as she waited on Chrissy to finish crying.

Silence then more sniffling, Finally, Chrissy said. "I'm good. Come over here right now."

Twenty-five minutes later, Kendall walked into Chrissy's house, and Chrissy led her into the living room.

"What happened?"

Chrissy hesitated before speaking.

"What did you see?"

"Yesterday when we talked, and I was telling you that you were being ridiculous and you were wrong for sleeping with Trainer Bae because I wanted your family to be together and I wanted Christian to grow up with his parents. I really wanted y'all to be a family," Chrissy whined.

Kendall became upset and annoyed, but at least she wasn't crying. "What happened?"

"I was on Facebook."

"Ok," Kendall prompted.

"Something told me to look up Catherine Smith."

"Something told you? What do you mean something told you? I thought she had made her page private."

"Her page is private."

"So how? What did you find and how did you find it?"

"When I searched Catherine Smith, I saw that someone had tagged her in some pictures..."

"What kind of pictures?"

"Girl." Chrissy looked like tears were about to well up in her eyes again.

Kendall said, "Don't start that bullshit again. What did you find out?"

"She and Dre are planning to marry."

"What do you mean they are planning to get married? How can they get married? Dre and I are legally married."

Chrissy said. "I know all of that, then she said Kendall "Follow me."

Kendall followed her to the other side of her room to her desktop computer. They plopped down in front of it, and Kendall's heart raced, trying her best to prepare for what she might see. Chrissy logged onto the computer then to Facebook. A video of a heavy set black man with blotchy skin wearing a chef hat appeared on the screen.

Chrissy laughed, "Did you see the video about black people Kool-aid vs white people's Kool-aid?"

"Ain't nobody got time for no goddamned Kool-Aid videos," Kendall waved her hand impatiently as if wiping it off the screen.

"I thought I would lighten the mood a bit."

"There ain't no goddamned lightening of no mood. Let me see what you're talking about."

Chrissy went to the search box at the top of the screen and searched the words Catherine Smith. Her page came up, and it was private. Chrissy tried to find the pictures she had seen the night before, but she couldn't find them.

"Oh wow she must have untagged herself. Now I can't see it but you believe me, right?"

"Of course I believe you. You're my best friend. Why would you lie about something like that?"

"Wait a minute, I forgot I took a screenshot of it."

Chrissy exited the screen and then she pulled up a screen shot of a picture that was on some woman named Megan Daniels' profile that said, "Congratulations to the new couple and their engagement." Dre smiled hard as his arm slinked around Catherine's waist.

Kendall burst into tears when she saw the picture. Though she'd felt like Dre might not have been the man for her, it still hurt like hell to see someone that she loved but was no longer in love with betray her like that.

Chrissy sprang from the chair, embraced Kendall, and handed her a Kleenex, erasing the tears from her eyes. Kendall buried her head into Chrissy's shoulder and sobbed. Chrissy caressed her head, and then they collapsed onto the floor.

Chrissy rubbed her back and said, "Get it all out. Keep crying, it is good for you."

Kendall cried as she kept repeating the words, "I feel so betrayed. I feel so hurt. How could this motherfucka do this shit to me? I don't know what I'm going to do. I don't know what I'm going to do."

Chrissy said. "I know what you're going to do. You are going to pick yourself up and you're going to be strong for Christian. Where are Christian and Dre?"

"I don't know where Dre is, but Christian is with Miss. Ortiz."

"Get yourself together. This is not the end of the world, you hear me?"

Kendall nodded, then sniffled, "But who's going to want me? I'm a woman with a child with no skills. Who is going to sign up for that?"

"Trainer Bae will."

"He has somebody."

"He loves you though?"

"He doesn't love me. He doesn't know me. It's lust," Kendall spat. "Plus I just need to work on myself."

"Are you going to confront Dre?"

"I don't know."

Chrissy made up Kendall's mind for her. "You don't need to see him right now. I think you just need to calm down before you go see him."

"You're right," Kendall agreed.

Chrissy handed her another Kleenex and said, "Fix your face, baby. I hate seeing you like this."

Kendall embraced Chrissy "Thank you. I don't know how I would get through his without you."

"One more thing. Go home, get your clothes and come back here. You and Christian can stay with me as long as you want."

* * * * *

Rashad laid on the bed as Layla prepared chicken in the crockpot while warming asparagus in a rice cooker when his phone buzzed with a text from Kendall: WYD?

Rashad: Nothing just laying down. Probably watch the game later on but right now just chilling. You?

Kendall: Over my BFF's.

Rashad: Tell Chrissy I said hey.

Kendall. K.

Rashad: Does she know about me?

Kendall: Of course she does, silly. She's given you a nickname. A name that I absolutely hate.

Rashad: I'm afraid to ask what it is.

Kendall: She calls you Trainer Bae.

Reahad: Trainer Bae? WTF? Im not even a trainer anymore. lol. What did you tell her about me?

Kendall: I told her you were a good guy.

Rashad: Where is Christian?

Kendall: With his dad.

Rashad: Just hanging out huh?

Kendall: I'm not going back with him. I just thought I would tell you. I don't expect you to come running to me. But me and Dre are over.

Rashad: Huh? Im confused. What happened?

Kendall: The man is planning a wedding.

Rashad: I thought you two were married.

Kendall: I thought so too. Can you talk?

Rashad: Not at this moment.

Kendall: Girlfriend there?

Rashad: ☹□. I'll call you tomorrow and maybe we can meet up.

Kendall: Okay.

The next afternoon, Kendall and Rashad met up at a Greek restaurant called Little Village Grill and had gyros and sparkling water.

He hugged her. "You've been crying?"

"Is it that obvious?"

"Yes. Are you okay?"

"I'd be lying if I said I were."

He took a swig of water. "Tell me what's going on."

"I miss you, Rashad." She looked at him; he was looking extraordinarily handsome today wearing a blue blazer, dark blue selvedge denim, and white trainers.

"Of course I missed you. Wanna tell me what happened?"

"Chrissy found some pictures of him and this girl Catherine that he's been cheating with on Facebook saying that they were engaged."

The waitress came and dropped their food and when she was gone Rashad said. "That's the part I don't understand. How can they be about to get married when you two are married?"

"I don't understand it either. It's obvious that he is about to file for divorce."

"Have you heard from him?"

"He called, but I didn't pick up."

"Why not?"

"There is nothing to talk about." She took a bite out of her side salad, then said, "I mean it's obvious this man is ready to move on."

"Are you going to contest the divorce?"

She shrugged. "Why should I?"

"You're right."

"What about custody of Christian?"

"I'm going to get sole custody."

"You know he's going to want joint."

She arched an eyebrow. "You think I give a fuck about what he wants?"

Rashad laughed, "Wait a minute. We're just having a conversation here. Don't get mad at me."

"I'm sorry, I just got a little heated thinking about him and what he's done to me."

"I know and I'm sorry for what he did to you."

Kendall shook her head. "It's not your fault."

He took a swig of water and saw pain and resentment etched in the wrinkles in her face. She didn't deserve that. He believed that she was a good woman.

"What's next for you?"

"I don't know."

"Well you can start back working on your business plan."

"I ain't thinking about no business plan. Only thing I'm thinking about is what in the hell is going to happen to my little family?"

"I feel bad for you."

"Don't. I was in denial for a long time and this is what you get when you're in denial about something that is painfully obvious."

"You were in love." he commented.

"Was I?" She paused. "I thought I was, but I think I was in love with the idea of love. The idea that I had a husband and a child. I don't know if I was in love, but that's besides the point. Now I have to start all over again with no skills or money."

"I'll give you money to find a place," he offered. He took a bite off his gyro and she watched his sensual rosewood colored lips as he chewed. She remembered those lips. She wished they could just go get a room, so he could place those lips on her clit again and she could forget about the pain for a moment, but she had to stay focused.

He sat the gyro down on the plate, scrunched up his face, then removed the sliced onions. "I said no onions."

She laughed.

"What's so funny?"

"The face you made when you said, 'I said no onions.' like onions are the worst thing in the world."

He challenged. "Name something worse?"

"I love onions, so I'd say heartbreak is worse, to me."

"You said you wasn't in love with Dre anymore."

She nodded. "I'm not"

"But you said heartbreak is worse."

"Heartbreak for me, is realizing when something isn't meant to be."

"Like you and Dre."

"Well, like me and Dre, and also like me and Rashad."

"I think I loved you."

"Loved? Past tense?" she inquired. "I love you."

"You do? Do you love me because you are available or because you can't get your family back?"

"My heart was never into it."

"Why did you do it then?"

"Because of Christian," she explained. "Because I wanted my son to be with his father. When you have children, sometimes you have to make sacrifices."

"I guess." He looked sad, and she could tell he was thinking about his deceased daughter Mya.

"Look, I'm sorry."

He took a bite of the gyro, then said, "It's all good."

They sat in silence for a few moments before her phone buzzed. Dre sent a text message: Are you okay? What the hell is going on? Why didn't you pick up the phone?

She stuffed the phone back in her purse. She didn't want to deal with him right now.

Their eyes met, and Kendall asked, "Do you remember what you said the other day?"

He narrowed his eyes and blinked twice. "What are you talking about?"

"The day when we made love in your apartment."

"I said a lot that day."

"But you said that if I wanted to be with you that you would leave her."

"Yeah, I remember."

"Does that offer still stand?"

He sighed, "She's moved in with me. We're living together."

Kendall sighed, too. "That was fast."

"She saw the hickeys on my neck. I admitted that we'd slept together, and I guess she felt insecure so she moved in." He pushed his plate aside and apologized. "I'm sorry, Ken."

"So what you said to me during sex was bullshit?" She paused, thinking about it. "Of course, it was bullshit because you were inside of me, and you felt like you had to say some dumb shit to keep me around, to turn me on, to have me wanting to make love to you and have me fall in love with you. You're just like the rest of them. Actually, you're worse than Dre. You knew I was vulnerable, and you listened to me. You knew the right things to say to make me fall, and now, the girl you said that you didn't love is back in your house. Bullshit."

He rested his elbows on the table and tried his best to make eye contact with her, but she refused to look at him. "Ken, it wasn't like that. I would never lie to you. I meant everything I said."

"Well if you meant it, go home and tell her to get the fuck out of your house. Tell her that you want to be with me. Go tell her, Rashad."

"I can't do that."

"Why can't you?"

"Ken you broke things off with me and told me that you were going to be with your baby daddy. Told me that you were trying to work it out with him, and here you are right now telling me that you want me to go home and tell my girlfriend to get out. What if you decide tomorrow that you want to be with Dre?"

"If what you said was true and you really want to be with me, what difference does it make?"

"I can't do it."

Kendall stood.

"Do you still want the money?"

"What money?"

"I was going to pay for a place for you to stay for a year."

"And why would you do that?"

"I love you."

"I don't believe you. You think I am supposed to jump for joy because you offer to give me some money? Rashad, I'm not a gold digger. Yes, my husband has money, but I was with him when he didn't have shit, and you have lots of money, so I'm sure it's nothing for you to do those things for me."

"You're right. I mean, I was just suggesting if you needed it. The offer will always be on the table."

"That's good to know." She shot him a fake smile "Good luck with your girlfriend." Kendall darted through the restaurant past the hostess station until she reached the door and exited in a hurry. When she was inside the car, she called Dre back.

"Finally! Where you been?" He asked.

"I've spent the last two days at Chrissy's."

"You didn't think to call me and let me know?" He paused. "Wait a minute, I called her."

"I told her not to answer the phone."

"What the fuck is going on, K? Christian has been asking about you. Every day, it has been 'Where is my mommy?'"

"So now you know what I've been going through when you pull your all-nighters," Kendall sneered. She started the car, and her phone auto-connected to the Bluetooth speaker.

"Is this what this is all about? You still trying to get revenge on me?" Dre asked.

"Dre, cut the bullshit. Just tell me when the goddamned divorce papers are coming. I won't contest it. I'll sign the goddamned papers, and you and you little white girl can go on with your lives."

"What are you talking about?"

"Yeah, you think I didn't know about her. I saw you smiling like hell with your little engagement party announcing that you two were planning on getting married, but the one little problem that you have is that you are already married. Luckily for you, I'm going to give you an uncontested divorce."

"What?"

"Look, Dre, I really don't feel like discussing this shit. It's only going to make me angrier. Get your attorney to draw up the paperwork. I'll sign it, and that will be that. I will talk to you in a couple of days."

"Okay. Don't you want to know why it's come to this?"

"Does it even matter?"

He shrugged though she couldn't see him. "I guess not."

"Where's Christian?"

"He's with my mom."

"I want to talk to him later tonight around eight. Can you call me so we can Facetime?"

"Okay."

"Goodbye, Dre."

"Goodbye." He ended the call.

CHAPTER 18

Dre's attorney was a red-faced, potbellied man named Harold Mankins. Mankins was dressed in blue seersucker suit that struggled to contain his big ass belly. She sat down beside Dre. Mankins extended his hand and Kendall shook it.

"Pleased to meet you," he said in a gentlemanly southern accent. Mankins was the type of white man that would address a lady as ma'am and give up his seat if she needed it. She could see all of that just by the tone of his voice; she'd seen his type many times before.

"Ma'am, I'm sorry to meet you under these unfortunate circumstances."

"Who said they were unfortunate?" Kendall said.

There was a long silence in the room as Dre cut his eyes over at her.

Kendall explained, "I mean, I don't think it's unfortunate at all if you are with the wrong person and you find out it's the wrong person before the end of your life, especially if you are young like Dre and I are. We have a beautiful son, and that's one good thing that came out of the situation. So I'm happy about that."

"Right," Mankins exhaled, then let out a hearty chuckle. "Hey, I always say best in a bad situation."

"Is this really bad though?"

Dre interjected, "Look, can get on with the process?"

Mr. Mankins cleared his throat, then asked Kendall, "Is there something that you feel like you're entitled to? Let's see if we can work it out and not have to go to court."

"I'm not entitled to anything. I came in this relationship with nothing, and I'm leaving with nothing."

Dre said, "Well I paid off your Range Rover, and you can have the house in Hyatt Park. I'll make sure you get the deed to that."

She turned to Dre and thanked him. "Thanks, that's more than enough. I didn't expect that."

Mankins smiled, then chuckled and grabbed the pocket square from his suit pocket and rubbed his forehead with it. "Looks like this one is going to be a smooth one. I'll get the papers drawn up, and you two can come by tomorrow around the same time. We can get the papers signed, and you can be on your way."

"What about child custody?" Kendall asked.

Mankins looked at Dre, who turned to Kendall and said, "I was thinking joint custody."

Mankins said, "You two can try to work out custody, but the courts will have the final say."

Kendall nodded and then stood and asked Mankins, "Are we done here?"

Mankins extended his hand and nodded. "As far as I'm concerned."

Kendall thanked Mr. Mankins and darted through the mahogany colored door without looking back. In the parking lot, Dre called out her name.

She turned and faced him. "Yeah."

"I'm sorry." He said, but he really wasn't but it seemed like the right thing to do.

She bit her lip and nodded. "Hey, it's really okay."

He rocked from side to side. She remembered when they'd met in high school and he had approached her locker. His friend Trayvon had dared him to talk to her.

"It's okay, Dre."

Dre bit his lip. "I don't understand. Why are you so cool with this?"

She leaned against her Range Rover. "This relationship was over a long time ago. I've been mentally checked out for a while. I knew it was going to come to this."

"I see."

They locked eyes for a moment, neither wanting to look away. Finally, he cut his eyes toward the rear tire of the Range Rover. "You need some air in that tire."

"Yeah, I noticed."

"I'll follow you to the gas station up the street, and I'll put the air in the tire for you. That is, if you want me to." He smiled.

She shook her head. "No, I can do it myself."

"I'm just trying to be helpful."

"Look, you've helped enough. I appreciate you paying off the Range, and I appreciate the property. That was enough. She stood and nodded to him and said. "I need be going."

"Before you go, I want to ask you something."

"What?"

"Did you sleep with the trainer?"

"Huh?"

"Come on, Ken. There is no way you can be over me that fast unless it's somebody else."

She shook her head again. "There is nobody."

"I don't believe you."

"What difference does it make at this point? I'm divorcing you, and you can get on with your life."

"Well if there really is no one, I'm sorry."

"Don't be. I'm young. I have better days ahead of me."

"I'll always love you."

"Look, Dre, if you don't want to talk about me picking up my son, there is no reason for us to talk." She climbed into the Range Rover and thought of that motherfucker saying that he'd always love her. He was divorcing her to marry someone else, leaving her with basically nothing, but yet he'd managed to muster up the words that he'd always love her.

"Hey, don't forget to put some air in that tire."

She ignored his silly ass.

* * * * *

The following day, Kendall signed the divorce papers. The day after that, she called Dre to ask him to meet so that she could pick up Christian. They would go home and pick up some clothes to take back to Chrissy's, and she, Chrissy, Cato, and a couple of other guys they knew from high school would move her into the house that Dre had given her in the divorce settlement. Dre didn't pick up.

She called again. No answer. She drove to the house alone. When she opened the door, the house was almost empty. There was nothing in Christian's room. She entered her and Dre's old room, and the bed was gone, but there was a dresser—the dresser that she used. When she opened the dresser drawer, she saw her things. Her socks, underwear, and lingerie were all there. Inside the walk-in closet, all of her shoes and handbags that Dre had bought her over the years were still there. She didn't understand. Why did Dre take Christian's things? She called him again, and there was no answer. Then, she called his mom.

"Mrs. Walker, have you seen Andre?" Kendall and Mrs. Walker didn't have the best relationship, but she still respected the woman for the most part. However, what she didn't like was that she always sided with her son, and Kendall vowed that when Christian became old enough to date, she'd call him out on his bullshit if he was wrong—something that Mrs. Walker never did to Andre.

"I'm minding my own business." The older woman said, then ended the call abruptly.

I'm minding my own business? What the fuck was that supposed to mean? Kendall thought.

She dialed Chrissy's phone number, and she picked up.

"I'm at home, and all of our things are gone." Kendall cried. "Everything is gone. All of Dre and Christian's belongings."

"Did you call Dre?"

"I've been trying to reach him. No answer. He didn't say shit about this. I called him and didn't get an answer. I called his mama, and all she had to say is 'I'm minding my own business.'"

"What the hell is that supposed to mean?"

"That's what I wanted to know."

"I'm five minutes away from you. I'm coming over."

"I'll be here. I'm getting a few items that I need."

* * * * *

The doorbell rang, then Chrissy stepped in and looked in amazement at the empty home. "Damn, I can't believe he left like this. I mean I knew he was going to leave, but I can't believe he took Christian's shit, too."

Chrissy passed Kendall a business card.

Kendall looked at the card strangely. "What is this?"

"I don't know. It was in the door."

"I wonder how I missed it." Kendall murmured.

"I don't know."

Kendall looked at the card that read "Teasha McKenny. Department of Social Services."

"D.S.S.? What the fuck?"

Chrissy asked, "You think Dre is trying to take Christian? Maybe he put D.S.S. on you."

"That motherfucker. He's the one that wanted joint custody."

"Don't worry. There is no way D.S.S. is going to take Christian. This doesn't make sense for Dre to call D.S.S. on you."

Kendall dialed the number on the card.

A woman answered the phone on the first ring.

"Hi, is this Ms.McKenny? My name is Kendall Walker." She tried to sound as pleasant as possible despite the situation. "I found a card on my door this afternoon."

"Yes, that is me. What did you say your name was again?"

"Kendall Walker." she repeated.

"Hold on a second, let me look you up." After a moment, she continued. "Oh yeah. You live on 2525 Brandywine Lane?"

"Yes, that's me."

"Can you come by my office tomorrow at 1pm?"

"Yes, but first, can you tell me what this is about?"

"I will tell you everything tomorrow." With those words, Ms. McKenny ended the call.

CHAPTER 19

Teasha McKenny was a short, black woman with green adult braces. She looked to be around thirty years old, and she had attended North Carolina A&T according to the degree hanging on the wall. Yolanda Adams' song "Open My Heart" played in the background. There was a picture of Teasha and a couple of her friends on the desk drinking. Kendall assessed that Teasha was a fake Christian; she'd seen her type before. Teasha was talking on the phone when Kendall walked in and Teasha pointed to a chair for her to sit in front of her desk.

Five minutes later, Teasha had finished the call.

"Good to meet you, ma'am."

"Same here. Can you tell me why I'm here?"

"Well, there has been a report of child abuse on your son. Christian."

"Child abuse? I don't know where my son is. If that motherfucker has touched my son, I swear to God, I'll kill him."

Teasha said, "Can you refrain from using profanity in my office?"

"Do you have children Ms. McKenny?"

Teasha McKenny glanced at a picture of a Maltese sitting on a desk.

"Don't you dare try to compare my son to a goddamned dog."

"Profanity."

"I'm saying, unless you have children you wouldn't understand."

"I have a nephew and a niece."

"That is not the same. Nobody wants to hear about their kid being abused."

"I can believe you."

"Can you tell me what happened?"

Teasha McKenny took a sip from a red and white coffee mug and said, "The allegations are against you, Mrs. Walker."

"What?"

"Yes."

"This is crazy! I've never abused my son. What the hell are you talking about?" She laughed. "I mean he's a toddler. I might have popped his hand or something, but abuse? That's crazy."

Ms. McKenny scribbled on a legal pad, then said, "According to my reports, you whipped him until he bruised."

Kendall was confused. "What are you talking about?"

"Would you like for me to read the reports?"

"Read the goddamned reports! Please read the reports." Kendall ordered.

"On or about June seventh, Kendall Walker whipped 3 year old Christian Walker until she bruised his hands, arms, and legs, revealing purple and blue welts. The report says the child was playing and the dog was barking, and you were pissed because he was running around playing and pissed at the dog for barking too loud, so you beat Christian and kicked the dog clear across the room."

"Now that's a lie."

Ms. McKenny presented her with a picture of Christian's bruised arm.

"I remember that day, and trust me, it's not what you say it is."

"And that is why I called you here, to hear your version of the story."

"My version of the story?" Kendall laughed. "My version is there was never any abuse. I've never abused my child ever."

"Do you want to tell me what happened?"

"Christian was playing near the wall socket sticking something in it, and I popped his hand."

Ms. McKenny made more notes in her legal pad and commented, "I understand the wall socket was child proof?"

"It was." Kendall nodded.

"So the child wasn't in any danger?"

"What are you getting at?"

Ms. McKenny dropped the pen on the yellow legal pad. "Was the child in any danger of getting hurt? I asked a question. Just give me a yes or no answer."

"It's not that simple."

"Yes or no?" McKenny sighed before rolling her eyes.

"He wasn't in any danger, but I didn't want him to think it was okay just in case he was at my mothers or Dre's mothers house. Those houses are not child proof."

Ms. McKenny said "So the answer is no?"

"So did you hit him with an open hand or did you use your fist?"

"I would never use my fist on my son. He's a toddler."

"Open hand or closed fist?"

"I popped him. You've been popped before as a kid, I'm sure."

"This isn't about me, this is about Christian. Answer the question, please."

"Open hand."

"How many times did you hit him?"

"Once."

"But there are two bruises on him."

"I might have popped him twice."

Ms. McKenny took down some more notes and asked, "Was this a whipping? Bruises like this are consistent with a whipping."

"It was not a whipping. A whipping is when you hit a child repeatedly."

"Correct me if I'm wrong, but you just said you hit him and then you hit him again."

"What the fuck?" Kendall stood and Ms. McKenny raised her eyebrow. "Are you leaving?"

Kendall sat back down when she realized that she wasn't helping her situation; she was actually making it worse.

"I hit him."

"Then you hit him again."

"Maybe."

"Two bruises."

"Okay, I hit him again."

"That was a whipping."

Kendall scoffed, "I see I cannot win."

"Listen, this is not personal. I have to write down the facts."

"These are not facts."

"Did you curse at Christian?"

"I might have said a curse word, I don't remember, but if I did, it wasn't directed at him."

Ms. McKenny scribbled on her paper, then grinned, flashing her disgusting green braces. "I have no further questions."

"What is going to happen to my son? Where is he?"

"He is with his father until the courts decide where he will go."

Kendall stood, thanked Ms. McKenny, left her office, and cried.

* * * * *

Kendall had gone by the house to pick up some of her clothes and was walking out the door, carrying an overnight bag full of things when Carlos appeared. She stepped back and grabbed her chest. "Damn, Carlos, you scared me."

He flashed a smile. "I didn't mean to do that."

She smiled back. "I know, it's not a big deal."

Carlos peeked inside the empty home before she could close the door. "Are you moving?"

"It's a very long story. But the short version of it is. Dre and I in the process of divorce. He came and took my son along with everything in the house, except my things."

Carlos thought about the sexy ass white girl that Dre was residing with, then he looked at Kendall in those tight ass jeans and her nipples peeking through her blouse. He decided he'd rather fuck Kendall, though Kendall might have been a headache to deal with.

"So what brings you here?"

"I was looking for Dre."

"He don't live here. Hell, I don't live here now."

"I see."

"Have you seen him since the last time you were here?"

"I saw him once, no twice."

"He didn't tell you where he was living?"

Now how was a nigga supposed to answer that question? He couldn't flat out tell her that he'd been to Dre's house with his mistress. The simple answer was "No." The truth was he'd just left there and the nosey ass neighbor had come outside on the steps with her handgun. He'd snickered at the old bitch under his breath before she told him that Dre and Cat were gone and she hadn't seen them in a few days.

"So what's going on, Ken?"

She looked confused. "What do you mean?"

"How did it come to this? Did you cheat on Dre?"

She shot him a nasty look and snapped, "What do you think?"

"I was just kidding."

"It was the other way around. Just ask him about it when you catch up with him."

"I will." His eyes met her thighs. Damn, he'd like to console her right now. Ordinarily he wouldn't ever think of fucking his homeboy's wife but A) He'd just gotten out of prison, and B) This was the same homeboy that owed him a shitload of money, so fuck him.

"So, why are you chasing Dre?"

Although he didn't want to put Kendall in he and Dre's business, she'd been around for a long time. She used to come with Dre when he would give Dre drugs. She already knew all about his and Dre's prior relationship.

"Look, Ken, Dre owes me some money, and I need it. It's very serious. I don't know if you can get in touch with him or not, but just tell him to give me my money so I can go away, and if he don't give me the money, things can get really bad for him."

"What kind of money?"

"Seven figures."

"Damn. I will tell him if I can get back in touch with him."

"Thanks, Ken."

* * * * *

Chrissy was gone when Kendall arrived at her house. She disappeared into the guest bedroom and tried to call Dre, but the number had been disconnected. She closed her eyes and prayed to God. *God, I know that everything happens for a reason, and I'm sure You're testing me and things are going to work out the way they are supposed to. I've never questioned You before, and I won't start questioning You now. Though I've lost a lot, I want to thank You for what I have. I am so thankful for my son, and I'm thankful for my best friend Chrissy who has been there for me since day one, and I thank You for my loving mother and stepfather. God, right now I just ask that You send me a sign to let me know not to worry, and I will not worry. Thank You, God, and I love You, God. Amen.*

The prayer made Kendall feel a lot better. She stood, then disappeared into the kitchen then returned with a bottle of water before she noticed her phone was buzzing with a text from Rashad.

Rashad: You okay?

Kendall: I'm fine.

Rashad: I was a little worried about you. I know the last time we spoke it wasn't on good terms.

Kendall: I know I acted a little emotional and I'm sorry.

Rashad: Don't be. I just want you to know that I would never lead you on.

Kendall: Hey, it's not your fault.

Rashad: So how are things going with you and Dre?

Kendall: It's over.

Rashad: How do you feel about it?

Kendall: To be honest with you I wasn't going to say anything. I'm really fucked up right now. Dre put D.S.S. on me and right now he has custody of Christian. I popped the boy one day and he welted up and Dre or his white woman took pictures of the welts and took it to D.S.S and now they trying to portray me as an unfit mother.

Rashad: Please tell me you're lying.

Kendall: I wish I was.

Rashad: I miss you.

Kendall: likewise.

Rashad: Send me your bank account number and routing number. I'm going to put that money in your account that I promised you for the apartment and the Range Rover payment.

Kendall: The Range Rover is paid off and Dre gave me a house.

Rashad: Send me the account number still I want to help you.

Kendall: That's nice of you.

Rashad: I want to see you.

Kendall: Let me get settled and then we can meet up.

Rashad: What do you mean get settled?

Kendall: I need to move out of Chrissy's house. Soon as I move out and I'll text you and maybe we can meet up. If your girl don't find out lol

Rashad. Okay.

CHAPTER 20

Catherine and Christian were dressed in matching black peacoats with gold buttons, and Frank wore a Louis Vuitton dog coat. Christian had begged Dre to go walk Frank, but Dre had business to attend to, and Catherine had agreed to step in. After her conversation with Dre, she was starting to get used to being a step-mother. She just had to get used to people staring at her, probably wondering what in the hell this white woman was doing with a small black child that wasn't biracial. They'd probably thought she'd adopted him from Africa and decided to give the kid a better life. If Christian had been biracial, at least they could have believed that he could have been hers. But she was used to the stares that she received when she was with Dre, mostly from white men and black women. She tried her best to understand what the fuck was those women's problems. It was not like Andre was the last black man on earth. Or hell why couldn't they just get a white man? But it wasn't her problem. She loved Dre, and he loved her.

Frank was acting particularly unruly today, and Christian could barely hold on to him. She took the leash from the toddler and grabbed his hand as they walked toward the dog park. She hoped like hell she wouldn't see the goofy Indian Prakash, who always wanted to have a conversation about dogs. Yes she was an animal lover, but did the subject of dogs fascinate her? Hell no. She'd much rather be talking about vacationing or beauty products or even making money. And it seemed like every time she showed up at the dog park, this man would come from out of nowhere. He swore to God that Frank had a crush on his dog, Precious.

They arrived at the park five minutes later, and sure enough there he was talking to an old Indian man, she assumed about dogs, breeds, and all kinds of boring shit. Frank started barking when he spotted Precious, and Christian pointed "Frank friend."

"Yeah," Catherine mumbled.

Catherine led the toddler and the puppy in another direction, avoiding the talking Prakash.

"We're going to go another way today, ok Christian?"

"Ok Step-mommy."

She smiled. She was warming up to the idea being a mother, and she loved when he called her Step-mommy. They had exited the park, and she looked over her shoulder. Out of the corner of her eye, she saw Prakash leaving the park, waving and trying to get her attention, but she was not in the mood to talk to him today. Frank smiled at his girlfriend because he was barking and trying to lead her back toward Prakash. She finally picked Frank up to lessen the struggle and held onto to Christian's hand tightly. They were walking swiftly up the sidewalk, when Prakash screamed out, "Wait!"

Catherine and Christian sped up.

Christian asked, "Step-mommy, why are you walking so fast?" They made it to the corner of the street, when a white Promaster Van pulled alongside them. Three armed men jumped in front of them waving handguns, and before Catherine could scream, one of the men yanked Christian. The child screamed before the assailant covered his mouth with a gloved hand.

Catherine yelled, "I'm going to call the police," and one of the men shoved her skinny ass to the ground. Prakash let go of the leash and ran toward the melee, then he yielded a pocket knife and one of the men laughed then fired a shot that whizzed right past Prakash's head.

"Drop the knife."

Prakash closed his eyes. "Oh my god."

The man stepped toward Prakash and slapped him with the butt of the gun. Prakash dropped the knife.

The driver of the van said, "Get the dog, and let's go."

The assailant that had pistol whipped Prakash yanked the dog from Catherine's grip. They jumped into the van and sped away. The last words Catherine heard was Christian yelling "Step-mommy!"

Catherine didn't know what else to do, so she called Dre and told him what happened, who ran down to the scene of the crime.

Catherine was breathing hard, and when she spotted Dre, she ran into his arms.

"Start from the beginning and tell me what happened?" Dre asked, then he turned to Prakash, who had retrieved his dog and was now standing holding his dog while talking into his cellphone.

"We were walking up the side walk when a big van pulled up alongside us and two or three men jumped out of the van and took Christian! Catherine wailed.

"Who took Christian?"

"The men."

"What men?"

"There were four men in a white passenger van. Two or three of them jumped out and snatched Christian and Frank."

"What?" Which way did they go?"

Catherine pointed in the direction that the men sped away in.

Prakash hung up the phone and announced, "The police are on the way."

Dre asked. "The police? Why'd you call them?"

"I asked him to call the police. She lied. That's what you do when something like this happens."

"I wish you hadn't asked him to do that."

"Andre, you sound ridiculous."

Dre sensed the irritation in her voice and said, "You're right, but I gotta find my son. You stay here and give the police report. I gotta go."

"Are you being fucking serious right now?"

Without answering her, Dre sprinted in the direction of their home. While he was running, he wondered who could have taken Christian. He'd owed his connect a shitload of money that he'd been slow to pay, but there was no bad blood, and he had assured him that he would send the money next week. Then, he thought about Carlos and realized that it must have been Carlos. He called Carlos, and the phone went straight to the voicemail.

He would have to find Ken to tell her what happened. This would be one of the toughest conversations that he would have to make in his life. How in the fuck was he going to tell her that his son and *her* baby was missing? This would not bode over well. He dialed her number.

"Hello."

"Where are you?"

"I'm at Chrissy's. Why?"

"I need to see you."

"Look, if it does not pertain to Christian, there is nothing for us to talk about."

"It does."

"Good. Are you bringing him with you?"

"Yeah," he lied.

"Ok, I will see you when you get here. How long is it going to take?"

"About twenty minutes."

Dre pulled into Chrissy's drive away thirty minutes later. He looked down at his phone, and he'd saw he had six missed calls from Catherine. He returned her call.

"Hey."

"Where are you?"

"I had to go see Kendall."

Catherine scoffed, "Why do you need to see her?"

Dre stared at his phone. Was this bitch being serious right now? "I'm here because I had to tell her that her son is missing. What the fuck do you think I'm here for?"

"You will not use that language speaking to me."

"Look, I'm sorry, but I have a missing son right now."

"The police want to talk to you."

"I don't want to talk to them. I told you that."

"I gave them your number."

"You what?" Dre all but yelled into the phone.

"I had to give them your number."

"You *chose* to give them my number."

"I will see you when you're done with her I suppose."

"I'm coming home right after I break the news to Kendall."

* * * * *

Kendall answered the door and invited Dre in; however she didn't offer him a seat. She frowned when she realized that Christian wasn't with him.

"Where is my son?" she demanded; that was his only reason to be here.

"I didn't bring him."

"Dre, why are you playing games with me? Where the fuck is my son?"

He avoided her eyes.

"Where is Christian?" She placing her hands on her hips before repeating, "Where is Christian, Andre?"

"He's not here."

"I can see that." She paused. "Is he with your little snowbunny?"

"No." He looked away then made eye contact with her, and she noticed a tear rolling down his cheek.

"What the fuck has happened to Christian? Did that bitch do something to him? Is he in the hospital?" Kendall's mind raced as she contemplating every possible situation her child could be in.

Dre took a step forward her. "Calm down, Ken."

"Calm down, my motherfucking ass! Where is my son?"

"Someone took him."

"Dre, stop playing with me. Don't try that bullshit with me, Andre."

"I'm not playing—someone took him. He was with Catherine. They were walking the dog, and someone pulled up and took him and Frank."

"I don't believe that shit," Kendall fumed, her eyebrow now raised skeptically. "That bitch did something with my son. She wants you all to herself. I know you don't believe someone just up and took Christian and the dog. Don't you watch court tv motherfucker? White people be doing all kinds of weird shit." She stepped toward Andre and slapped him as hard as she could.

He grabbed her and held her arms. "You need to calm the fuck down, Ken!"

She wrestled free from his grip. "Don't you ever touch me!"

"It's true! Three men in a van pulled up and snatched Christian and Frank. There were other witnesses there."

"Witnesses like who? I want to talk to the motherfucking witnesses."

Andre knew Kendall was indeed pissed. He'd never heard her curse this much, but what mother wouldn't be pissed if her son had been abducted?

"There is this Indian guy named Prakash that lives in the area. We always see him at the dog park."

"So I'm supposed to believe Prakash from the dog park?"

"Yeah, it's the truth."

"Dre, I don't give a damn what you perceive the truth to be. I know that you better go out and get my son. That's what I do know."

Dre stared at Kendall for a moment. There was fire in her eyes, the kind of fire that let him know that she was going to do whatever it took to get to the bottom of this. There was no reasoning with this woman. The person that she loved the most was gone, and he knew that he'd better be prepared to do whatever it took to bring him back. He turned to walk away. Before he reached the door, she called out to him.

"Andre!"

"Yeah?"

"Why did you even bother to come here, and why the fuck did you have to tell me this?"

"It's the truth."

She collapsed to the floor and began to cry. He kneeled to try to console her, but she shoved him away. "Don't ever touch me, motherfucker."

He stood and walked out the door on a mission: He had to find his son.

Chrissy came in and found Kendall still sitting in the same spot crying.

"What is wrong?" She sat down beside her friend.

"Christian is missing."

"Huh? What do you mean he's missing? He's with Dre."

"No." She raised her head to make eye contact with Chrissy. "Dre just left here talking about how Catherine took Christian to the park, and some men in a van, jumped out and grabbed Christian and Frank."

"Who the hell is Frank?"

"The dog."

"Oh. And you believe that?"

"Yeah, I believe that someone took them, but I also think that Catherine is behind it somehow."

"You think so?"

"I don't know what to think."

Chrissy shook her head. "I don't think so."

"Why would someone take my baby?"

"I don't know."

Kendall's phone rang.

She scrambled to answer. "Hello?"

"It's Carlos."

Before he could ask, Kendall blurted, "I don't know where Dre is."

"Kendall, I have Christian, and he's okay."

"What do you mean you have him?"

Kendall heard Frank barking in the background. She's never been so happy to hear that annoying little shit eater.

Carlos said, "Christian this is your mother, say hi to her."

"Mommy?"

"Yes, sweetie, it's your mommy."

"Hey, Mommy."

"Hey, baby, how are you doing?"

"Great! Mr. Carlos bought me ice cream and is letting me play games. I'm having a lot of fun. Are you coming to get me?"

"Yes. Mommy is coming to get you."

Carlos took the phone. "Kendall, you know me. I don't want to do anything to your son, and I damn sure don't want to go back to prison, but Dre needs to pay me my money."

"How much does he owe you?"

"Just relay the message. Tell him to give you the money. I meet you and you get your son."

"I will tell him."

"Nothing is going to happen to the boy if you do this."

"Okay."

"No police, Kendall. Do you understand?"

"I know."

"Tell Dre that too."

He hung up, and Kendall immediately called Dre.

"Hey where are you?"

"I just pulled up to my townhome. There are some detectives that I have to talk to. Why?"

"Don't talk to them." Kendall ordered him.

"Why not?"

"Just don't. I know where Christian is. Come back and talk to me." Kendall said, not wanting to discuss what she knew over the phone.

"I'll be there in twenty minutes."

"Okay."

A half hour later, Chrissy opened the door for Dre, led him into the living room where Kendall sat drinking coffee, noticeably calmer than she'd been before he'd left.

He sat down beside her and asked, "What did you find out about Christian?"

"He's with Carlos."

"What?"

"Yeah, he called, let me speak to Christian, and Christian said he's having fun, that everything was okay. Carlos said he had no intention to hurt Christian, but he wanted his money."

Dre stood and ran his fingers through his hair.

"Dre, I don't know what you owe this man, but I suggest you give it to him."

"What else did he say?"

"That's it. And he stressed no police."

"Okay."

Dre removed his phone from his pockets and dialed the number he had for Carlos, but it had gone straight to voicemail. He tried again, but the call went straight to voicemail.

Dre looked at Kendall, who was a completely different woman right now after talking to Carlos, but of course she was; she was confident that he was going to handle the situation. He asked her, "What was the number he called from?"

"The number was private."

"So how do we get in touch with this dude?"

"He said he would get in touch with me—just have the money ready."

"Okay, but I need to talk to him."

"What the fuck is there to talk about? He wants his money, and I want my son."

"Yeah I know but…"

"But what?" Kendall was fuming again. She had gone back to being the crazy woman that he'd spoken to earlier.

"I just need to speak to him, that's all."

"He spoke to you, Dre. He came to you like a man when he got out and asked you for his money. For whatever reason, you didn't pay the man, and here we are. We're right here."

"Yeah, I know, Ken. I should have paid him, but I didn't have the money right then."

"How much do you owe him?"

"A million dollars. Well, over a million dollars, but he told me that he would take a million and be done with it."

"I know you have the money. Give him the money, so Christian can come home."

"It's not that simple."

"What? Dre I've seen you count millions of dollars. What do you mean it's not that simple?"

"I'm just saying that I don't have the money. It's tied up."

"I suggest you untie it because if you don't, I'm calling the police."

"Didn't Los say no police?"

"Do you think I give a fuck about the police or a beef between two dope boys? All I care about is my son."

"Let me know when he calls."

"I will, meanwhile you need to get that money up. Now."

* * * * *

Stacy called Layla and asked her to come to room 1854 in the Ritz Carton downtown. She had been on her way to the gym, but she told him that she would come for a few moments. When she walked in Stacy was seated across from a middle aged white man with thinning, brown hair, and bloated face and drooping mouth. He wore a really expensive looking tight blue pinstriped suit.

"I didn't know that you had company."

"No, it's okay. We were just discussing some business issues, and since you're going to be one of my managers, I don't mind you being here. Layla, meet Brad Spritzer, my attorney. Everything that I do has to go by him first."

Brad stood and extended his hand, and his eyes traveled Layla's whole body in a creepy way, but it weirdly aroused her.

Layla sat in an armchair next to the sofa that Brad and Stacy were sitting on.

Brad said, "Like I was saying, this deal is unprecedented for an entertainer. This deal is similar to the James Harden Adidas deal. You're about to be set my friend."

"I still can't believe it."

"Why, you certainly deserve it. You're a trendsetter; everybody is noticing your 'Glow-up.'"

Stacy turned to Layla. "This is the woman that deserves the credit."

"I don't deserve no credit. I just helped him tweak his style a little bit."

"You helped him tweak his style a bit?" He echoed.

"I just started posting pics, and then when the last record came out, it took off. Then, GQ did an article on their website titled '8 Things We Can Learn from Rapper Drive-by'"

"Now, Abezas sneaker company came calling."

Layla looked confused. "What sneaker company?"

"Abezas." Stacy said.

"I've never heard of them." Layla said.

"They haven't been around but for a couple of years. A couple of tech geeks started the company, and it's mostly worn by skaters and hipsters. They're supposed to be the next Vans."

"And they picked you?" Layla grinned.

"Yeah, I wore a pair from the subscription box that you had given me. Somebody took notice of it, they had read the GQ article, and then they got in touch with Brad. When they found out I had a top ten hit, they wanted me to be the face of the brand."

"Wow, that's amazing."

"And what's even more amazing is the money they offered Stacy." Spritzer said.

Layla remembered the James Harden shoe Adidas deal; she'd even remembered right after the deal, she'd seen him at a club and waited around to try to talk to him and get to know him better, but some thirsty bitch with a sheer dress held his attention the whole night. She could also still remember how he'd cut his eyes at her seemingly wanting her to save him from the thirsty ass hoe. Layla had eventually got tired of waiting on him and settled for another player who sat on the bench with a two million dollar salary and no sneaker deal.

"Yeah, the deal is comparable in a lot of ways, not quite the money that James Harden is getting, but it's pretty damn close." Spritzer said grinning.

Brad stood and gave Stacy a pound before nodding to Layla. "Nice to meet you, Layla. I'm sure we'll be seeing more of each other."

"Yeah, nice to meet you too, sir."

Stacy and Layla watched Brad leave before Layla squealed, "Congratulations, man! You're a big deal."

He disappeared behind the bar and poured himself a shot of Patron and then poured her a shot.

"Let's celebrate."

"Of course." She walked over toward the bar with him, and he watched her tight black yoga pants, and his tool came alive.

He then passed her the drink. "Did you notice how Brad was looking at you?"

"Yeah, I did notice that."

"Do you know him?"

"How would I know that man?"

"I don't know. I just got a weird vibe that you two knew each other."

"Are you jealous, Stacy?"

"Why would I be jealous? I'm the one with the shoe deal. That man works for me."

"Right."

"That white man wanted some of that ass. I don't blame him though."

She winked at him. "You don't, huh?"

"No, I don't. Not at all."

Layla looked around and noticed she hadn't heard anyone else in the apartment. "Where is your little girlfriend, today?"

"Out of town with her mom."

"Why did you check into a suite?" Layla asked. "You have a place."

"Plumbing problems, so the rental office put me up here until they get it fixed."

"Nice."

"Drink up," he said.

She smiled, "Let's toast."

"Toast to what?"

"Toast to your new contract, silly."

He grinned and held his glass up. The glasses clanked together, then they both threw down the Patron.

"Another?" he asked.

"No. Are you trying to get me drunk?"

He smirked, "Maybe."

She made her way back over to the armchair. He watched her and wanted to see her out of those workout tights.

She caught him staring. She smiled then picked up a luxury magazine from the coffee table. She could feel him staring.

"What are you thinking?" She asked, without looking up from the magazine.

"I didn't really get a chance to appreciate your body."

"Huh, where did that come from?"

"The other day. You know, the threesome."

"Oh, yeah."

"Did you like it?" He asked.

"It was unexpected, but I did. What I didn't like was your girl's attitude the next day."

He frowned, then closed his eyes shut. "What did she do?"

Layla shrugged nonchalantly. "She just made it clear that you belonged to her."

"I don't belong to anyone."

He walked over to her and sat on the sofa, then he peeled his shirt off, and she stole glances at his thin but muscular frame and those tattoos. She had to admit the young boy now had sex appeal, and the fact that he had just gotten signed to a multi-million-dollar shoe deal didn't hurt either.

He removed a marijuana pen from his pocket and turned it on. "You mind if I smoke?"

"You're good, as long as I don't leave out of here smelling like weed."

"I got the vape pen like you suggested."

She grinned. "Glad you listened, but you really should quit all together."

He laughed then grinned. "You know you're bougie as fuck."

"You like it."

"Just a little."

"Just a little." she mocked.

He took a drag from the pen. "Come over here and sit beside me."

She walked over and plopped down beside him on the sofa.

"I almost forgot. I have something for you."

"A gift?"

"Yeah."

"I love gifts. What is it?"

"Some coconut oil."

She frowned. "Some coconut oil? What the fuck kind of gift is that? Are you saying I'm ashy or something?"

"No. I was just kidding. Go in the bedroom, there is a Neiman bag on the bed. Look inside."

She was smiling hard as hell. What did the young boy know about Neiman Marcus? She peered inside the bag, and there was a black Celine bag in there. She put it over her shoulder and paraded in front of the full-length mirror. She loved it; she had been wanting one in that color. She brought a brown one a few weeks ago after she'd asked her IG followers if she should get black or brown and they had voted brown. How did he know this? The young boy must have been following her IG account.

"I love it, Stacy!"

"Good. I'm glad you're happy. Now come back in here to keep me company."

She came back inside the room, and she found that he was now sitting on the edge of the couch, his jeans down to his ankles, and stroking his long slinky cock.

She laughed "What the hell are you doing?"

"What does it look like I'm doing?" He flashed a grin. "I'm pleasing myself."

"I can see that."

"I don't want to cum fast when we do it, so I want to bust one really fast, so I can last longer later."

"Do what?" Layla asked.

"You know."

"Who says we're going to do it?"

He frowned.

She plopped down beside him, then took possession of his stiff penis. She stroked for a minute before getting down on her knees. She stared at his penis; she loved the look of his skinny dick, but what she loved more was he'd just become a multi-millionaire. She took him deep inside her mouth and tried to suck the soul out of his body. He came really fast and hard, and she swallowed every bit of his multi-million dollar seed. And three minutes later his dick was standing back at attention ready for round two.

CHAPTER 21

A 8x5 framed image of John Smith and Donald Trump sat atop John's desk, but that didn't surprise Dre; Catherine had actually admitted to voting for the man, and though Dre didn't vote for anyone, he despised everything Trump stood for, so he and Catherine had agreed not to talk about politics. John Smith was wearing a blue wool suit and a crisp white shirt and a red tie, he was surely an All American white man and Dre was sure he hated the fact that he was fucking his daughter, but he had to admit the man hid his true feelings about him very well. Dre shook John's hand before taking a seat across from the desk.

"So what brings you here, Andre?"

"I need some money."

"What kind of money?"

"I need to take a million dollars out of the investment pool."

"A million dollars?"

"Yes."

"So you want me to write check for a million dollars?"

"I would prefer you get me cash."

"I'm afraid I can't do that right now."

Dre looked at that motherfucker like he was crazy. "What the fuck do you mean you can't do that right now? We are talking about my money. This is the money that I gave you."

"Listen, I'll tell you what we will not be doing. We will not be swearing in my office."

Dre stood and paced. He wanted to beat the brakes off the old white man, but he was Catherine's father.

"Have a seat please, Andre."

He asked, "Can I get my money or not?"

"So you want me to go in the bank and withdraw a million dollars?"

"Yes."

"Look, it's going to take me a month to get that money to you."

"I don't have a month, I need the money right now."

"Sit down and explain to me what's going on." Mr. Smith said calmly.

Dre looked John Smith in his ice blue eyes and saw Catherine in them.

"Catherine didn't tell you what was going on?"

"No."

"My son."

"Your son?" His voice rose a couple of octaves; clearly, the man was surprised.

"You do know I have a son, right?"

"Catherine may have mentioned it, so what about your son?"

Dre was still standing, trying to figure out the right way to tell the man that his son had been abducted and was being held ransom by a guy that had just gotten out of prison, a guy who had connected him to his plug. There was no way this white man would understand the rules of the street. There was no way he would understand why Carlos had taken Christian and how could Dre explain why he'd chosen not to notify the police.

"You don't have to tell me what's going on."

Dre shook his head gratefully. "I'd rather not."

"Fine, but right now I cannot give you the money, but I can go ahead and get the ball in motion, so that we can have the money in a few weeks."

"That's not going to help me."

"Fuck!" Dre said.

"What's going on, Andre?"

"My son has been kidnapped."

They stared at each other for a moment before John Smith said, "You have got to be kidding."

"Now why in the hell would I kid about something like that?"

* * * * *

Layla and India decided to meet up at the food court in SouthPark Mall. India was eating a chicken burrito bowl when Layla walked up. Layla dropped into the seat across from India.

India immediately noticed her friend's worried disposition and asked, "What's wrong?"

"I missed my period."

India dropped her fork, then took a swig of water. "When were you supposed to get it?"

"Almost a week ago."

"Just wait a couple of days. Mine came late a couple of months ago, and I told my mom. She was happy and hoped that I was pregnant—you know how parents are, they want grandkids—but then it turned out to be a false alarm. I was ecstatic. I did not want to have a kid by the dude that I'd been fucking."

"Why were you having sex with someone that you wouldn't want to be your kids' father, especially at this age?"

"You want to know the truth?"

"Yeah."

"You really want to know the truth?"

"Of course."

"Because he has some good dick."

"Okay, but's wrong with him?"

"He don't even have a car."

"What the fuck? How could you fuck with a dude that don't even own a car?"

"He's my homeboy from high-school. We'd been smoking one night, and I was high and decided to give him some." India closed her eyes, thought back to the night, and smiled.

"Damn, it was like that?"

"Girl, the way he eats pussy needs to be outlawed, and I was like damn who knew? So from that day on, he'll hit me up and we'll smoke and chill, and he'll fuck me to sleep. But when I tell you this dude ain't got a pot to piss in… I mean he calls himself a hustler, but he be hitting me up for a couple of hundred dollars to re-up."

Layla rolled her eyes. "I've heard those broke dudes are the ones with the good dick."

"You want to hear my theory on that?"

"Yeah, why not?"

"They know they don't bring nothing else to the table, so they may as well bring their pipe game."

"That's true. I never looked at it like that."

"I like him, I just wished he made a couple more hundred thousand dollars a year, but he's cool hanging out between his mom's and baby mama's playing PlayStation all day."

"Not one of those," Layla groaned. "I'm sick of hearing 'bout these grown ass boys, playing PlayStation all day, especially when they ain't got shit."

India ate more from her bowl. "Back to you, I really don't think you have anything to worry about."

"I hope not."

"Well, at least Rashad will be happy."

"That's just it—I don't know if it's Rashad's, I mean Rashad and I fucked around the same time I fucked Stacy but Rashad didn't come inside me."

India spit her food into her bowl. "Hold on, wait a goddamned minute, what do you mean you don't know if its Rashad's?"

Layla avoided her friend's eyes and explained, "I went there with that young boy a couple of times."

"Bitch, and you ain't tell me?"

"I don't kiss and tell."

"You're kissing and telling now."

"That's because I'm concerned. I don't know how this shit is going to play out."

"You have to quit thinking the worse."

"I know," she said, biting down on her bottom lip.

* * * *

Kendall had been up pacing. There was no way that she could fall asleep until Christian returned. In the past couple of days, she slept for a total of two hours, and she taken six melatonin tablets, but even then, she had the craziest dreams that Christian was an angel who had super powers and incredible strength—he'd even picked up her Range Rover and carried it on his back while she was inside. She had no idea what that dream meant, but she was glad that Carlos had given her updates twice daily. Pictures of Christian eating cereal, playing on a swing with Frank at the park. But he also said if he didn't get his money, he was going to take Christian to Mexico and sell him to the cartel. They had three days to come up with the money.

It was 1:15 am when the phone rang; it was Dre.

"Hey, I'm outside."

"Come in."

"I don't want to wake Chrissy up."

She huffed, "I'll come outside, then."

She came outside wearing a blue loungewear set. The car was running, and 21 Savage played on the radio. She sat on passenger side.

"You look tired," he said.

She looked at his stupid ass but decided to ignore that comment. How the fuck was she supposed to look? She didn't know where her son was.

"You really need to get some rest," he continued.

She sighed, "Okay Dre, did you come here to tell me how bad I look, or did you come to give me an update on Christian?"

"I'm sorry."

"Apology accepted, so what is going on with the money?"

"I don't have it." He avoided her eyes.

"What do you mean you don't have it? I can't believe it, Dre."

"Do you really think if I had it I wouldn't gladly give it up for my son?"

She knew that Dre loved his son and though she'd come to realize that there was a lot of things that Dre had done in the past year she couldn't quite believe, she knew that he must not have had the money, but knowing that did not help her at all.

"What happened Dre, where is the money? Where is your money?"

"Tied up in real estate investments."

"You don't have cash?"

"You know I was trying to go legit, and I lost two shipments, so now I don't have cash. I was trying to get some money from the investments, but it's gonna take at least a month to get it."

"No cash?"

"I got about a hundred thousand."

Kendall's legs trembled as she thought about Christian being dropped off somewhere in Mexico with God knows who.

"Borrow it from the connect."

"I called him, and his loyalty is with Carlos. Carlos gave me the connect."

"And why the fuck couldn't you just do right by Carlos, Dre? He gave you the plug and made it so that you can live this great fucking life. Now you got all your money tied up in stupid ass real estate with some dumb ass white chick."

"I know."

"But this is not making any sense Dre, why didn't you just pay Carlos?"

"I was going to pay him, but he asked me for it at the wrong time."

"He said you stopped giving him what you were supposed to give him years ago."

"I know. I know. I'm a fucked-up person." Gucci Mane burst through the speakers. Kendall looked at Dre and wondered what she had seen him in the first place. Who would have thought that she would have had a child by a fuck-boy?

"Where is the hundred thousand?"

"What are you going to do?"

"I'm going to work it out."

"How?"

"When he calls, I'm going to tell him that we have the hundred thousand and the house that you gave me." She'd figure out where she was going to live later.

"I'll go get the money I have and bring it back in the morning."

"Okay, Carlos has been calling me twice a day, usually first thing in the morning and then around ten, so I'll need it by then."

"You spoke to Christian?"

She nodded. "He seems to be doing fine."

"Good."

She opened the door. He lowered the volume on the radio. She was about to step out of the car when he called her name. She turned to face him.

"I'm sorry. I really am."

"Yeah." was all she could say. What was she supposed to say and what was he really sorry about? Was he sorry it didn't work out or was he sorry that this had happened to Christian?

She closed the door and skipped up to Chrissy's step. He watched her until she closed the door.

CHAPTER 22

It was 9:30 am when India opened the door for Layla, who was wearing a white robe and clutching a coffee mug tightly. India quickly invited Layla in. "You better have a great goddamned excuse for showing up at my house unannounced."

"Your phone kept going to voicemail."

India narrowed her eyes. "That means I was sleepy or busy girl."

"I forgot you're not a morning person."

"Not at all."

"It's important."

"What is it, girl?"

Layla paced, then ran her fingers through her hair. "I'm pregnant."

"What?"

"Yeah, I took a test and it was positive, bitch. Can you believe that?"

"Tell me you're lying."

"I'm not. I wish I were."

"Hey babe, did you have to go to Columbia to handpick the coffee beans or something?" A nappy-headed shirtless man appeared wearing only black boxer briefs, but his body was shredded as fuck, his huge package lying to the side. Layla stole a glance then turned away. She was in enough trouble as it was.

The man said "Oh, I'm sorry. I didn't know you had company."

India passed him the coffee. "This is Layla, my best friend. Now take ya coffee and get out of here."

Layla nodded to acknowledge him. As he walked away, she stole a look at his ass, then his tiny waist and thought this must be the dude that didn't have a car. He was in incredible shape, but what else did a broke motherfucker have to do other than go hang out at the gym all day?

India said, "I'm sorry for him interrupting."

"Is that the guy you were telling me about?"

"Yeah." She smiled.

"What's his name?"

"Myron."

"He's not bad looking."

"I know, but he was supposed to be at a job interview this morning at eight. You see where he's at. No ambition at all." India shook her head.

"So I'm pregnant. What the fuck am I supposed to do?"

"I don't know the answer to that."

"I think I'm going to get rid of it."

"No."

"Why not?"

"You're fucking thirty! Who the hell has an abortion past age thirty? Who fucks somebody by mistake and gets pregnant by mistake?"

Layla stared at her and thought, So says the woman with the broke ass arm candy in her bedroom.

* * * * *

It was almost noon when Kendall's phone rang with an unknown number. She figured that it must have been Carlos, because he had always called from an unknown number. She answered it right away.

"Good morning, Kendall."

"Hey. How is my boy?"

"Had a rough night last night. He cried a little and had nightmares, and he peed in the bed when he finally went to sleep, but he's okay now. He's playing with Frank. I just fed him grits and bacon. That boy loves himself some grits."

Kendall smiled remembering how her son loved grits and bacon."

"Dre came over."

"Did you tell him what I said?"

"What *did* you say?"

"About Mexico."

"Would you quit saying that!" Kendall screamed.

"Hey. Hey. Hey! Kendall will you calm down? I have no intentions of harming Christian. You know what I want."

"Yeah."

"When the fuck is he going to have my money?"

"He left some money with me."

"Okay good. I will call you later today and we can arrange a time where you can drop the money off, and I will have someone bring Christian home."

"How do I know you're going to do what you said you are going to do?"

"Have I harmed him yet?"

"I don't know. Have you?"

"You're pissing me off, you know, you really don't sound like a mother who wants her child back."

She was almost offended. "I was just saying. Just wanting to know how do I know if I give you the money that you will do what you say you will do?"

"I guess you'll just have to trust me."

"I guess so."

"Going to call you back in a few. Pick up the phone please."

"Carlos."

"Yes?"

"I don't have all the money." Kendall confessed.

"What?"

"Yeah, Dre only brought part of the money."

"How much did he bring?"

"I only have a hundred thousand."

"What the fuck? A hundred thousand? You are kidding me right?"

"Dre didn't bring all the money. Saying something about his money being tied up. I was pissed too when he told me, believe me."

"Kendall, you and Dre are making this shit hard."

"Look we're going to get the money. I swear to you, we are going to get the money."

"Kendall, you have two more days."

"I have a house, and I think it's worth $275 thousand. We have the deed to it. I can sign it over to you."

"I want cash."

"Okay, we'll come up with the money. I swear."

"You know you're realer than your bitch ass ex-husband."

"My son means the world to me, as I'm sure you meant the world to your mother."

"If and when you come up with nine hundred thousand, I'll give you your son back."

"We're going to get the money up, don't worry."

"I'm not worried. Why should I worry? I'll get what I want either way."

* * * * *

Layla tossed the pregnancy test on the bed, and he picked it up and examined it. "What are you trying to tell me?"

Layla had a wide grin plastered on her face. "You're going to be a father!"

Rashad sprang from the bed, embraced her, kissed her, and then caressed her belly that was still very flat, though he knew it was still in the early stages. "This is great."

"Yes. It is." She sat on the edge of the bed. "I thought you would be excited, but I didn't think you would be this happy."

"I'm going to be a daddy again. Of course I'm going to be happy!"

"And I'm going to be a mommy again."

He sat down beside her and gazed into her eyes. "How do you feel about it?"

She shrugged. "I don't know how to answer that."

"I know you didn't want to be a mommy right now." He paused. "I know you had all these dreams of being famous and being a brand ambassador, whatever the hell that means. Doesn't this ruin your plan?"

"I thought about that. I want to have this baby while I'm still young and healthy, and I'm sure you going to get me the things I need to get this body right."

"The things you need?" He asked, confused.

"A chef, a personal trainer. Or you can be my trainer."

"We'll worry about all of that later. Right now, let's go out and celebrate. I'm so happy."

"I'm glad you're happy." She smiled.

He leaned into her and kissed her again. He was getting his family.

* * * * *

Rashad stepped inside the house. What Layla was wearing accentuated her skin tone perfectly. Her breasts were pushed up nice and high, and her ass looked like two volleyballs jammed together.

His bottom lip dropped. "You are one sexy motherfucker."

"Thank you."

"What's the occasion?"

"I want to celebrate."

"Celebrate what?"

"The baby, silly. It was your idea."

"Of course."

She loosened his tie, then unbuttoned his shirt and rubbed his chest. Then, she unbuckled his belt and wrestled his penis free from his boxer briefs, and his dick rose to the occasion. Long and chocolate, the color of a candy bar, she fell to her knees and took him deep in her mouth as she toyed with his balls. She looked up at him seductively, her eyes the color of grass. He usually hated colored contacts on black girls, but this color actually looked good on Layla and aroused him even more.

She removed his tool from her mouth briefly and said, "Cum in my mouth, Zaddy."

"I don't want to."

One thing that annoyed her about him is he always tried to be respectable, but she wanted to be man-handled and treated like a slut.

"Cum in my goddamned mouth!" she commanded, then resumed slurping his tool.

He frowned. "It's harder for me to cum from head."

"Fuck me on the balcony and treat me like a ho."

"Are you drunk?"

She stood, grabbed him by the hand, and led him out onto to the balcony. The building across from him was hosting a BBQ.

"Fuck me right now."

"But there are people outside on the balcony right across from us!"

"Who cares? They've fucked before. Everybody has fucked before."

He removed his pants completely, and his dick was now limp. She placed it in her mouth and pulled it until it stiffened. She kneeled over the balcony, the yellow thong climbing in her ass cheeks. He pulled it aside and entered her.

Layla gasped, "Pull my hair! Pull my hair!"

He twirled locks of hair around his wrist as he stroked her, but he couldn't help but think of the people at the BBQ and wondering if someone would report them? He gazed into crowd; they were all laughing and having a good time, nobody seemed to be caring about what he was doing on his balcony.

"Fuck me harder."

He kept stroking.

"Treat me like a porn star."

"Huh?"

"I want you to choke the shit out of me."

He didn't remember Layla being this daring, but he liked the new Layla's sexual prowess.

She placed his hand on her neck, forcing him to apply pressure. "Choke me Daddy."

He looked over at the BBQ. Nobody seemed to notice. What the fuck was going on? He saw there was a DJ there, but he didn't hear any music. Then, he spotted the headphones. It was a fucking silent party.

She forced his hands to squeeze harder. She released his hands and closed her eyes, gasping for air.

He let go of her. "Why'd you do that?"

"Huh?"

"No. I'm okay. Quit treating me like I'm some kind of princess and fuck the shit out of me!"

He kept stroking. She forced him to apply pressure to her neck again, and it pissed her off because there he was with that soft bullshit again.

"Manhandle me, Daddy."

"But the people at the BBQ."

"They ain't thinking about us, and I ain't thinking about them."

He gripped her neck and all he could think about was this couldn't be healthy for the baby. Perhaps the baby wasn't getting enough oxygen.

"The baby."

"What about the baby?"

"I can't do this."

"Well fine. Don't choke me, just fuck me."

He kept humping.

Someone from the BBQ yelled, "They're fucking, look!"

And the crowd from the BBQ looked over and started clapping their hands.

"So what do we do now?"

"Cum inside me."

"I can't." He panted.

"Why can't you?"

"I'm nervous."

"Don't be."

"I am"

"Don't be. It's going to be okay."

He closed his eyes, and she was right; he no longer thought about the people at the BBQ. They were all pointing, and he could smell grilled chicken. Now he could hear music, and he thought that was quite weird since it was a silent party but then he realized the music was coming from the balcony next to them. "Where Ya At" by Future was playing on the balcony next to them, meaning that they had more guests.

He relaxed a little.

"I want you to cum for me, Zaddy."

"I'm about to cum."

She disengaged herself from him and stroked his dick. He needed to cum. He had came too far not to. She plopped to her knees, and he exploded in her mouth. She slurped it all up and licked her lips.

The next day, Jeremy came over and said, "You're a motherfucking star, my man."

"I'm a star? Of course I'm a star."

"A motherfucking porn star."

"What are you talking about?"

"So you know about the sex tape?"

"What sex tape?"

"Exactly what I mean. The sex tape was on all the blog sites. Saying Instagram star and her boyfriend sex tape." He laughed. "Bruh, you've gone viral."

"What?"

"Everybody is talking about your sex tape."

He narrowed his eyes, then raised the left eyebrow.

"My nigga, think about your girl. You go viral, she gets more followers, and we both know that's what she cares about."

"You think she did it?"

"Fuck yeah, bro."

"I have to see the tape."

"What do you mean?"

"There were people at a BBQ perhaps one of them could have recorded it."

"I don't know, bruh. You could hear the sounds and everything. I mean she was telling you to choke her."

"Where can I find it?"

Jeremy pulled it up on his phone and Rashad heard himself say, "What about the baby?" He frowned.

Jeremy asked, "What were you talking about when you asked about the baby?"

"She's pregnant."

"What?"

"Yeah."

"When were you going to tell me?"

"It's not like I was keeping it from you," he said defensively. "I just hadn't had time to tell you." He placed his hands atop his head, then decided to call Layla. She picked up on the second ring.

"Come home right away."

CHAPTER 23

The sound of rain bounced off the roof as India and Layla sipped chai latte's in India's living room on opposite ends of the sofa. India had her feet propped up on the living room table. "I hate weather like this unless—"

"Unless bae is here, right?"

"I don't have a bae," India corrected.

"You could have fooled me! In here making breakfast for a nigga the other day."

"Hey I walked to the Keurig to get him coffee. That does not qualify as me making breakfast for him, though I did whip up some cheese grits and turkey sausage after you left."

"That man eats grits?"

"Yeah... Why?"

"With a body like that, I was sure all he ate was salad."

"Actually, he don't eat healthy at all. His metabolism is just crazy."

"I hate people like that."

"Yeah, but that's not my bae."

There was a flash of lightning then thunder roared; they looked at each other.

"India, I don't know what I'm going to do."

"What do you mean?"

Layla rolled her eyes. "Bitch, I'm pregnant."

"I know, I don't think you should keep it."

Layla looked at her like she was crazy. "Didn't you just tell me the other day that I should keep it?"

"Yeah, but the more I thought about it under these circumstances, it might not be a good idea."

"What changed your mind?"

She sipped her latte, then the thunder roared again "I'm just thinking about how Rashad would feel if he found out the baby was not his."

"So I'm supposed to take a life because I'm worried about how a man would feel?"

"Well, I just know the history of you two, how you lost Mya and how much it would hurt if you had a baby by another man. A younger man. A richer man."

Layla admitted, "I didn't think about that, but I can't kid myself either. Rashad and I love each other, and I think we'll always love each other, but it's not right."

"So who do you think you're right for, Layla?"

"I don't know. I don't know if that person exists."

"Have you told young boy?" She laughed. "I can't believe you got me calling him young boy."

"No. Do you think I should? You know him better I do."

"Oh, no, I don't."

"You know what I mean."

"I wouldn't tell him."

"I have to tell him."

"Did you tell Rashad the kid was his?"

"Yes, but I know it's not."

"So now you're going to tell Stacy that he's going to be a father at the height of his career. This is not going to go over well. You know he's going to accuse you trying to trap him though it was him who decided to go raw. He's going to say that you planned this and you're a gold digger."

"That's nothing new. I've been called that before, and I'm sure you have, too."

They laughed their asses off, then India said, "I've been called it so much now I think of being called a gold digger as a compliment."

"Girl, just stop right now."

* * * * *

The concierge in Stacy's building was a hulking black man named Zeke with a bald head. He wore a blue suit and white shirt with a red tie. Layla approached the desk and sweetly said, "I'm here to see Stacy Cooper."

"I'm sorry. Mr. Cooper is not seeing anyone today."

"I really need to see him."

"Are you a relative?"

"Yes."

Zeke studied Layla's face. "You know what, you must be his Mom."

Layla winced. "No the fuck I ain't."

"I'm sorry."

"I'm only thirty!"

Zeke held his hands up "Hey, I'm sorry."

"It's okay."

"Who are you to him?"

"I'm cousin."

"You have to be immediate family."

She dug into her purse and removed a one hundred dollar bill. "Can you let me up?"

"Fifty more and I can make that happen."

"Are you being serious right now, Zeke?"

"How'd you know my name?"

"Bruh, it's on your name tag."

"I got three kids. Every little bit helps."

"I only got twenty-five."

"That'll do." He grinned, revealing some very childish-looking baby teeth. Yuck! She hated grown ass men with kid teeth.

She took the elevator up to the 46th floor before exiting. She exited the elevator, and as she walked to his condo, she replayed all the different outcomes in her head. A) Maybe he would be ecstatic, she would have the child, and she would get twenty thousand dollars a month in child support for the next eighteen years. B) He would be pissed and claim that she had set him up and tell her to get the fuck out. C) Claim she was lying. D) Tell her to get an abortion real fast. E) They could co-parent in peace. Her gut told her that E was probably not going to happen.

She knocked on the door.

Malika answered the door wearing some ratty ass wool pajamas, her hair wrapped in a lavender silk scarf. Layla was not expecting to see that bitch, but she was his girlfriend and this was probably why baby-teeth Zeke didn't want to let her up; he couldn't really believe that she was really related to him.

Malika placed her hands on her hips and asked, "How did you get up here?"

"Good morning to you, too."

"Don't good morning me." She rolled her eyes. "How the fuck did you get past security?"

"You mean the concierge?"

"You know what the fuck I mean."

"Is Stacy here?"

"Quit avoiding the question, ho."

"I'm here now, so that is irrelevant."

Stacy came out shirtless drying his hair with a towel. "What's going on?"

"Your little girlfriend somehow managed to get past security. She wants to talk to you, but anything she got to say to you, she can say it in front of me."

Stacy laughed, pissing Layla off. Clearly, he was amused.

"Hey, Stacy. I see this is a bad time for you, just give me a call whenever you're free. I had some questions about the contract. Perhaps me, you, and Brad can go over it."

"There won't be no going over shit without me being there." Malika said.

"Hey, how do you deal with this?" Layla asked, waving a hand in his girlfriend's general direction.

"Yo, why don't you just get the fuck out of here?" Malika said.

Stacy wedged himself in between the ladies, then said. "I will call you later."

"Okay." Layla said, then turned and opened the door. Malika slinked around Stacy and pushed Layla out, then slammed it hard behind her. Layla was fuming. She'd wanted to beat the shit out of the little hood rat if she ever got the chance.

Later that evening, Layla was driving home when the phone rang. Stacy.

"Hey," he greeted her.

"I guess you can talk now? Your little pitbull must not be around."

He laughed.

"I don't find that shit funny," Layla snapped.

"Hey, what was so important that you showed up at my house unannounced?"

"I'm pregnant."

"Congratulations, I think you'll make a great mom."

"I don't think you understand." Layla bit on her bottom lip.

"I guess you came to tell me that you won't have time to be my manager."

"Stacy I'm pregnant by you."

"What the fuck do you mean you're pregnant by me? You have a man. I'm telling you right now I'm too young to have a baby."

"What?" She stared at the dashboard, thinking, This is what you get when you have sex with an immature ass kid.

"What about your man? I know you must fuck him."

"A man that I barely fuck. When I count back to the last time I had sex, it was with you. I'm sure it's yours, plus the last time I had sex with him it was just head." She lied though she was almost certain that she wasn't pregnant by Rashad because he'd came in her mouth and not in her VJ."

"I ain't going for that."

"Huh?" She was annoyed as fuck. "You ain't going for what?"

"I don't believe that baby's mine. I fuck my girlfriend raw all the time, and she's not pregnant. Get the fuck out of here with that."

"What... You can't be serious right now."

She pulled her car into the parking lot of the nearest gas station. She was becoming upset and didn't want to crash her car.

"Stacy I just called to tell you this. I didn't call to argue."

"You might as well call the nigga you're living with, because like I said, I ain't trying to hear that shit."

* * * * *

Terry Stowers was five-three with skin the color of almonds, he had a pointy nose and large bucked teeth and he resembled a Rat, thus earning him the nickname Rat-Boy. Rat-Boy paced outside the room where Frank and Christian were being housed. Christian was lying on a sheet-less twin size mattress crying his head off as Frank barked. Rat Boy was instructed to guard the room and to make sure neither Christian or Frank left the room. Christian was cried out, "I want my mommy! I want my mommy! I want to go home!"

Rat Boy opened the door and yelled, "Will you shut the fuck up? Mommy can't save your little ass now!"

Christian turned to the side of the mattress and stuck his thumb in his mouth. He'd never sucked his thumb before. The thumb had become a crutch for him, a coping mechanism for the absence of his parents. He looked at Rat Boy who was grinning, taking sick pleasure in the child's misery.

"You're a mean man." Christian said.

"And you're a spoiled ass little brat."

"Quit cursing."

Frank growled and ran up to the edge of the room and barked, but he wouldn't go closer to Rat Boy, who had kicked the dog clear across the room two hours earlier.

"You two are going to shut the fuck up or—"

Carlos stepped into the room and when he realized Christian was crying, he slapped the fuck out of Rat Boy.

Rat Boy held his jaw. "Hey what did you do that for?"

"I've told you two times to quit cursing at the little boy."

"You act like you care about him."

Carlos narrowed his eyes. "You know I have a soft spot for children and old people. Yell at him one more time, and I'll shoot you in both knee caps with my .380."

Rat Boy held his hands up. "All right. All right."

Carlos dialed Kendall's number.

"Hello?"

Christian was crying in the background.

Kendall said, "What in the hell have you done to my son?"

"I haven't done anything to him!" Carlos spat.

"Why is he crying then?"

"He wants his mommy. He's been saying that for the past two days, so I hope you have the money or else we're headed to Mexico."

"I will have the money by the end of the day."

"I better have the money by the end of the day too. Give me the money or this little piss-ant kid is gone forever."

CHAPTER 24

etectives Michael Hearns and Ian Forrester sat on opposite ends of the Birchwood table. Hearns and Forrester made quite the odd pair with their different styles, Kendall thought, but they both seemed very knowledgeable and concerned.

"This guy is very smart. There was no way we could get a location of his cellphone." Hearns said.

Forrester said, "Yeah, he's probably using some sort of VOIP phone service or an app."

Kendall legs trembled as she thought about Christian crying and imagining all the horrible things that could be happening to him.

"What are we going to do? He's threatening to take him to Mexico."

Hearns said, "He's not going to take him to Mexico—I can tell you that right now."

Forrester agreed, "Yeah he's bluffing, the guy is too smart to telegraph his next move."

Kendall found a little relief in the two detectives' confidence that her son was not going to be in Mexico somewhere. "He wants money."

Hearns asked, "Why do you think he believes that you have the money? A million dollars, at that. Not many people have that just lying around."

"I don't know." Kendall lied.

"Makes no sense. There is something you're not telling us." Forrester said.

"I told you. I knew him before he went to prison. We used to kind of mess around, you know."

"So you used to sleep with him?" Hearns said.

"Do I have to spell it out?"

"Yeah."

"Well I used to fuck him, then." Kendall lied.

"So you used to sleep with him, and he's kidnapped your kid?"

"Yes."

Hearns didn't believe shit she was saying. He removed a Kleenex from a box on the desk and blew his huge snout, then tucked the tissue into his suit pocket. "There has to be more to this story."

Kendall thought hard. "After he was in two years, he'd found out that I'd moved on. I'd met someone and gotten pregnant, and he'd written me a letter vowing to kill me."

"Because you had a child with another man?" Forrester asked, and Kendall watched his mouth, thinking, *Damn this was one goddamned fine ass white man.* For a second, she wondered how Dre would have reacted if she was fucking Forrester. *That* would piss him the fuck off.

"Yes," she said.

"Okay, so he gets released, and he finds your child with his father's girlfriend and takes him and the dog?"

"Yeah, he must have been following me when I dropped him off over there or something, I don't know how he got their address."

"I didn't ask you that." Hearns said.

"But you were going to ask me that." she snapped.

Hearns removed the tissue from his pocket and blew his nose again. "What makes this man think you have access to a million dollars?"

"Because after, I started dating a rich man."

"Your son's father?"

"No, a much older man, around fifty. He would buy me things and take me on exotic vacations. So I guess the word got back to Dre, and now he's pissed."

"Dre?"

"I mean Los."

"Who is Dre?"

"My son's father. I've told you his name earlier when I first came in."

Forrester studied his notes. "Andre, your ex, and his wife's name is Catherine."

"Yes."

"So Carlos finds out you have this rich sugar daddy, and now he thinks you can get the million dollars from the sugar daddy."

"Do you have to use the word sugar daddy?"

"Well an old man that helps a young woman out is a sugar daddy."

"Well, its sounds so dated."

Forrester cut in. "I've been skimming over these police reports, and I see the day this happened, Andre never talked to the police, and this is the first time that you have been in touch with us? Am I correct?"

"Yes."

"Okay your son got kidnapped four days ago, and you reach out to the police four days later?"

"Am I being interrogated here? We need to be working on getting my son back before it's too late!" Kendall began to tear up. She was faking, but they didn't need to know that.

Her phone rang again. She answered and put it on speaker.

Carlos said, "Kendall."

"Yes."

"I have a final offer of three hundred thousand dollars or else I'm leaving tonight for Mexico."

"Tell him you have the money." Forrester whispered.

"Hey I have the money."

"Good."

"Thank you, Carlos."

"You know, I really like this kid, and he shouldn't have to suffer because of Dre's punk ass."

"Right."

"I'll call you in a few to tell you where to meet my girlfriend. You're going to give her the money, and later in the day I'll drop him off somewhere safe."

"Of course we'll give her the money."

* * * * *

Layla looked seductive in the lavender Under Armour tights. Rashad was lying on the sofa when she entered the condo. He sat up on the sofa and asked, "Where have you been?"

"The gym, duh."

"Duh, you're pregnant. You don't need to be going to the gym. I'm a trainer that don't believe in all that pre-pregnancy workout stuff."

"Well this is my body, and I want to snap back." She smiled. "Why are you in such a sucky mood?"

"We need to talk."

"Oh my god. Did I do something wrong again?" She sank down on the black armchair across from him.

His serious face made her nervous.

"What's wrong babe?"

He sighed, "Have you heard about the tape?"

"What tape? Like scotch tape?"

"Video."

She laughed, and it annoyed the fuck out of him.

"Why are you laughing? What's so damn funny?"

"I was just laughing because who uses the word 'tape'? That is so nineteen eighties. That word went out with VHS."

"You knew what I meant."

"You were asking about a video?"

"Yeah. A video of us fucking has gone viral."

"So?" She smirked. "Who cares? Everybody fucks."

"So you already knew about it?"

"I might have heard something about it."

"Did you leak it?"

She crossed her legs and rubbed her chin. "Leaked it? I didn't know it existed until today."

He stood. "Who the fuck recorded it then?"

"Wait a minute. You think I recorded the video? Now tell me, how did I record the video that I starred in."

Rashad shrugged. "I didn't say you did."

She licked her lips. "First of all ,who would be interested in a video of me and you?"

"Perhaps your little social media fans. I don't know. I do know that your fans have more than doubled since."

"What you talking about?" Layla narrowed her eyes.

"Your Instagram followers, Snapchat friends. I don't know."

"I don't have contacts at any blogs, so it wasn't me."

"Really?"

"I didn't do it." She lied.

"Who did it?"

"How would I know that? It could be anybody. Like you said, I have a little social media fame—people know who I am." She paused then said. "You know it could have been somebody from the balcony. I really don't know who filmed us."

"Whatever, bruh."

"First of all I'm not a 'bruh,' but you can believe what you want to believe."

"Somebody did it. Somebody filmed us and leaked this bullshit video."

"Why are you so upset about it?"

"I'm a businessman. How do you think it looks for me, a business owner, to have my naked ass all over the internet?"

"Relax. You know how the world is. Somebody is going to do something stupid, and people will forget all about you. Trust me. There will be more dumb shit going on in the world by tomorrow and we will be old news."

"That's not the point."

She raised her eyebrow. "What is the point?"

"I don't need the unwanted attention."

She stood and said, "I'm not about to argue with you about something I didn't do. I'm getting in the shower."

* * * * *

It was 12:31 a.m. when Rashad's phone vibrated. He glanced at it before sending it to voicemail. He wasn't in the mood to chat. Jeremy called again. Then a picture came through of Layla and India at a lounge, champagne glasses in their hands. He called Jeremy.

"Where are you?"

"I'm at Club One."

"Layla is there, huh?"

"Bruh, that's what I'm trying to tell you."

Rashad stood, grabbed the robe from the door then he stepped outside onto the balcony. His heart raced. He couldn't believe this bitch was out partying while carrying his baby.

"How long has she been there?"

"I don't know. I just got here like twenty minutes ago. She was definitely drinking. I wanted to go slap the fuck out of her, but I didn't want any problems with you."

"You should have."

"I'll go slap the ho right now just give me the word."

"No!"

"What do you want me to do?"

"Stay there. I'm going to put on some clothes, and I'll be there in a few minutes." He ended the call, threw on a white t-shirt, a pair of jeans, and white trainers and headed out the door. He jumped into his car and sped to the club, arriving in fifteen minutes. The big light skinned bouncer with freckles named Tank stood in front of the door. Tank was speaking into some microphone around his neck when Rashad approached. Tank stopped him then ordered one of the other bouncers to come to the front of the club, then he looked at Rashad and said, "I'm sorry homeboy. I can't let you in dressed like this."

"Like what?" He eyed his outfit but couldn't find anything wrong with it.

"You need to have on a shirt with a collar."

"You can't be serious." Rashad groaned.

Tank shrugged and said, "I just work here, man."

Rashad dug into his pocket then slipped Tank a one-hundred-dollar bill. "Can you work this out for me?"

Tank stuffed the money into his back pocket. "You still have to pay the twenty dollar cover."

"Really?"

"The demand."

"Look, bruh, I appreciate that. What's your name?"

"David, but everybodycalls me Tank."

Jeremy was at the bar with a curvaceous Puerto Rican girl with blotchy skin named Myra. Jeremy introduced Myra to Rashad.

Rashad nodded to Myra then turned to Jeremy.

"Just tell me where the fuck Layla is so I can get outta here."

Myra pouted. "You just got here."

Jeremy said, "That's the most non-partiest nigga in the world."

"Non-partiest. Is that a word?"

Jeremy laughed. "It is when you're high as a motherfucker like I am."

"Where the fuck is Layla?"

"You should have just let me slapped that ho, bruh."

Rashad was getting annoyed with Jeremy's drunk ass. "Tell me where she is."

"I'll show you where she was. I don't know if she's still there or not."

Jeremy and Rashad pushed through a small crowd until they reached an area with plush blue suede sofas. Jeremy pointed to two cornball looking dudes. One was wearing a blue pinstriped suit and the other wore a dark grey wool blend suit. They both had on expensive cap-toe oxford shoes. "She was over there with those computer geeks."

"Where is she now?"

"I don't know. You didn't tell me to watch the her.

Rashad scanned the club looking for any sign of Layla."

Layla and India returned from the bathroom, marched past Rashad and Jeremy, seemingly oblivious to them and settled back at the table with the computer geeks.

Jeremy said "Okay there she is, bruh. What are you going to do?"

"I can't believe she walked right past me."

"She didn't see you." Jeremy whispered. "But the question is now that you see her, what the fuck are you going to do?"

"I don't know."

"What did you even come here for if you don't know?"

"Because you said she was drinking."

"And she was, but why is she in here in the first goddamned place? She is pregnant with your seed. This is no place for a pregnant woman. "Go grab her ass and pull her out of here, now that's what the fuck I would do."

Myra girl grabbed Jeremy's hand "Stay out of it."

Jeremy wrestled his hand free and said, "This is between me and my brother."

"And your brother is going to handle it the way he wants to handle it, not the way you want to handle it."

"Let me ask you a question?" Jeremy asked.

She was silent.

"Did you or did you not see her drinking."

"I did, but this is a lounge. Everybody is drinking."

"Everybody is not pregnant."

"I didn't know she was pregnant."

"Well, keep your motherfucking mouth shut then."

"Why are you disrespecting me like this?"

Rashad snapped, "Will y'all just chill?"

Jeremy turned to Myra and kissed her forehead. They observed Layla, India and the computer nerds for a while.

One of the computer nerds poured Layla a glass of champagne as Kanye West's "All Of the Lights" came on.

Layla and India started dancing on each other, and Layla sat back down. India was grinding on Layla before she reached over, grabbed the champagne flute, and held it to her mouth.

Rashad ran over to the section and slapped the champagne flute out of Layla's hand, glass shattering everywhere. The nerd with the blue slim fitting pinstriped double breasted suit approached Rashad, and Jeremy wedged himself between them, facing the nerd. "Bruh, you don't want to get yourself involved."

"What's going on?"

Jeremy gritted his teeth and warned, "Let it go, bruh."

"Why is he disrespecting the lady?"

Jeremy punched the geek, and the man stumbled back, holding his eye. The other guy stepped toward Jeremy, Jeremy open hand slapped him, then grabbed him and body slammed his nerdy ass on the table, shattering the bottles of champagne.

Rashad yanked Layla by the arm and was leading her out of the door.

The bouncers bum rushed the section as Jeremy stomped the fuck out of the brave ass nerd.

Two huge bouncers—a black one with a bald head and a hoop earring in both ears and a big white guy with gel spiked hair and a tribal tattoo on his forearm—surrounded Jeremy. Jeremy picked up a champagne bottle. "I wish one of you fat motherfuckers would grab me!"

A third man unfastened the velvet rope and tackled Jeremy from behind. The three men restrained Jeremy and carried his ass out of the section, escorting him to the back of the club while he screamed to be released.

Layla yelled. "Rashad, will you please let me go?!"

India said, "You fucking asshole, you're hurting her!"

Rashad ordered India, "You stay the fuck out of it!"

Tank, the bouncer that Rashad had given the tip, came and approached him. "What's going on, bruh?"

Layla yelled, "He's hurting me!"

Tank grabbed Rashad's other hand. "Let her go, bruh."

The owner of the club, a tanned white man with yellow linen pants and slicked back graying hair, said, "Restrain him. We're calling the police."

Tank turned to the white man and said. "I know him, I'll calm him down."

"Well, you better talk to your friend, then."

Tank led Rashad to a section near the bar. "Look, man, I don't know you, but this asshole Lenny will have you arrested. I see it every night."

"Who is Lenny?"

"The owner. That white man with the greasy hair."

"That's my girl, and she was in here with some other niggas."

"I know and that's fucked up, but you are going to have to let it go, bruh. Matter of fact, I'm going to lead you out of the back door, and you need to get in your car and go."

"What about my friend? I can't leave him here."

"He's probably in the back handcuffed, but I'll go back there and see if I can get him out before Lenny calls the police. Lenny will sometimes listen to me. What's his name?"

"Jeremy."

"I'll pretend like I know him, too."

Tank said, "Follow me."

Rashad said, "Where the fuck are we going?"

"I'm getting you out of here, bruh."

"What about my friend?"

"I told you, I'll see what I can do."

Rashad dug into his pocket, removed two more one-hundred-dollar bills and a business card and passed it to him. "Get him out of there and come see me tomorrow. I'm going to give you a job. It's obvious you don't like this Lenny dude."

"Thanks." Tank stuffed the money and the card inside his wallet, then led Rashad to the exit through the back of the lounge.

Rashad gratefully said, "Thanks, bruh. Call me tomorrow."

"Get away from here. I'm telling you, I've seen Lenny lock a lot of brothers up. I'll go get your friend. I'll tell him I know him and that I saw the other guy throw a drink on him or something."

Rashad dashed across the street to the parking lot and waited until Jeremy was released. Jeremy got into an Audi A8 with his date and Rashad drove home.

CHAPTER 25

Layla had spent the last two days staying with India in her two-bedroom apartment. She and Rashad had communicated mostly through text. She hated that she'd given up her apartment to live with Rashad because she was sure that India was growing tired of her camping out on her sofa, invading her and that bum ass nigga's privacy. He'd been there for the past two days, and she was starting to believe that he was more than a fuck buddy. It was 7am when India strolled into the living room wearing a white robe, and Layla was flipping through pictures on Instagram. Layla looked up and smiled. "Good morning, princess."

India sat on the armchair and smiled. "How did you sleep?"

"I was sleeping pretty good until—"

India blushed. "Were we loud?"

"You were more than loud." Layla laughed. "Damn he must have some good dick."

"I know, right?"

"I think you're falling in love."

"Who, me? Never. I'm telling you he's just something to do for right now."

"But he's over here every night."

"What's wrong with getting good dick every night?"

"Nothing at all," Layla said. She was now on Stacy's IG page admiring his style. It was amazing how he'd developed so much swag since the day that she met him.

"I see you on Stacy's page. Somebody is in love."

"No," Layla sighed. "Well, I told him about the pregnancy."

"And what did he say?"

"Says he's too young for a baby."

"You should tell Rashad that it's not his kid."

Layla looked at the bitch like she was crazy. "Wasn't it you just the other day telling me that I should abort it? First, you tell me I should have it, then you tell me I should abort it, and now you are telling me I should tell Rashad it's not his."

"Girl, did you see how mad he was at you at the club?"

Layla nodded. "I was there."

"He cares about this baby that ain't even his."

"I know."

"What are you going to do?"

"I'm going to abort the kid, then tell him I miscarried."

"You think he's going to believe you?"

"Now is the perfect time to do it while he's mad and I'm not there. You're going to help me, right?"

"How?"

"I need you to verify that I lost the baby."

"Anything for you, sis."

"Thanks. I'm going to need to be here for at least another 4 days after the procedure." Layla said, then grabbed a Louis Vuitton clutch from the table, removed a thousand dollars, and passed it to India. India refused to accept the money. "I can't take money from you, sis."

"Take the money. I don't believe in freeloading. You know me."

India finally accepted the money.

Two days later, India and Layla left the abortion clinic after the procedure. India had given up her bed to Layla for a couple of days, but on the third day, Layla resumed her position back on the sofa after Myron had brought his broke ass back over one morning. India came and sat on the armchair beside the sofa. "Hey, sis."

Layla looked up; she was doing much better today. She was still kind of sore, but not as sore as before. "Hey what's up?"

"You okay today?"

"Yes. I got up to pee earlier, but it didn't hurt as bad as it had been before. Thanks for asking."

India smiled, "Of course, sis."

"I don't know how I can thank you enough for all that you've done for me."

"Look, I love you. Don't worry about that. I know you would have done the same for me."

"Of course."

"But I do have a small favor to ask of you."

"Anything."

"Do you think you can give me another thousand dollars?" India asked.

"Yeah, sure, I'll go to the bank today and give it to you later."

India smiled. "You're the best, sis."

* * * * *

Carlos had called Kendall, and she picked up on the first ring. Seemed like she was always within arm's reach of the phone since the kidnapping.

"Hey."

"Hey."

"Are you ready?"

"Yeah. I'm just waiting on Dre to bring me the last twenty-five thousand dollars, and then I'll meet your friend at the Publix parking lot."

"Cool."

"Describe her."

"Biracial girl with freckles around her nose, blond dreadlocks, and a nose ring."

"Okay, what's her name?"

"Just call her Onyx Moon."

"Onyx Moon? What the fuck kind of name is that?"

"Look, her name is not important."

"Okay I'm to give her the bag, right?"

"Yeah, I've already told you this. Are you alone?"

"Yes." She lied.

"Alright I don't want to no bullshit, Kendall. I don't want anything to happen to little Christian, okay?"

"Where is he?"

"In his room."

"That is not his room."

"You know what I meant."

"Is he with that man who was yelling at him?"

"What are you talking about?"

"Remember? I spoke to him the other day. He told me about some man that was yelling at him and Frank."

"No, that is under control. Nobody is yelling at Christian."

"Okay, Dre should be here in twenty minutes. Can I speak to Christian?"

"You'll have plenty of time for that later."

* * * * *

The Charlotte SWAT team used the battering ram to burst through the door of the eighth-floor apartment.They were able to locate the aparment using Frank's G.P.S. collar. Carlos sat between Onyx Moon's legs, getting his braids picked out. He tried to grab the gun beside him, but a fat Native American cop named Lightfoot placed a gun under his throat. "Hands up motherfucker!"

There was a loud commotion in the back room, followed by a dog barking. A black man named Lyons and two white officers charged the bedroom where they found a man holding up a child as a shield with a gun to his head.

Christian cried, "Put me down! I want my mommy! I want my mommy!"

"Give me the kid, and you walk out of here alive." Lyons said.

"Fuck you. Kill me, bruh! You're going to have to kill him too, 'cuz I ain't putting him down." Rat Boy pressed the steel barrel against the child's head. "Ever seen kid brains?"

The black officer dropped his gun, then tiptoed into the bedroom and looked back at his white counterparts. He said, "Let me talk to him for a moment," then shut the door.

Lyons was from the streets of Atlanta. He'd moved to Charlotte after college, but most of his family had been in some kind of trouble; they dealt drugs, ran numbers, and sold guns. You name it, they'd indulged in it, but Lyons had wanted a better life for his family. So, he moved to Charlotte and joined the police force. He'd often found himself as a liaison between young black men and white police officers. He related to both worlds.

One of the white officers peeked in and said, "Look we don't need you to go and play hero, Lyons."

Lyons closed the door, ignoring the man.

"Drop the gun, bro. I will walk you out of here alive. Just do what I say."

"Fuck you."

"Do you really want to die?"

"I'm not going to die alone, I can promise you that."

"Nobody has to die. Think about your children."

"I don't have any. I don't have anybody, so I don't give a fuck about the shit you're talking about."

"You have a life in your hands. Don't do it, bruh."

"I ain't trying to hear that police academy bullshit bruh!" He was sweating, while at the same time pressing the barrel further into Christian's temple, as Frank continued to bark.

Someone tapped the door and yelled, "We're coming in if you can't get him to drop the gun."

"Look man, these white boys come in here and they're killing everything in here. Maybe even me. It's not worth it. Let the kid go, and give me the gun."

Carlos was now in handcuffs as he sat on the floor. "Fuck," he muttered as he thought about going back to prison. Hell, he hadn't even been out a year, and now he was on his way back on kidnapping charges. He heard all the commotion in the next room, and he thought about little Christian. He'd grown to like the little piss-ant, and he hoped stupid ass Rat Boy wouldn't get himself or the kid harmed. He asked the officer "Is there a way I can talk my friend out of doing something stupid? I don't want anything to happen to the kid."

Lightfoot, the officer who arrested Carlos, asked the oldest white cop, who then said it was okay.

Lightfoot picked him up and led him to the bedroom door, his hands still cuffed behind his back. He entered the room. The sudden movement startled Rat Boy and he applied pressure to the kid's neck until he saw Carlos.

"Put the goddamned gun down, Rat Boy, and let the kid go."

"I'm not doing shit."

"You want to leave out of here in a bodybag?"

Christian was crying.

"It's going to be okay, Christian." Carlos assured the kid.

"Let him go," Carlos pleaded. "Let Christian go now!"

He and Rat Boy stared at each other for a long time. "I don't want to go back to prison bruh. You told me that it was going to go smooth. You told me that I was going to make a hundred thousand dollars. Now, I'm fucked."

"I'll take the rap for it."

"With my record, you think they give a fuck about you taking the rap for it?"

"Well, you need to quit running your mouth and let the kid go."

They made eye contact for a few more seconds before Rat Boy lowered the kid to the floor, and Christian ran to Carlos, who was still handcuffed. Carlos said, "Christian, go in the other room."

The boy did what he was told.

Lyons entered the room and ordered, "Put the gun down." He ushered Carlos out of the room, then continued, "Put the gun down, and you live."

Rat Boy lowered the gun before pulling it back up and firing two shots into Lyons' chest. Lyons crashed face first to the floor, he wasn't dead, he was still breathing thanks to his body armor

"Officer down! Officer down!" the walkies screamed. The SWAT team rushed the room, and Rat Boy fired more shots before jumping out the window, falling eight floors, his skull smashing against the pavement.

CHAPTER 26

ive days after the abortion, Layla felt much better. She still had not gone back to working out, but she was walking. She was about to go for a walk when India burst through the door, smiling.

"Looks like someone is doing good."

Layla forced a smile. "I'm feeling a lot better today."

"It shows." India frowned, "But I hope you're not going to the gym."

"No, I'm just taking a little stroll around the neighborhood." She grabbed her water bottle from the kitchen counter and started for the door. "You should come with me."

"No, maybe some other time." India's frown deepened.

"Is there something bothering you?"

"Well, there is something."

"What's wrong?"

"I really don't want to bother you with my bullshit."

"What is it, sis?"

"I was going to ask you for some money, but if you can't give it to me, that's okay."

"What? Now wait a minute, I gave you a thousand dollars the other day. As a matter of fact, I have given you two thousand dollars in less than a week. What the fuck is going on?"

"Are you going to give me the money or not?"

"What's the money for?"

India was silent.

"Is it for your rent?"

"No."

"Car note?" Layla suggested.

"No."

"Your mother needs it?"

"No."

"What is it for?"

"What difference does it make? Can I have the money?"

"Tell me what it's for, and it's yours."

"What if I don't want to?"

"Then I'm not giving it to you."

"So you can come live with me and it's no problem, and now I can't get a thousand dollars?"

Layla stared at her and thought, *Was this bitch crazy? Did she just actually fix her mouth to say that bullshit?* She had given this woman two thousand dollars in the past week.

"Are you being serious right now?"

India said, "Look I'm sorry. I just need the money."

"What is the money for?"

"It's for Myron. I'm helping him out; he lost his job a couple of months ago."

"Oh no, baby girl, you are helping this grown ass man, the same man that a few days ago missed his job interview, but I can't help you. If it was your situation, I would give it to you. Even if it was your parents, but not this nigga who you claim you don't love. I've been here the past week. I see how late he gets up. A man that gets up that late does not want a job. He's bullshitting you."

"So you're not giving it to me?"

"I'm not giving it to him."

"It's like that, huh?"

Layla sipped her water and nodded. "I'm going for my walk now, and when I come back, I'm going to pack my shit and leave."

* * * * *

Rashad was lying on the sofa, watching First Take, when Layla casually walked into the house. He looked up at her for a second, then resumed watching his show. She sat down on the opposite end of the sofa. They made eye contact, then she removed her denim jacket and asked, "So you're going to go on and pretend that I'm not here, huh?"

He cut his eyes at her again, still not saying anything.

She grabbed the remote from the table and lowered the volume.

He used an app on his phone to raise the volume again.

"Rashad, talk to me."

He powered down the TV.

"I know you're upset with me," she said.

"You think so?" he said, the anger evident in his voice.

"Rashad, I was having a good time. What's wrong with that?"

"You're pregnant."

"I know."

"And you were drinking."

"Who said that? Oh, I know your little snitch, Jeremy."

"What difference does who told me make?"

"It was one drink."

He threw his hands up. He was annoyed with her ass already.

"Tell me why you were so upset with me," she demanded.

"You were fucking feeding my baby alcohol."

"It was only champagne."

"I don't give a fuck what it was. It was not good for you or the baby."

"I know, and I'm sorry. I'm so sorry."

"Abort the baby and move out."

"Where would I go?"

"I don't know. Houston, I guess. Wherever you want to go. I don't care."

She was glad that he'd suggested that she abort the baby. Now she wouldn't have to concoct the whole story about a miscarriage. She could abort the baby, move out the house for a couple of weeks, wait until he calmed down, and move back in, and things would be back to normal.

She made a sad face. "I don't want to abort my baby." She'd lied. She knew she couldn't act like she was happy about the abortion of a baby that she'd pretended she wanted just a few days ago.

He looked serious. "Me and you are not meant to be."

"So that means that I need to abort my baby? There are plenty of people co-parenting out here."

"I don't want to do it."

"I'm having this kid with or without you." Layla said.

"No the hell you're not. Get rid of the baby and get rid of it right away."

"And if I don't?"

"You will." he stated plainly. "We won't worry about if you won't. You're going to do what I say."

Layla was pissed at his tone of voice. She crossed her arms and said, "You can't make me do anything."

"Layla, make the appointment for the abortion."

* * * * *

Kendall texted Rashad: Good news.

Rashad: Tell me please!

Kendall: Christian is home.

Rashad: That's great.

Kendall: I want you to meet him.

Rashad: Are you serious???

Kendall: Do you want to meet him or not?

Rashad: Of course I would love to meet him. Do you think I should meet Dre first?

Kendall: For what???

Rashad: Because Dre is his father.

Kendall: Fuck Dre.

Rashad: LMAO, you're a savage.

Kendall: no he's the savage

Rashad: When do you want me to meet him?

Kendall: Come over this afternoon. I'll make dinner. A real dinner. What have you wanted that you haven't had in a long time?

Rashad: What you making?

Kendall: You tell me you're the guest.

Rashad: I want pot roast. I haven't had that in a while.

Kendall: I can make a mean pot roast.

Rashad: We shall see if you can.

Rashad arrived at 6:30, and Kendall answered the door. Christian and Frank stood a few steps behind her. She smiled brightly but was nervous about how her son would react to a man that wasn't his father. She hadn't realized how much she'd missed Rashad. Rashad stepped inside looking dapper and smiled at Christian.

"You must be Christian."

"Who are you?"

"I'm going to be your new best friend."

"Are you a good guy or bad guy?"

"I'm a good guy." Rashad smiled. "Don't I Iook like a good guy?"

Christian shook his head. "No, you look like a bad guy."

Rashad and Kendall laughed their asses off.

"My name is Rashad."

Christian said, pointing to the dog, "This is Frank."

"Hey, Frank."

"Yesterday, I was walking with my step-mommy and some bad guys came and got me and Frank."

"Yesterday?"

Kendall whispered in his ear, "Well, it happened a few weeks ago. You know kids don't have a concept of time. He told Chrissy it happened ten years ago."

Rashad examined Christian. Christian and Kendall had the same eyes, but he didn't really resemble her. He must have looked like Dre. Then, he thought how cool it would be to have a son that looked exactly like him. He thought about Layla and how he was adamant about her having an abortion. Had he done the right thing?

Kendall led Rashad into the dining room. Rashad could smell the aroma of the food. He sat at the head of the table, and Christian sat beside him.

"You want to see my Pop It Pal?"

"A what?"

"A toy that lets you pop fake pimples."

"What? You can't be serious."

Kendall chuckled. "Hey it's the new toy like last year's fidget spinner; I can tell you're a man without kids."

"You want to see it?" Christian asked.

"Yes."

Christian disappeared before returning with what looked like a glob of flesh. He squeezed, and whiteheads sprang from it. It looked very disgusting to Rashad, but he said. "That was amazing, man."

Christian was smiling hard, glad he'd impressed his new friend.

"I can count to ten."

"If you count to ten, I'll count to ten."

"You go first," Christian said.

Rashad counted to five then appeared to be confused about what came next.

"Mom, he doesn't know how to count to ten," Christian laughed.

Kendall smiled; she was happy that they were getting along. "Help Mr. Rashad count to ten, Christian."

Christian counted to ten, and Rashad said, "You're amazing and smart."

"I know." Christian said.

Dinner was served. Rashad chomped down his food and Christian who had half eaten his food, left and disappeared to his new bedroom to play with Frank.

"Sometimes you have to get away from just eating spinach." Kendall said.

"Who in the hell just eats spinach?" Rashad said.

"It was a joke."

"Where is Christian?"

Kendall called him, and Christian came running. "Mr. Rashad is leaving now. Tell him goodbye."

"Goodbye, Mr. Rashad. Will you come back and play with me?"

"Yes, I'll come back and play with you, and you can teach me how to count some more."

Christian laughed.

Rashad said. "Take care of your mommy, okay?"

"Okay." Christian nodded.

"Give me some dap." Rashad held his fist out, and he and Christian fist bumped. Then, Christian disappeared back into his room.

"Why did you want me to meet your son?"

Kendall shrugged. "I don't know."

"I'm glad I got a chance to meet him."

"He likes you."

"He's a special kid."

"I know."

There was an awkward silence as they stared at one another.

"I missed you."

"Same here."

"I want to spend more time with you, but I have some things I have to work out."

"With your baby mama?"

He laughed "Yeah."

"We'll be here. Me, my son, and his dog."

CHAPTER 27

The sound of the blow dryer was coming through the bathroom door. Rashad opened the door of the bathroom, and Layla was blow drying her hair. "Please don't go."

She turned the blow dryer off and smiled. "What changed your mind?"

"People go through things. I know you, and you know me. We might not be exactly right for each other, but we laid down together." He avoided her eyes and gathered his thoughts. "Now you have this life growing inside of you that we both created, I think we need to do what's right by the kid and do what's right in the eyes of God."

"You mean you want me to stay because I'm pregnant with your child."

"Yes."

"But if it wasn't for the child, you'd absolutely want me out?"

"I don't know."

She picked up a brush and began brushing her hair. "What do you mean you don't know?"

"How am I supposed to know that?"

"You know if you love me or not."

"I do love you."

"You're not in love with me, Rashad." Layla sighed. "I can tell. Women always know."

"If you weren't pregnant and drinking, we would have never had the falling out."

She set the brush down on the sink and asked, "So you wouldn't have been pissed that I was with two guys?"

"Look, I don't want to deal with hypotheticals. This is where we are right now."

"Right."

"So what do you want to do?"

"What do you want to do?" She answered his question with a question.

"Have my baby."

"What changed your mind?"

Christian changed his mind, but he couldn't exactly say that he'd just left another woman and her son at dinner.

"I don't know—I was just giving it some thought, and I missed Mya. I remembered how cool it was when she was living how she'd come and get in the bed with us."

Layla smiled. "Yeah, I missed those days."

"Will you stay?"

"Yes."

* * * * *

John Smith's secretary Glenda came running back to the office. John Smith was on the phone and threw up a hand signal indicating that he wanted her to hold on a second. "But it's important!" she cried.

John asked his client to hold.

"What's up?"

"There are two gentlemen in the lobby saying they're with the F.B.I. and they need to see you."

"Huh, how do they look?"

"Like F.B.I. agents. Young around 30-ish, clean shaved, blue suits."

"What do they want?"

"They want to talk to you."

"Send them back."

John told the client on the phone that he'd call him right back. Seconds later, two young-looking men entered his office, but John was sixty; he didn't remember looking that young when he was in his thirties. The red-headed gentleman introduced the pair of them, "I'm Agent McDonnell and this is my partner, Agent Nelson." Nelson was carrying a briefcase.

The agents extended their hands, and John shook each of them, then offered them a seat.

"Do you know why we're here?" Agent McDonnell said smiling.

"No, but I have an idea." John answered.

"What do you think?" McDonnell asked.

"I'm assuming it's about my daughter's no good black drug dealer boyfriend. I told her that boy was nothing but trouble when she brought him home to meet me. Nothing but trouble! But then she'd accused me of being racist. Can you believe that? I'm not racist—I just don't think we're supposed to mix races. Does that make me a racist? What do you want to know about him? He's a loser, I can tell you that for sure. I'm not going down for him."

McDonnell and Nelson looked at each other.

McDonnell asked, "You want to guess again?"

"So you're not here about him?"

"Not unless he works for St. Morgan's National Bank."

"What are you taking about?"

"You sold a lot of houses last year."

John nodded slowly. "I sell a lot of homes every year. I'm in the home selling business."

McDonnell said, "You're a smart man, Mr. Smith."

"I think so, though not as sharp as I used to be."

"You know what a straw buyer is?" McDonnell asked.

"A what?"

"Come on, Mr. Smith, you're a smart man. I know you've heard the term." Agent Nelson said.

"Maybe." John said nonchalantly.

"Well just in case you haven't, a straw buyer is a person who consents for a mortgage company or bank to use their name or personal details for a mortgage for a house that they don't intend to live in." McDonnell said.

"I don't want to talk to you unless my lawyer is present."

"Feel free to call him." Nelson said.

John Smith picked up the receiver, placed to it to his ear, and then sat it back down without calling him.

"What do you want to know from me?"

"We want to know about your inside connection at St. Morgan's." McDonnell said as he stared at John with intense eyes.

"What makes you think I have some sort of 'inside connection' as you put it?"

"You know, Mr. Smith, in my briefcase, I have a list of more than thirty people or straw buyers who've falsified W2's to buy homes and are willing to testify against you." Agent Nelson said pointing at the black briefcase sitting on the floor.

"What do you want from me?"

"We want you to tell us what you know. Who helped you."

"I don't know what you're talking about."

McDonnell leaned forward and said. "Mr. Smith, you look like a man with a lot to lose. You have a loving family, and I'm sure you've made a lot of money. I'm sure you don't want to go to prison."

Nelson cut in for once. "I don't think you would do well in prison."

"I'm calling my lawyer." John said.

* * * * *

Rashad was getting a bottle of water from the fridge when Layla burst though the door with an ultrasound that she'd purchased online in her hand, she passed it to him. "Looks like another girl."

He passed it back refusing to look at it. "You know those things creep me out."

She laughed. "What is it about ultrasounds that creep you out?"

"I don't know they just look weird, my Dad is the same way."

"Seriously. I'm happy you decided that you wanted the baby."

He narrowed his eyes and squinted "Is that so?"

"Yeah."

"Why?"

"I'm older, I think I'm ready for a family. I'm ready for marriage."

"I think you just want to get married because you're pregnant."

"Well, I damn sure don't want to be a baby mama."

"This is what we can do," Rashad started.

"I'm listening."

"If things are going well a year from now, we can get married."

"Well if we're going to get married a year from now. Don't you think we should be planning the wedding?"

"I haven't proposed yet."

"But you are going to."

"You might not accept," he laughed.

"You got jokes." Layla posted a pic of the ultrasound on Instagram. She tried to tag India in it, but found that India had deleted her account, then she figured the attention whore wasn't going to delete her account. It quickly dawned on her that India had blocked her. Why would India block her?

She turned to Rashad and asked, "What do you do when you see a friend that's with someone that is clearly no good from them?"

Rashad was startled by the question. *Was she talking about her being no good for him?* he wondered but then dismissed the thought. She would never talk about herself. Layla's ego was too big to admit that she was ever a problem in a relationship.

"Who are you referring to?"

"I'm talking about India."

"What's going on with her?"

"She's with this dude. I mean I ain't going to lie—the nigga is super fine, but it's clear he's an opportunist."

"What makes you say that?"

"He borrows money from her."

"What's wrong with that? Let me get this straight: if I wanted to borrow some money from you, you wouldn't let me get it?"

"That's different."

"How? I don't see what's the big deal." Rashad shrugged.

"Dude is a loser."

He frowned. "We all get down on our luck from time to time."

"A loser. He's not looking for a job, he's missing job interviews, but some way somehow, he finds time to do the shit that he wants to do."

"Hey, why does that concern you? India is a grown ass woman. She can do what she wants."

"She was borrowing money from me to give to that nigga! I had to put a stop to that."

"But why do you care?"

"She just blocked me on IG."

"Oh, okay, I see." He laughed, "She hurt your little pride. She blocked you on IG. Whatever shall you do?"

"You think it's funny," Layla pouted.

"IG is not real life."

"You're not a girl. You wouldn't understand."

CHAPTER 28

John Smith sat behind his desk feeding documents into the paper shredder. Dre sat across from him, holding his ears.

When John was done, he asked. "How is your son?"

Dre's brow wrinkled, and he faked a smile. Did this man really give a fuck about his son or was it the right thing to do? He thought back to the day he'd marched into the office demanding his money. How indifferent John had been then.

"So do you really want to know what's going on with my son or are you just asking?"

"Catherine told me he's at home safe with his mother."

"If Catherine told you that, then that's what it is."

"I understand that I must not be your favorite person in the world right now."

"The main thing is that Christian is at home." Dre said, thinking motherfucker you have never been my favorite person.

"Yeah." John Smith said smugly.

"Is that why you called me to your office? You want to know about my son?"

"Look, I know you're in the drug business."

"Who said that?"

"Let's keep it real. Who has millions of dollars in cash to invest in real estate?"

"I used to be in the drug business."

"Okay... you *used* to be in the drug business."

"I don't want to talk about that."

"I just wanted you to know that I am sincerely sorry that I couldn't help you."

"Hey, it's okay. Like I said, the main thing is that Christian is okay."

"Yes. Thank God. I don't know what I would have done if one of my kids had gotten kidnapped by a rival drug dealer."

"Who said that it was a drug dealer that kidnapped my kid?"

"I was just assuming. Wasn't it a rival drug dealer?"

"Don't assume anything about me. I'm not in the drug business anymore."

"You're right, and I'm glad you left that life behind you."

"I have to go now."

John Smith extended his hand, but Dre left the man hanging.

* * * * *

Jeremy sat in the lobby of a car detail shop skimming through an old G.Q. magazine when a woman walked in wearing a tight red skirt and heels and the lavender notes in her perfume were intoxicating . He glanced at her and thought, *damn this bitch's body was ridiculous* but he kept looking through the magazine then could feel that she was staring at him and he'd made eye contact with her when she said. "Don't I know you?"

He smiled. "I don't think you know me. Yet."

"I do know you, you're Rashad's friend."

"Yeah, who are you?"

"Remember I'm Layla's friend. Remember we were doing the photoshoot on the rooftop and you beat up my two friends at the club."

"Hey I'm sorry."

She laughed. "They weren't really my friends, I just use them to buy me drinks when we go out."

He shrugged. "So did you snitch to Rashad and tell him that Layla was drinking?"

"First of all don't ever use my name and snitch in the same sentence."

"You know what I mean."

"Look Rashad is my brother. I would do anything for him, just like you would do anything for Layla."

"Hmph. Whatever."

"I would do anything for Rashad. "

"I know, I'm saying I thought me and Layla were cool but she turned out to be nothing but a selfish little bitch."

"Huh?" Jeremy said knowing damn well Layla was very selfish. He really didn't understand why Rashad had gone back to her in the first place. He wanted to milk India for all the information that she had.

He smiled warmly. "What happened? I mean I thought you and her were BFF's and shit." He tossed the magazine back onto the table. He knew this story was going to be far better than anything that G.Q. had to offer.

"She's just selfish."

"There has to be a reason you say that."

"You know Layla, Jeremy, you know she's selfish. She told me she's known you for years."

"How long have you known her?"

"Well when she lived here before, we worked together a few times for promotors, doing some liquor promotions. I thought she was cool and she was cool until she'd gotten with Rashad then she started acting like I was beneath her. After she lost the baby and moved to Houston, we stayed in touch, I would stay with her whenever I traveled to Houston."

"Tell me what happened."

"I can't."

* * * * *

Later that evening, Jeremy and India were back at his condo taking shots of Patron watching Den of Thieves. "You know what, you're cool as fuck Jeremy. I wish you would get rid of that man-bun, but other than that I think you're the shit."

He stood and carried the bottle of Patron to put it back on his liquor tray.

"You didn't think I would be cool?"

She unzipped her dress exposing a hint of cleavage. "The first time I saw you, you were acting kind of funny-style. I didn't like it but I don't know why but it turned me on kind of.

He laughed. "I was acting funny and you didn't like it but it turned you on a little bit? How does that work?"

"You know what I meant."

"I heard women like assholes."

"Are you an asshole Jeremy?"

He smiled. "The question is, do you think I'm an asshole?"

"I thought you were."

"I can be but that's what you like."

She winked. "Maybe, come over and have a seat beside me."

Jeremy made his way over to the sofa and plopped down right beside her.

She downed another shot of liquor and his hands were on her thighs. She pushed him away.

"What makes you think I'm going to let you do that?"

"Do what?"

"Feel me up?"

"Is that what I'm doing?"

"Yeah."

"I have a boyfriend."

"Okay." Jeremy thought what the fuck does that have to do with anything?"

"Do you have a girl Jeremy?"

"No."

"Who was that girl that was in the club with you the other night?"

"What other night?"

"The night you called Rashad."

"My friend." He smiled.

"Your friend? Okay, your friend."

"I have lots of friends."

"Do you sleep with your friends?"

"From time to time, I see nothing wrong with two consenting adults doing whatever they want." His hand was now on her thigh again, this time she didn't move it.

"I was just letting you know I had a man."

'I'm not worried about him. Neither should you."

She laughed.

He leaned over and whispered. "You ever been fucked on a kitchen table?"

He continued to massage her thigh then turned and leaned into her and she kissed him and Jeremy was thinking the bitch don't seem to be thinking about her boyfriend right now. He kissed her back, his hands gliding down her back, gripping her ass. She smelled like Vanilla Wafers. He unzipped her dress then removed it. Jeremy struggled with her bra. She unfastened her bra and huge breast implants revealed themselves. Jeremy took the left breast into his mouth and she ran her fingers through his man-bun. She collapsed onto the sofa and he made a trail of kisses down her stomach until he reached the top of her high waisted leopard bikini panties. He yanked those things down to her ankles band she opened her legs wide and he went in face first. His tongue darting in and out of her VJ. "Damnit. you feel so good," her legs now resting onto his shoulders. He massaged her clit with his middle finger.

"Jeremy I want you to fuck me. Damnit fuck me now!"

Jeremy wanted to laugh. He always got a kick out of the drill sergeant ass women.

He picked her up, her legs enveloping his neck, while still giving her the best oral that she'd had in a long time. He carried her into the kitchen, sat her butt on the edge of the table, knocking the artificial magnolia arrangement from table. He then slid her ass to the center of the table. She clawed his back as he entered her. He fucked her, forcing her to climax three times. Later that night they laid in the bed watching Black Panther on the jailbroken Firestick when she said. "Rashad is too good for Layla."

"I've been trying to tell him that for years, but hey he's a grown ass man."

"I know right. I'm just glad she decided to abort the kid."

Jeremy said "What do you mean decided to abort kid?"

Jeremy narrowed his eyes. "What did you just say?"

"Oh you didn't know that Layla had an abortion?"

"Neither did Dre."

"You know---." She stopped.

Jeremy raised his eyebrow."What were you going to say?"

"Nothing."

"You were going to tell me something . I can tell."

She stood from the bed avoiding Jeremy's gaze.

Jeremy said. "Look I ain't going to tell anyone."

"You expect me to believe you? You already told me that you and Rashad were like brothers." They locked eyes before she said "Fuck it! Layla has already proven she wasn't my friend." thinking about the money Layla had refused to loan her. That was her way of justifying what she was about to tell Jeremy.

"Tell me India."

"The baby was not Rashad's. She was pregnant by a young rapper."

"What do you mean it wasn't Rashad's?"

"Exactly what you think I meant."

"What the fuck?"

"I'm dead ass serious."

"What's the rapper's name?"

"I can't remember." she lied.

CHAPTER 29

The stench of marijuana smoke hung in the air of Jeremy's two bedroom apartment when Rashad walked in. Jeremy passed him the blunt that he was smoking, Rashad refused it. "You know I don't smoke."

"You might want to smoke after I tell you what I have to tell you."

Jeremy sat on one end of the leather sofa and Rashad sat on the other.

Jeremy coughed then set the lit blunt on the ashtray.

"What's on your mind."

"Layla bruh."

"What about her?"

"You 'member shorty that was trying to get with me that day during the photoshoot on the rooftop?"

"India, yeah what about her?"

"A few days ago, I ran into her and we hung out and she ended up sleeping with me and she told me that Layla wasn't pregnant by you." Jeremy picked up the blunt took another toke.

"What?" Rashad said with mouth now hanging. "What are you talking about?"

"Shorty said that she was pregnant by a young rapper, but she aborted the baby."Jeremy coughed.

"Get the fuck out of here man."

"I'm just telling you what India said."

"So she just volunteered that information to you?"

"No, she didn't want to tell me but I could tell that she was holding in that she wanted to tell me so I kept begging her and that's what she told me." Jeremy removed his cell phone from his front pocket then dialed India's number, the phone call went straight to voicemail."

He coughed again. "She's not picking up."

Rashad stood and paced. "This is fucked up. Real fucked up bruh." He looked Jeremy straight in his eyes. "What do you think I should do bruh? I want to kill that bitch."

"Don't do that. It ain't worth it, not over that."

Rashad took a seat again. "No, you don't understand, she knows secrets. Secrets that will get me killed. So I know I gotta cut her off for this shit, but what will she do when I cut her off is the question."

Jeremy said. "What kind of secrets? Shit that I don't know about?"

"I stole a shipment of coke from my old connect and nobody knows except Layla."

"Damn I see."

"I'm so fucked up right now. I swear to God I want to hurt that bitch."

"Look I'll go tell her to get her things and leave if you want, you don't need to see her right now."

"Okay, I'm crashing here tonight."

"Of course."

* * * * *

Later that evening Jeremy went to Rashad's place and found Layla lying on the sofa talking on the phone. She was stunned when she looked up to see him. She sat up then said "I will call you back later." To whomever she was on the phone with.

"Hey Jeremy. Just so you know I ain't mad at you for ratting me out that night at the club. You are Rashad's best friend and I would have done the same thing if I were you."

Jeremy sat in the armchair across from Layla and stared at her."

"Glad you are not mad."

"Water under the bridge."

"Huh?"

"Old saying." She laughed. "It just means leave the past in the past."

"Oh."

"So what brings you here?"

Jeremy leaned in placing his elbows on his knees. "Look Layla to be honest with you I came to tell you to get your shit and go."

"Excuse me? What the fuck did you just say?"

Jeremy cracked his knuckles and stared at her like he was going to punch her. He did want to but he wasn't. "Bruh knows that you were pregnant by your little rapper boyfriend and he knows that you have had an abortion and he's pissed the fuck off. I didn't want him to lose his temper and do something crazy, so I told him that I would come and deliver the message to you."

"And what message was that?"

Jeremy looked at the bitch like she was crazy. Had he just told her that she needed to pack her shit and go? "Look Layla you need to go."

"You can't put me out. Who the fuck are you Jeremy? If Rashad wants me to leave he needs to tell me. I don't listen to you."

Jeremy stood. "Oh yeah you're going to listen to me and you are going to get the fuck out "Jeremy lifted his shirt revealing a gun."

Layla laughed at him. "You think I'm worried about you killing me? We are in a secured building, fool. You can't scare me with that."

"I might not shoot you, but I will pistol whip the fuck out of you."

"You won't do a damn thing to me." Layla called Rashad on the phone.

"Hello."

"Did you tell Jeremy to put me out?"

"Yeah I told him to ask you to leave."

"Why didn't you just do it yourself." Layla rolled her eyes at Jeremy who was smiling at her.

"Look I don't want to talk about it, but can you just leave?"

"I'll leave, but motherfucker don't think I won't get in touch with our little friend."

"Do whatever you gotta do. I want you gone."

"And I will wait here until she leaves." Jeremy said as he took a seat back on the sofa.

* * * * *

Dre stood in line at Highland Bakery waiting to get a lemon pastry and water. He'd been walking to the bakery every morning since he'd discovered it. There was tall, voluptuous black woman cutting her eyes at him from the line parallel to his line. She cut her eyes at him and smiled and he would return the gesture. Though he loved sex with Catherine, he had to admit he very much missed the curves of a black woman, and the woman that stared at him was very attractive. Her amber skin glowed, slight freckles circled her nose, and she had large, pouty lips and her figure was unmatched. She possessed the tiniest waist he'd seen in a while, and her ample ass was very pronounced.

Glancing at her hand, he didn't see a wedding band. She smiled at him again. Maybe he'd say hi when they left the bakery. But damn this woman was divine. Why was she checking him out though? Women rarely openly flirted with him unless they saw his car or if he was wearing a Rolex; then, there would be the gold diggers that would say something to him, but even that rarely happened. He arrived at the register the same time she arrived at hers. He paid for his pastry, and she was still eyeing him. He politely smiled and received the lemon pastry before deciding to have a seat at the table next to the door. He would hold the door open for her, then ask for her name and number when she was heading out. She paid for her pumpkin scone and was walking in stride to the exit. He jumped from his seat to hold the door for her.

She nodded smiled and thanked him.

He smiled back and asked, "What's your name?"

"Andre, I'm Agent Angela Roberts with the F.B.I."

What the fuck did she just say? He thought.

Before he knew it, he was surrounded by F.B.I., I.R.S., D.E.A., and U.S Marshals.

"Get down on the ground," a tiny Asian agent commanded, pointing a .40 caliber at Dre's chest."

He collapsed to the ground, covering his head afraid that one of the trigger happy white boys was going blow his goddamned brains out. All he could think about at that moment was Christian. He didn't want to die.

He was then taken to the courthouse, arraigned, and charged with money laundering, drug conspiracy, and tax evasion. Bond was set at two million dollars. He called Catherine but couldn't get her on the phone. His next call was Kendall, who accepted the call immediately. He told her what he knew about what was going on and that he couldn't get in touch with Catherine. He also suggested that he might need her to help him make bond.

CHAPTER 30

Later that night Rashad called and said he needed to see her and Kendall dropped Christian off over at Chrissy's house and they met down at a hookah lounge called Crave. She hugged him when she saw him and she noticed that he looked very upset so she asked "What's wrong?"

"I've been played." She inhaled the hookah. "What happened?"

"Layla had gotten pregant by someone else, while I was with her, lied to me like she was pregnant by me, aborted the kid, but lied like she was still pregnant, but turns out she wasn't pregnant and if she were the kid wasn't mine."

"What the fuck?"

"She's been sleeping around with some twenty-two year old rapper."

"What the fuck? Are you serious?"

"I'm so serious right now."

"You look hurt."

"I feel deceived you know."

"Can't say that I'm surprised. I wish I could say that I'm surprised, but I'm not. But I'm sorry this happened to you."

He took a drink from his glass. "You ever just want to kill somebody? I mean just get rid of them? Somebody that not only just hurt you, but knows all your secrets?"

"Yeah, but it's not worth it. You're young. Just cut her off and move on."

"You don't know how bad I'm hurting right now." He downed his Cranberry vodka and ordered another, this time a double.

Kendall stared at him trying to figure out what could be so bad that Rashad would want to kill her. What did she know? Was he that much in love with her? Was he still in love with her? She thought about how she'd felt when she had found out about when Dre was sleeping with Catherine.

She'd certainly wanted to kill his ass, but in the end she knew she couldn't go through with it. Maybe Rashad was just talking.

"What does she know about you?"

"Everything, even how I got my money."

"But you're legitimate now right?"

"Of course."

"You think she'll rat you out?"

"No."

"Talk to me."

He looked away.

"You don't want to talk about it?"

He resumed eye contact with her. "Years ago my plug sent a shipment over and they thought it had been confiscated, but I saw it as an opportunity to get a win."

"Get a win?"

"The connect sent over 2 million dollars worth of shit. He thought he'd lost it but I got it and started my own business and I was able to get out of the business."

"Why'd you do it? Doesn't seem like the kind of thing that you would do."

"We'd just had our daughter. I wanted my daughter to have a man that she could look up to. I didn't want her to know no parts of my prior life."

Kendall admired that about Rashad. Unlike Dre, he thought about the consequences."

"You're a smart man Rashad and you don't have to throw your life away because of her. Let her go, Karma will get her ass trust me."

"You think so?"

"It's a fact."

"Did Karma get Dre?"

"Feds picked him up a couple of days ago."

"You're lying."

"I wish I was for the sake of my son. He's been asking about his Daddy. I don't know if I'm going to take him to visit his father in jail or not."

"Naw, don't take him there. If he was in prison it would be different, it will be sad and I think it will be too much for you to handle."

"That's why I respect you so much Rashad. You had a daughter and you didn't just think about yourself you thought about everybody involved"

"I don't even know if Mya was my daughter or not." He smiled. "Yeah she was mine, she was mine, everybody says she was my twin and she was stubborn as hell just like me."

"Rashad you're going to have to get over what happened to you. She was an opportunist. Sometimes we pick the wrong partners in life, but we move on."

"You're right. He grabbed the hookah and took a toke. I wish I'd met you a long time ago. Damn you're the perfect woman."

"Nobody is perfect, but we're here now."

He leaned into her and kissed her.

* * * * *

At seven in the morning, Layla banged on India's door. Myron opened the door in a pair of boxer briefs, his dick print looking very prominent. He invited Layla in. India watched his half naked ass walking back to the bedroom thinking what kind of self-respecting man would open the door half naked for his girlfriend's friend. There were people out there that didn't believe that she was a self-respecting woman, but fuck those people. India marched out of the bedroom, bags under her eyes and still half asleep.

"Why'd you just pop up at my house like this?"

"Look I'm sorry, but we have to talk."

"Talk about what? Something better be wrong. Somebody better be dead."

"Why the fuck did you tell Jeremy that I was pregnant by Stacy and that I had aborted the baby?"

"I didn't tell him that."

"Stop the lying. There was only one person that knew this information and it was you." India, glanced over her shoulder trying to make sure that Myron wasn't listening, the last thing she needed was him to find out that she'd slept with Jeremy."

"Can we take this outside?"

"We can take it wherever you want to take it."

Layla followed India outside the door and when the door slammed. Layla said. "Don't you worry I'm not going to expose that you fucked Jeremy."

'I did not fuck Jeremy."

"What the fuck ever, ho I know you. You think you're better than me but you're just like me. Why'd you tell Jeremy that I was pregnant by Stacy?"

India was silent. "I'm sorry, that was my bad."

"Why did you do it?"

"I don't know. I'm sorry. I was mad because you didn't give me the money and I knew you had it."

"That's fucking wack India and now I have nowhere to go and I'm broke as fuck!"

India dropped her head. "You're right, I'm sorry. I know things are fucked up for you and it's all because of me."

"Damn right it's because of you."

"I'm sorry. Please you have to accept my apology. I shouldn't have done it."

"I forgive you, but I can never trust you again with my personal business."

"Look you can stay here as long as you want." India said then her eyes lit up. "Look, what if we can convince Stacy to pay you to abort the baby?"

"What are you talking about, the baby is gone."

"Stacy doesn't know."

"So want him to pay for the abortion?"

"No bitch, I want him to pay you to have the abortion. Make him think you're going to have the baby unless he pays you."

"You know that might work unless your dumb ass has already told him that I've had the abortion."

"I haven't told him shit. You're going to split the money with me right?"

"If we get it. Damn right."

India embraced Layla.

* * * * *

Rashad left his phone on the nightstand. Kendall picked it up and then realized it was a Samsung Galaxy. Rashad owned an iPhone. Whose phone was this? Maybe Rashad had left one of his friends' phone. She called Rashad to tell him about the phone, but the call went straight to voicemail. She called again, still no answer. She decided she would call the last number back on the phone. There was only one number in the phone, an initial "J." Strange. This was either a burner or this was a phone that Rashad used to call other women. There were only a few apps on the home screen like Facebook and Twitter—standard apps that came with damn near every phone. There was one app she didn't recognize: Signal App. She googled the app on her tablet and found out that Signal was a secure messaging app, used for messaging on a secure server. This person J was the only other contact in the messaging app. She clicked on the conversation and read

J: I've got the heat and the silencer.

Me: Good. How much do I owe you?

J: You don't owe me shit, just looking out for Fam you feel me? Me: I appreciate it.

J: Just don't go out there and get yourself caught up.

Me: I got this bruh

J: You sure you want to do this?

Me: Why do you keep asking me this, you know I want to do it.

J: I would have thought you would have calmed down by now, you were always the level headed one, this is some shit I would do for sure, but not you. I know your pride is hurt, but think about it. I can tell you from personal experience once you do this, you'll never be the same.

Me: I got this bruh. I know where she's been living I can handle it.

J: I'm going with you. Meet me downtown at 9pm

Me: Aight.

Kendall couldn't believe what she'd just read. This conversation between Rashad and this J person—they were plotting to kill someone! She assumed the person that they were going to kill was Layla. She couldn't let this happen, and she would not let him ruin his life. She called him but he didn't pick up. She called him twice more and still no answer.

Five minutes later, he called her back. "Hey, what's going on, babe? What's wrong? Why are you blowing me up?"

She didn't want to talk over the phone, especially implying that he was going to kill someone. She lied, "It's Christian."

"What's wrong with Christian?"

"He was outside playing, and now he's gone!" Kendall cried.

"What do you mean's he's gone?"

"He's not here." She tried her best to sound as hysterical as possible. "I don't know what I'm going to do. I called the police already, but I don't know if I can go through with this again. I need you to come over. I need someone to talk to."

"I'm coming."

"When?"

"I'll be there in twenty minutes."

Rashad hung up the phone then turned to Jeremy who was dressed in a black leather jacket and black turtle neck and Stan Smith Adidas.

"What the fuck is going on, bruh?"

"I gotta go."

Jeremy's eyes widened. "You gotta go? You gotta go where?"

"Kendall's son is missing."

"Bruh, we need to handle this tonight."

"Just ride with me over to her house, let me calm her down, and then we can go out."

CHAPTER 31

When Rashad and Jeremy arrived at Kendall's house, Kendall called for Rashad to come upstairs. Rashad told Jeremy to have a seat, telling him there was food and liquor in the kitchen and to make himself at home.

Kendall was lying across the bed wearing a leopard print thong when he entered the bedroom.

He licked his lips, confused. "What the fuck?"

She patted the bed four times. "Lay down beside me."

He sat down on the edge of the bed. "I guess Christian is not missing."

"He's at my mom's." She sat up and shook her head. They locked eyes. "Let it go, Rashad."

"Huh?"

"The situation with Layla."

"What are you talking about?"

She tossed him the burner phone and explained, "I read the conversation between you and J. I'm assuming it's Jeremy."

Rashad didn't respond.

"It's not worth it, Rashad."

"Why were you reading my texts?"

"I love you, Rashad. I don't want you to go to prison. So what she got over on you? She may not have even loved you, but it happens." She paused.

He lowered his eyes to her breasts and felt a stirring in his pants. "You're making it hard for a nigga to leave here tonight."

She smiled, "I had to use my super powers."

"Is that what it is?"

"Yeah. You didn't know I had super powers?"

He massaged her thigh gently. "I know now."

Their eyes held for a while before he leaned into her and kissed her.

She said. "You have too much to lose."

"Nobody is going to find out."

"But if they do?"

"I go to prison."

"Do you want to go to prison? Your life is that insignificant to you that you will just accept the fact that you're going to prison?"

"I don't want to go to prison."

"Nobody does."

"Including Jeremy?"

"What are you saying?"

"You think he'll go down for you?"

"If he has to—that's my brother."

"And you'd risk your brother's life with something that can be prevented?"

Rashad was silent.

"We love you, Rashad."

"We?"

"Christian and I."

He raised his eyebrow. "Christian?"

"Yeah, all he talks about is since Daddy is at work, if Mr. Rashad could come over and play."

"I love that little boy."

"I want you to be in our life. I want us to take our relationship to the next level. You're who I'm supposed to spend the rest of my life with. Now, do you want to spend your life with me or inside a prison with 2000 other men?"

"Of course, I'd rather be with you."

"You have to let it go, then. You have too much to lose."

"I hate that bitch."

She massaged his shoulders. "I know you do, bae."

He nodded. "I'm going to let it go."

She smiled. "You're going to be okay." She massaged his chest before they kissed and helped him remove his shirt. She stood and dropped his pants, his erection already bulging. He dove onto the bed, and their mouths met again. She was lowering her underwear when he stopped her. She frowned.

"It's Jeremy, he's downstairs."

"So?"

He laughed his ass off. "You don't care, huh?"

She shook her head and smirked.

He stood, put on his underwear, and raced downstairs to tell Jeremy that the plans had changed. When he returned, she was naked. He lay in the bed beside her. Her hands were now on his chest again, but he wasn't responding to her touch.

"What's wrong now?" she asked.

"Nothing is wrong? I was just thinking about how lucky I am."

"I'm the lucky one."

"No, I am. I have a wife and a son."

"A wife?"

"I want you to marry me. I know this is awkward, but I also know it's right. That is, of course, if you want to marry me."

She was caught off guard. Who the hell proposes in the middle of sex? "Of course I want to marry you, but right now, can you just put it in, nigga?"

He chuckled, then pecked her forehead. She took possession of his dick and forged it inside of her.

After they had made love they lay in the bed facing each other and she said "You look worried."

"Can you read my face?"

"Yeah, what are you thinking about?"

"Just thinking if she calls my old connect and tells him about the shit that I took."

"Why don't you call him before she does?"

He stood and began to pace. "What will I say?"

"I don't know maybe you can say that you fell out with her and she's out to get you."

"Are you saying to tell him that she might lie on me?"

"No, that would be stupid. Look this shit happened years ago right?"

"Yeah."

"Just call him see how he's doing and just mention that you tried to make it work with her but it didn't then maybe allude to the fact that she's in trouble and she wants to save her own ass. Drug dealers hate informants."

"You want me to lie?"

"You've already stole from the man, I know you're not trying to be a boy-scout now."

He laughed his ass off then sat on the edge of the bed.

She passed him the phone.

"I ain't calling that motherfucker on the phone that's in my name."

"Call him on the burner."

"I don't have his number, come to think of it. It's been years since I've spoken to him." then he rubbed his chin. "I know what, I'll reach out to one of his kid's mother's on Instagram."

"I'll do it for you. What's her name?"

"Melody Snow and the plug goes by the name of Low-Down."

"Low-Down. What the fuck?"

"He's an ex banger out of Watts."

"Melody Snow's name is very common."

"She's from South Central but she lives out in Orange County now,"

"I will find her."

Kendall's phone rang. A private number. She answered and the recording came on from the jail.

Rashad said. "Do you want me to leave the room?"

"No. Please stay, you're my man."

Kendall accepted the call.

"K."

Rashad laid his head in Kendall's lap and she ran her fingers through his beard.

"How are you doing Dre?"

"I'm doing good. Can I speak to Christian?"

"He's not here."

"Where is he?"

"He's at my moms."

"Look K, I need you. Do you think you can come see me tomorrow?"

"What time?"

"Visitation is from 3-5."

"I will see."

"Look, I know I did a lot of fucked up things and I don't deserve your forgiveness, but if you can I come see me I would really appreciate it."

"I will see. I'm not making any promises."

"Okay that's all I can ask of you."

"What time will Christian be home?"

"Tonight."

"Okay I'll call again in a couple of days. "Come see me if you can."

"Okay." She ended the call.

Rashad sat up and looked her in the eye. "I want you to go see him."

"What?"

"Yes, you have a son with him and you two have been through a lot together, go see him."

"If you say so."

He took possession of her hand and stroked it. "Go Ken."

He stood from the bed again and made his way to the bathroom. "I'm gonna take a shower and leave."

"Well damn."

"Look Ken, we have a lifetime to be together. I have some things I have to take care of."

The next day Kendall called Rashad. "I found Melody Snow last night."

"What did she say?"

"Said Low-Down got murdered six months ago and she was glad that you reached out, she was trying to reach you."

"What?"

"Yeah I went to her page and there are pictures of him and all kinds of Rest In Peace comments."

"Damn I wonder who killed him?"

"She said some young punk from Compton, trying to make a name for himself."

"Damn. Text me the number and I'll call her."

"Okay."

"What are you doing?"

"Getting ready to go visit Dre in jail."

"You're a good woman Ken, I know I keep saying this, but I'm lucky to have you."

"Yes, you are." she laughed.

* * * * *

Dre wore an oversized orange jumpsuit and his hair was unkempt and he looked as if he hadn't shaved in a few days. A plexiglass window separated them, as Kendall sat down and picked up the phone receiver and seconds later Dre did the same. There was a long silence before either of them said anything. "I'm glad you decided to come." Dre said.

"The least I could do." Kendall said avoiding eye contact with Dre.

"I wish you would have brought Christian."

"I don't know if I want him to see you in here."

"I can understand that, but I'm his father."

"Yes, you are, but right now I don't know if it's a good idea."

310

Dre bit his bottom lip. "I know you hate me Ken."

"I don't hate you Andre. I love you and I always will."

"Can you handle my legal fees?"

"With what, I'm broke."

"I have a couple of antique cars and I was thinking that if you could take out a home equity line on the house, you could cover the legal fees."

"I will think about it, but I have to also think about where me and our son are going to live. I don't have a job yet."

"I know. You know what? You're right. Scratch that, you and Christian come first."

"You heard from Catherine?"

"Yeah right."

"Do you think she gave you up?"

"No, but her father did. He lied on me." Dre said, knowing that the phones were tapped

"I'm sorry."

"No I'm sorry for all I've done to you. I fucked up, we were supposed to make it."

Kendall smirked. "Yes we were, but that's old news."

"You just said you loved me."

"I do love you, but I'm not in love with you Andre."

"Are you involved with someone?"

She looked in straight in the eyes. "Yes and I'm very happy."

There was an awkward silence before Dre stood and dropped the receiver then picked up the receiver again and said. "I wish you nothing but the best." He lied.

He blew her a kiss and she stepped outside the visitation room, where Rashad was waiting on her. He embraced her and held her before whispering "It's gonna be okay."